The Design

R.S. Grey

Published: R.S. Grey 2015
authorrsgrey@gmail.com
Editing: Editing by C. Marie
Cover Design: R.S. Grey
Stock Photos courtesy of Shutterstock ®
ISBN: 1508481938
ISBN-13: 978-1508481935

"All journeys have secret destinations of which the traveler
is unaware."
- Martin Buber

Prologue

Five years ago

Grayson watched the lights dance above his head. Neon blue, green, pink. He was two drinks past sober and the club's lights were starting to become more interesting than the dancers below.

Brooklyn took a seat beside him and he nudged her with his shoulder.

"How ya holding up, champ?" he asked, eyeing the young pop star as if she was about to pass out on the spot.

Everyone else had deserted them for the dance floor a few minutes earlier and the two of them were alone in the booth, so he hoped she'd speak the truth for once.

"Fine," she said.

He nudged her again, a little harder this time.

"I'm really worried about my sister," she said, hiding her face against her shoulder.

Before Grayson spoke, he surveyed the crowd around them. They were the young Hollywood type: sons and daughters of media moguls. The most they had to worry about in a day was whether they wanted their $8 coffee with or without an extra shot of espresso. Not Brooklyn.

After she lost her parents at eighteen, she'd become the sole guardian of her little sister, Cammie. It was obvious that she felt the weight of that burden every day, even though it'd been nearly ten years since their death.

"What's wrong with her?" Grayson asked. The few times he'd been around Cammie he'd seen a wild streak lurking beneath the surface. She was beautiful and sharp, there was no denying it. Something about her had Grayson enamored from the very start. A fact, he tried to deny every time she slipped into his thoughts.

"I have a lot of people supporting me—my managers, my assistants, and my friends—but it seems like Cammie has no one. She ditched her old friends one by one after our parents' accident and I'm just scared that I'm not enough for her." By that point, tears were slipping down Brooklyn's cheeks and Grayson wrestled with how to best console her. They were just friends, nothing more, but he'd known her for years and it still hurt to see her upset.

Brooklyn turned to him with determination in her eyes. "She's so smart, Grayson. She wants to study architecture, just like you did, but I think it might be too late. She's been so...unfocused these past few years."

Grayson nodded, already appraising the answer starting to claw its way to the front of his thoughts. Immediately after the car accident, he had thought about stepping in to help Brooklyn and Cammie, but he hadn't had the resources to affect any real change. Now, things were different. He had the connections to really make a difference in Cammie's life.

A few drinks later, Grayson's mind was made up. He'd step in and help Cammie. He told himself that he was doing it for the right reasons, though deep down he knew that not to be true. He wanted to be close to Cammie any way that he could, but taking advantage of a young, vulnerable girl wasn't something his morality would let him get away with. To keep temptation at bay, he'd help her from afar and keep his distance whenever possible.

Even with the utmost precautions in place, he knew his morality was bound to fail him one day. After all, the moral high ground does get awfully lonely.

Chapter One

Cammie

I dreamed of leaving. I dreamed of filling a giant backpack with the essentials (my sketchbook and my favorite Black Keys album) and setting off for destinations unknown.

I was one week out of college, where I'd completed a combined bachelor's and master's degree program in architecture. After all the long nights, I wanted to change gears and travel, finally check off a destination or two on my bucket list.

I already had a plan in place. I just had to work long enough to save up a little nest egg. From my calculations—*assuming I didn't turn to prostituting myself in Europe*—I'd need to work for about three months before I could purchase a one-way ticket to Paris.

Technically, I didn't need to save at all. My parents had left Brooklyn and I with plenty of money after the car accident, but I hadn't touched my portion yet, and I wouldn't. I wanted to board that plane to Paris knowing that I was doing it completely on my own.

While my plan seemed to be coming together, I had no clue what I'd do with myself once I actually got to Paris. There was a 50% chance that I'd immediately cave and fly back home…right back into Brooklyn's waiting arms.

Brooklyn was my big sister, mother, father, sidekick, best friend, and most importantly, my security blanket. She didn't know about my plan to leave for Paris, but there was no way around the deceit. If she found out that I was planning to move across the world, she'd lock me up inside of her condo. (*Which, for the record, wouldn't be that bad. She had satellite TV and her fridge was always stocked with fancy cheeses.*)

"Have you been practicing any interview questions for tomorrow?" Brooklyn asked as she bent over to finish painting my toenails.

I sighed and sunk into the couch cushions even further.

My interview.

My interview at Cole Designs—one of LA's largest architecture firms.

I'd managed to forget about my impending interview for all of five minutes, but now it was right back to the forefront of my mind.

"Yes, I've practiced, but I doubt Grayson will even bother asking me questions. He'll just stare at me from across his desk hoping that I'll spontaneously combust…or start crying."

Brooklyn rolled her eyes and twisted the lid back onto the red nail polish. She liked to play devil's advocate when it came to Grayson, but I knew better. He actually was the *devil*, with no advocate to say otherwise. He might have been her friend for the last ten years, but he was *not* a nice guy. He'd proven that to me on multiple occasions, and I was content with where our relationship was. I.e. non-existent.

"Give him a chance. He's under a ton of stress. Don't take his curtness personally."

I grunted. *Curt was putting it lightly.*

"All right. No more Grayson talk. I need food," I said, patting my stomach like a jolly Santa Claus. "When is that man slave of yours getting back with the fajitas?"

"Jason is my *boyfriend*, not my sex slave," she corrected with a threatening stare.

"Whoa Ms. Freud, you dropped your slip," I said, reaching for my phone so I could check my email for the one-thousandth time that day. There was probably nothing new, but I didn't want to miss any last minute changes concerning my interview in the morning. For the last week I'd kept my phone attached to my hip as if it would alert me about the apocalypse at any minute. Seriously, I'd been in the shower earlier, trying to talk myself into actually shaving my legs, when my phone vibrated on the bathroom sink. I scrambled for it, slipped, and ended up inches away from hitting my head on the bathroom tile. (*Thank goodness I missed, because the paramedics would have had to use the Jaws of Life to hack through my leg hair to save me.*)

To say that I was nervous about my interview with Grayson Cole was an understatement. Homeboy held the keys to my future. Landing a job at his firm would be the crucial first step in my plan to move to Paris. See detailed outline below:

1. Land a job.
2. Work until I have a nice little nest egg.

3. Ignore the fact that Grayson Cole is the sexiest architect in all the land. *He's my boss, he's my boss—* I'd have to just keep repeating that mantra until it stuck

4. Buy my ticket to Paris and fly far, far away - thus proving that I can go through life on my own, without living in Brooklyn's shadow.

5. Gloat with sexy Frenchmen.

6. Eat lots of French bread.

• • •

Later that night, I laid out an outfit for my morning interview. I had more than enough clothes to choose from since Brooklyn had taken it upon herself to surprise me with a work wardrobe earlier in the week. She was annoyingly confident that I would land the job. I, on the other hand, was happy to have the new designer duds. If nothing else, I'd look killer as security hauled me out of the building for karate chopping Grayson in the face.

I slid my hand over the fabric of a dark red wrap dress. I'd already tried it on earlier, loving the fit. It fell a few inches above my knees and the soft belt knotted to the side of my stomach, just above my hip. The sexy color would afford me at least half the confidence I'd need to step into Grayson's office. The other half would come from my sky-high nude heels.

After checking that my four cell phone and two clock alarms were turned on and set to the exact pitch of a wailing newborn, I crawled into bed, willing sleep to take me fast.

Shocker: it didn't.

7

Instead, I laid on top of my sheets, tossing and turning for hours, replaying every encounter I'd had with Grayson from the very beginning. My goal was to pinpoint the exact moment when he'd started to despise me.

The first time I'd ever laid eyes on Grayson, I was a senior in high school—a baby in his eyes considering he was already two years out from completing his master's degree at MIT. Brooklyn had dragged me to a dinner with some of her friends. He'd been there, at the opposite end of the table, his brown hair long on top with a bit of wave he didn't bother trying to tame. His dark eyes were focused on the girl beside him, but I didn't mind. I had a perfect vantage point to take him in. His wardrobe was far more relaxed in those days. Even still, he somehow made dark jeans and a gray t-shirt look edible.

There were plenty of other people to focus on, but my gaze kept landing on Grayson. I'd catch a hint of his smile or hear the tale end of his laugh and lose myself in imagining what it would be like to date a guy like him.

We didn't speak once at that dinner, yet over the following two months, he morphed into the perfect hero in my mind. He was the Mr. Darcy to my Elizabeth Bennet, the Prince Charming to my Cinderella, and most importantly, the Ron Weasley to my Hermione Granger. I'd find myself thinking of him, recreating his appearance from that dinner, pretending I was the dark-haired girl sitting beside him. My fantasies were more than enough to tide me over until one day when Brooklyn brought him over to our condo and I didn't have to imagine him anymore.

The front door of the condo opened and Brooklyn breezed inside with Grayson on her heels. He looked effortlessly cool with two-day stubble, a flannel shirt, jeans, and worn brown boots. I was in my pajamas, stuffing popcorn into my gullet when he glanced through the doorway and saw me. I wanted to melt into the couch from embarrassment. Brooklyn, of course, hadn't warned me about his arrival. With a seven-year age difference, we shouldn't have even been on each other's radar, but he was the only person on mine.

He came to sit down on the chair beside the couch and turned toward me just as a popcorn kernel got lodged in my throat. I turned away and tried to pound my chest to get it out. *Please, God, take me. This is the worst moment of my life.*

"You okay?" he asked, drawing my attention back toward him. There was a hint of a smile hidden somewhere beneath his hard exterior.

The first time we'd met, I hadn't seen his features up close. From my seat on the couch, every contour of his sculpted cheekbones, straight nose, and angular jaw were like my own personal siren call. Dark brows framed distant eyes—the sort of eyes that did a better job of keeping people out than letting them in. But it was his lips, *his lips* that completely did me in. When those lips hitched into a suggestive half-smile, I realized I'd failed to respond to his question.

"I'm fine," I muttered, my face enflamed with a blush that didn't want to recede.

"Oh, Grayson. This is my baby sister, Cammie!" Brooklyn cooed, reaching over the back of the couch to grab my shoulders. "She's a senior in high school this year."

I'd never wanted to strangle my sister more than I did in that moment. Sure, I was wearing pajamas pants with baby sheep jumping around on them, but she didn't need to drive home the point that I was practically a toddler in Grayson's eyes.

His brow arched as he regarded me from his armchair and I inwardly groaned at what he was probably seeing. Had I brushed my hair *or* my teeth yet that day?

Before the situation could get any worse, I stood with my popcorn bowl and left the living room with a whispered grumble about needing to get my homework done. Brooklyn was probably seconds away from telling him that I'd wet the bed until I was six or that I'd only had my braces removed the year before; I was *not* going to stick around for that kind of mortification.

I locked myself in my room, pulled out my sketchbook, and started to draw Grayson on the first few pages. Every single detail of his appearance was still fresh in my mind and I didn't want them to fade before I finished.

I sketched with my back against my bedroom door so that I could be sure to hear if Brooklyn was approaching my room. I'd have rather eaten my entire sketchbook than let her see the drawings I was working on.

Just as I was almost finished, I heard Grayson speak up in the living room, his deep voice penetrating my bedroom walls. He was talking about his job as an architect at a firm downtown. He explained to Brooklyn how he wanted to branch out on his own and design things without some failed-architect-turned-manager constantly hovering over his shoulder. I stood there with my ear pressed to my door as he talked about what his firm would be like and the kind of buildings he wanted to design.

An architect.

At the time, my future career hadn't been my top priority. I was too busy trying to grasp onto anything I could find easily: boys, partying, alcohol, drugs—none of which had succeeded in replacing what I had lost when my parents had died. I kept floating farther and farther away from my old life while Brooklyn tried desperately to reel me back in. Just three weeks before I'd told her that I didn't want to graduate from high school knowing our parents wouldn't be there to watch me walk across the stage. I didn't want to move away to college knowing our parents wouldn't be there to help me unload my car. So, I'd pushed everything out of my mind.

It'd been incredibly easy.

Too easy.

Until that moment.

I remember sitting against that doorframe and daydreaming about becoming an architect, just like Grayson. I'd loved to draw. I had sketchbooks filled to the brim, and when I was younger I'd dreamed of going into a creative field. *Was it too late?*

I grabbed my laptop from my bed, slunk back down onto the floor, and researched architecture programs in Los Angeles for hours. My options were limited, but I still had time to make something happen before graduation.

I hadn't realized it then, but that night was the first time I'd started to think about my future since the day my parents had passed away…and I had Grayson to thank for it.

For the next few months, I brushed off requests to party. I pushed aside the bad influences and locked myself in my school's art room after the final bell rang each day. I had a portfolio to build and hardly any time to do it.

The next time I saw Grayson after he'd unknowingly changed my life was at Brooklyn's twenty-second birthday party. I knew he'd be attending, so I'd tried to dress up my seventeen-year-old frame in a way that screamed "precocious chic". I had too much make-up on and wore a dress that was fighting to cut off circulation to my lungs. I teetered along on high heels I had no business wearing.

When we arrived at the party, Grayson was already there with a gorgeous blonde girl hanging on his arm. She looked like she'd just stepped off the catwalk in Milan and as she smiled wide, pressing her palm to his chest, my hope deflated. I paused at the front entrance of the restaurant as every question I'd planned on asking him, every conversation starter that I'd brainstormed over the last few days slipped away along with my naive hope.

I remember feeling so silly standing there in a dress that gapped around my hips—where seductive curves should have been.

I'd done a stupid thing by putting my faith in an absolute stranger. For those last few months, since he'd first appeared in my life, I hadn't done a single reckless thing. I'd made curfew, I hadn't sneaked out at night, and I'd told my sister exactly where I'd be when I was going out. Grayson had been my reason for changing, but as I stood there and watched him with that woman, a beautiful woman *his own age*, I had a sudden yearning to do something crazy, to get out of my own head for a few hours.

I slipped over to the side of the restaurant and gave my friend Darren a call. He was a guy from my high school, someone known for walking the line between right, wrong, and Class C misdemeanor. With his holier-than-thou attitude and his ever-present pair of combat boots, even I couldn't stand the idea of being around him for very long, but he would work just fine for one evening of fun.

When Darren arrived, he stood at the entrance of the restaurant wearing a Ramone's t-shirt and a bored expression. He didn't even bother stepping inside. It wasn't his style. He waited for me at the door as I hugged Brooklyn goodbye. She begged me to stay and whispered that she was worried about me leaving with Darren. I pulled out of her grasp as a sinking feeling started to take hold inside of my gut. *You're better than this. Stay. Don't do something reckless.* There was no point in doubting my decision; my conscience was fighting a losing battle. At that point in my life, I wasn't worried about anyone but myself. I didn't care that it was my sister's birthday. *I needed out.*

I felt Grayson's gaze on me as I walked away. Just before Darren took my hand and pulled me through the front door, I turned back and locked eyes with him.

His gaze was cold and hard. There was a darkness in his expression that hadn't been there before. His jaw was locked tight and his brows were knit together. He shook his head once, and then turned away from me—back to the blonde staring up at him with doe eyes.

Annoyed, I stormed out of the restaurant's front doors, ripped off my heels, and sped off with Darren to a college party down in the Valley. I can't recall if I even slept in my own bed that night.

After that night, a few years passed before I saw Grayson again. I'd done my best to forget the part of my life when I'd been completely obsessed with him. Instead, I focused on my goal: becoming a licensed architect. I was in the second year of my architecture program and I was already in love with the field.

Then, one day, I glanced up from writing "*Guest Lecture Series - #3*" in my spiral notebook and saw him standing at the front of my college lecture hall.

I didn't believe it was him at first. He looked different than he had before: all grown up in a navy blue suit, complete with linked cuffs and shined shoes. His rich brown hair had grown out a little on top, but it was styled back, highlighting his strong bone structure. His red tie fell perfectly down the center of his broad chest and his hands were clenched into fists by his sides as his eyes locked with mine. *Oh, it was him all right.* He'd given me that same exact stare the last time I'd seen him.

I did my best to pay attention during his lecture. The class was absolutely silent as he spoke. The girls all leaned in to hear each syllable he uttered, while the guys tried to dissect how he was able to captivate a room with zero effort at all.

After weighing the pros and cons, I'd worked up the courage to talk to him after class. It'd been a few years since I'd last seen him and I felt like I'd grown up a lot in that time. I wasn't Brooklyn's little sister. I was Cammie Heart, architecture student. (*I mean, I'd traded my sports bras in for the real thing, and I knew how to style my hair properly. How could he resist me?*)

So, after the lecture, I joined the line other students— all conspicuously female—who wanted to have a chance to speak with him. I craned my ears to hear him speak to each one of them. He was quick, but polite. He offered them real advice and encouraged them to apply for summer internships at his firm.

The line continued to move until I was one person away from getting to talk to him. I knew he saw me standing in line behind the girl he was chatting with, but just before they finished talking, he smiled down at her and gestured for her to lead the way out of the classroom. I was left standing there like a fool as I watched them leave. He had his hand on her lower back and his gaze focused on the door. A part of me wanted to yell after him, but I knew it was futile. To Grayson Cole, I was as good as a ghost. He might have humored me around Brooklyn, but whatever politeness he'd once shown me was long gone.

From that point forward, I attempted to block Grayson from my mind. I did my best to ignore him whenever we saw each other, and he did the same. We had an unspoken agreement to pretend the other person didn't exist.

That is…until a few days ago—the day of my college graduation. I'd just arrived at the restaurant for my celebratory brunch when I saw Grayson waiting for me on the sidewalk, wearing his classic navy suit. I was shocked to see him—I hadn't invited him to my graduation, obviously. Yet, there he stood, turning heads on the sidewalk and forcing my heart to kick into overdrive.

"Could I speak with you for a moment, Cameron?" he'd asked, ignoring the other four people in my group altogether.

I froze with his confident gaze on me. Actual conversation was against our unspoken rules. I couldn't recall him ever asking to speak with me privately.

Despite my nerves, I agreed, and once we were alone, he stepped forward and presented an offer I couldn't refuse: an interview at his firm, Cole Designs. The exchange was brief—he turned back to his car as soon as I'd accepted— but the fact remained: he'd gone out of his way to offer me an interview.

So tomorrow morning, I'd sit across from him with every bit of confidence I could muster, all the while wondering how he could hate me so much yet still consider hiring me.

Chapter Two

The dynamics of an architecture firm harken back to the stone ages. *No, really.* Over my morning coffee, I browsed the employee section of the Cole Designs website. Out of fifty-five employees, there were thirteen females. Of those thirteen females, seven were in the interior design department, three of them were in the accounting department, two were in reception, and yep—you guessed it—there was ONE female architect in the entire firm. Her name was Gina and she was an older looking woman with graying hair and a flat smile. According to her profile, she'd been with the company since it was founded a few years back.

I'm sure the disparity in gender wasn't by design, but due to the fact that architecture (or rather, solving differential equations for systems of cantilevered beams) doesn't excite most young girls. Even in my graduating class of one hundred students, there were only fifteen females. I'd known all along that I was entering a world dominated by men. I'd even had one asshole professor ask me if I honestly thought I'd be able to delegate orders to general contractors or supervise rowdy construction workers. I'd walked out of his classroom without gracing him with an answer, fighting away the urge to flip him the bird. Six weeks later, I'd received my final grade and it was the highest one in the class. *"How 'bout them apples?"* (Psst…thanks, Matt Damon.)

I smiled at the memory and closed my laptop with a newfound sense of resolve. There was less than an hour and a half until my interview, just enough time to prepare and get across town.

• • •

As I sat in the back of a cab on the way to the interview, I attempted to snap a photo of my dress to send to Brooklyn. It was hard to get the right angle, but she'd get the idea.

> **Cammie**: Does this scream "Confident, worldy architect?"
> **Brooklyn**: It screams "I could out-design your flat ass any day. So give me this job *with* a signing bonus."
> **Cammie**: Ha. With the sleep I got last night, I'd settle for a signing latte.

I didn't get the chance to read her response because we were already pulling up in front of the Sterling Bank Building. I'd never actually ventured inside of it before, but it was one of the tallest office buildings in downtown Los Angeles and I'd seen it countless times. Its black metal frame paired with its imposing shiny black glass gave the building an industrial, masculine feel. Even the heavy doors served to intimidate guests as they entered the pristine lobby.

I paused just outside of the front doors and took a deep breath, trying to get my bearings. I was twenty minutes early for my interview. My outfit was still wrinkle-free and fit like a glove. My padfolio was filled with extra copies of my resume and reference letters, and I'd rehearsed every question that Grayson Cole could possibly ask:

Greatest weakness? *My inability to settle for anything less than what I deserve. I'm stubborn and persistent.*

The honest answer? *My inability to overcome my schoolgirl crush on you even though you're a self-righteous ass.*

I would NOT be giving him the honest answer.

I reached for my phone to check the suite number of Cole Designs just as a businessman yammering into his cell phone, bumped into me from behind. I lost my balance and in a matter of two seconds, my padfolio went flying across the concrete and I had to think fast to catch myself on my hands and knees. The asphalt rushed to meet me and I hissed as my kneecaps caught the brunt of my weight. The sound of ripping tights was the icing on the cake.

"Watch where you're going," the man snapped, not even bothering to help me up or apologize for bumping into me. "Jesus. No, I'm still here," he barked into his phone. "Go on."

I ground my teeth together as I pushed to sit up on my heels, and then I reached to collect the papers that had slipped out of my padfolio. Once I'd stuffed them back inside, I stood and flinched at the feeling of blood running

R.S. Grey

down my tights. I had nothing to clean it off with and my tights were already stained down to my shin.

Awesome.

I straightened my dress as best as I could and assessed the damage. Other than the small amount of blood, there were two giant holes in my tights directly over my kneecaps. I knew the fabric would continue to split as I walked, but my dress would look too sexy without the added cover the tights afforded me. I was early, but not early enough to run home and change. My only option was to trash the tights and pray no one noticed my short hem and skinned kneecaps. I'd have to distract the interview panel with my sparkling personality if I had any hope of making it out of there with a job.

With my chin held high, I pushed through the front door of the building just in time to see the rude man step onto one of the elevators. He turned and I caught a better sight of him. He was middle-aged with thinning hair and a greasy forehead. His beady eyes narrowed when he spotted me across the lobby, as if he were angry with *me* for the accident out font. *The audacity.*

I purposely waited until he was long gone before I made my way over to the elevator bank. While I waited for the next elevator to arrive, I pulled out my phone and checked the confirmation email from an assistant at Cole Designs.

"Cole Designs, #1160"

It seemed easy enough. I took the elevator up to the eleventh floor, slipped off my tights without flashing the security camera, shoved them into my purse and then watched the numbers change above my head. *This was it.* Cole Designs was the premier design firm in Los Angeles and I had one shot at landing a job there. I just had to prove to Grayson Cole that I was a capable architect. MORE than capable according to most of my professors, but their letters of recommendation probably wouldn't be enough to sway Grayson Cole. *No, I'd have to really impress him during my interview.*

The elevator doors slid open and I stepped out onto the eleventh floor with a confident smile and a walk that belonged on a runway. (*Y'know, a runway that didn't mind bloody kneecaps.*) The elevator opened up to a small waiting room with a petite blonde sitting behind a mahogany desk. She was facing away from me, chatting with another employee. I didn't recognize either of them from the employee section of the Cole Designs website, but I couldn't really see their faces.

"No. Seriously, the teenager swore that she'd never been sexually active," the employee whispered, much louder than she probably intended.

"Was her mom in the exam room with you guys?" the receptionist asked.

"Yes! That's why she didn't want to tell us the truth."

"So what happened?"

"We figured out what was causing the problem. She had like ten condoms stuck up there!"

"No!" the receptionist gasped.

"I swear."

What the hell had I walked in on? I cleared my throat as they continued their private conversation. The moment the receptionist noticed my presence, she swiveled in her chair and smiled wide, trying to cover up the fact that she'd just been gossiping in front of me.

"I'm so sorry! What's your name?" she asked.

"Cameron Heart. I'm here for an—"

"I don't see your name on the schedule," the receptionist cut me off with a frown.

"Oh, um, I received an emai—"

She stood, cutting me off again, and shoved a clipboard at me so that the sharp metal clip jabbed into my stomach.

"Just fill this out and give it back to me. Do you have any pain? Any UTI symptoms?"

I narrowed my eyes, trying to figure out why those questions were relevant in any way. Then I glanced down at the paperwork. A few questions jumped out at me right away:

"What's your sexual orientation?"

"Are you currently taking birth control?"

"What was the last day of your menstrual cycle?"

I blanched. *Nope. No.* Oh dear god, I was *not* in the right office. I dropped the clipboard onto her desk and bolted toward a side door off the main waiting room. Once I was outside, I glanced back to read the placard that I'd missed on my way in.

"Dr. Donald Fitzpatrick, OB/GYN #1160"

Shit. Shit. Shit.

I reopened the email from Grayson's receptionist, cursing myself for reading the suite number wrong. But when it opened, I found the same number staring back at me: #1160. *What the hell? Was this a joke?* I groaned and pulled up the Cole Designs website. At the very bottom of the black screen, it listed the firm's address and suite number: #2160. *NOT #1160!* I was ten floors short of the Cole Designs offices.

I took the stairs up two at a time, not bothering to go back through the doctor's waiting room to call for an elevator. The rage I felt toward Grayson's receptionist was boiling up inside of me and I used it to fuel me up the ten flights of stairs.

By the time I'd reached the correct floor, I was breathing far heavier than I should have been. Sweat was collecting under my arms. The cuts on my knees hadn't started to scab over yet, and blood was still trickling down my knees. In a matter of ten minutes, I'd gone from put together professional to homicidal hobo lady.

I stared at the placard for Cole Designs as I collected my hair in one hand and fanned my neck with the other. Most of it had fallen down from my updo, but there wasn't much I could do about it without a mirror. A quick glance at my phone informed me that I was a minute away from being late, and although I wanted to run home crying, I knew I had to pull the door open and face my interview head on. I gave myself three seconds to calm my heart rate before pulling open the door and walking into the Cole Designs lobby.

It felt like I was walking into my own personal version of hell, but I pushed the feeling aside and forced my feet to move forward, one after the other. The moment I crossed through the threshold, chaos erupted before me. There were at least twenty applicants sitting in the waiting room. They filled every possible chair, and even overflowed onto the floor. Like me, they all had padfolios. Unlike me, they all looked cool, calm, and collected, save for the skinny boy in the far corner, who was talking to himself and rocking back and forth. *He* might have been even more nervous than I was.

I turned toward the reception desk, ready to explain my tardiness, only to find a frazzled woman shoving everything from her desk drawer into a cheap cardboard box.

"Smug, no good—" she mumbled beneath her breath as I stepped closer, unsure if I was meant to check-in with her or stay far, far away. Up until a moment before, I was ready to growl at her for sending me the wrong information, but now it looked like she might have been having an even worse day than I was.

"Excuse me," I spoke, trying to get her attention as quietly as possible. She had a pencil shoved into the messy bun atop her head. Sugar—*or some other white substance*—coated the top of her cardigan, and her red lipstick was smeared across her teeth. When she looked up, she gave me a plastic smile and aimed the stapler she had clutched in her hand right at me.

"I'd *love* to help you out," she said. Her tone insinuated otherwise. "It's just that I am no longer *employed* by this company or by its *prick* boss."

My mouth fell open while my brain tried desperately to catch up. I was about to ask for clarification when a new woman stepped out of the door behind the reception desk. She had a clipboard in one hand and a pen in the other. She was beautiful in a non-threatening sort of way, like a chic French girl. Her skin was a rich dark brown and her eyes shown just a few shades lighter.

When she caught sight of the receptionist in the midst of a public meltdown, her eyes widened and she quickly tried to reign in the situation.

"Kelly! That's enough," the woman said, putting her hands on Kelly's shoulders. "Here, just let me…" The new woman tried to gently pry the stapler from Kelly's hand, presumably to keep Kelly from firing it off at me.

"Beatrice! THAT'S MY STAPLER! It's not company property and neither am I so get your damn hands off of me!" Kelly sassed, as she tried to keep Beatrice from clawing the stapler out of her hands.

Just when I thought an actual brawl was about to break out, Kelly paused.

"No wait," Kelly said, huffing from the exertion of fighting Beatrice off. "Actually, the *staples* aren't mine. So here, have them." Kelly then proceeded to punch every single staple out onto her desk as Beatrice and the rest of my fellow applicants looked on. Each staple hit the desk with a soft clap. I wasn't sure what the hell I was supposed to do, so I just stood there. *Was this whole office building full of crazy people?*

When the stapler was empty (and no longer in danger of going off in one of my eyes), Kelly went back to packing her things and Beatrice turned to me with a bright smile. *She clearly had practice in dealing with crazy.*

"Hello. I'm Beatrice, Grayson's personal assistant. Interviews haven't started yet so you can take a seat with the other applicants and then we'll begin shortly."

She was attempting to salvage the situation as best as possible, but her smile was tight and I knew she was mentally cursing her job.

I found an empty spot on the ground near the front door and sat, while the applicants did their best to size me up inconspicuously. I could practically hear their thoughts. *Is that blood?* Yes. *Is that sweat or a design on her dress?* It's sweat, you judgmental cows.

They were exactly the type of people I'd been expecting: Ivy League prodigies with a creative flair. There were two other girls in a sea of men, one sitting directly beside me on a chair and another one on the other side of the room who kept giving me death stares whenever we made eye contact. *I guess she didn't believe in the whole "you go girl!" mantra.* Most everyone seemed to be about my age or a few years older. A boy across from me had on a tweed jacket and thick black glasses, and he was flipping through flash cards at lightning speed.

What was he even memorizing at that point?

Now that I was at least in the correct office, I finally had a moment to piece together my appearance. I tried to wipe off most of the blood with tissues from a side table and then I combed through my hair with my fingers, but it was almost too far gone by that point.

"You look like you could use a cup of coffee," said the girl next to me, interrupting the layer of silence that had covered the waiting room before that, save for the stray curse word uttered by Kelly every now and again.

I peered over to take in the girl beside me. Her smile said, *"I'm not your enemy"* but her power suit said, *"Or am I?"* I decided to test the waters with a friendly smile of my own.

"You wouldn't believe that I started this morning off thinking everything would go just as I had planned," I said.

The girl laughed. "It rarely does." Then she reached her hand out toward me. "I'm Hannah by the way."

I liked that name. Mean girls didn't have names like Hannah.

I returned her handshake. "I'm Cameron, but everyone calls me Cammie."

"Nice. Are you a recent grad?" she asked, eyeing the leather of my padfolio like it would belch out all of my secrets.

"Yeah. First interview. You?"

She grunted and leaned back against her chair, glancing up toward the ceiling as if recalling distant memories. "Nah, I've been out of school for about three years. My firm had layoffs a few months back so I've been looking for a job every since."

Great. She was older than me and had more work experience. Not to mention, she was gorgeous. Her blonde hair fell straight past her shoulders, her tan skin glowed, and the smoky eye effect she'd done with her makeup looked killer. I glanced down at my already-chipped nail polish and my red dress that had once made me feel sophisticated, but now just made me look like a sweaty Twizzler.

"Was your old firm in LA as well?" I asked.

"Nope. If this interview works out, I'll need to find a place to stay. I've been crashing on a friend's couch while I look for a job."

I smiled. "Same here. Well, I'm from LA, but I have to move out of my dorm in a week. I either have to find a roommate or crash with my sister."

Hannah peered over at me from the corner of her eye. "Well, good luck. Hopefully we'll both be starting here soon."

A few minutes later, Hannah's name was called from the front of the waiting room and we both looked up to see Beatrice standing behind the desk, gesturing for Hannah to stand up.

"You'll be our first candidate," Beatrice said.

With a final "here goes nothing" smile, Hannah stood and walked to meet Beatrice while Kelly simultaneously picked up her full cardboard box from the reception desk. Her personal items shuffled around inside the box, announcing her departure to the quiet waiting room.

When she passed me, she stopped and glanced down.

"Here," she said, starting to rustle through her box. "If you end up working here you'll need this."

She pulled out a small object and tossed it onto my lap before proceeding to the elevator. I looked down to find a blue stress ball with the words "Grayson Cole" written across the latex in black Sharpie.

I smiled and picked it up, wishing there was a picture of his beautifully annoying face on it. Maybe if I did land the job, I'd modify it.

• • •

I sat in that waiting room for three hours. As each applicant's name was called, they stood and made their way through the double doors behind the front desk, one by one, until I was the only one left. It was excruciating to have to sit there, even after I'd finally landed a coveted seat. (*My ass had gone numb from sitting on the ground, or maybe from the blood loss from my knees. Whatever.*)

To pass the time, I alternated between checking my phone and squeezing the stress ball. In the end, I sat there with my arms crossed, staring up at the ceiling and wondering for the hundredth time that morning, just how cruel Grayson would be that day. Surely he intended on actually interviewing me; it couldn't all be some cruel joke.

"Ms. Heart," Beatrice spoke.

I looked up in time to watch the blonde guy with glasses—I'd dubbed him Flashcards—make his way through the waiting room with tears streaming down his face. *Oh, jeez. Grayson made him cry?*

"You'll be our final applicant," Beatrice said with a bright smile, seemingly unconcerned by the blubbering young man passing by her.

My walk to join her at the door seemed far less dramatic than it should have. In hindsight, a violin should have been playing a sad song to accurately portray the tone of the moment: *dead man walking.*

"Don't worry, Grayson always likes to save the best for last," Beatrice assured me.

Chapter Three

I highly doubted that Grayson was saving me for last because he I thought I was the best applicant. There were many possibilities for why I was last:

> 1. He wanted me to sit and sweat, torturing me slowly. (In which case, joke's on him, because it took about 3 hours for me to *stop* sweating from my sprint up the stairs.)
>
> 2. He wanted to have ample amount of time to criticize my resume and everything listed on it.
>
> 3. He'd actually forgotten I was even there for an interview.

Beatrice held the door open for me as I walked through, and then I got my first glimpse at the company Grayson had built from the ground up. The office was shaped like a giant square with four arms branching off at each corner. The main room itself was the biggest space in the office. It housed the architects, dividing them into small teams of four or five. It was a collaborative work environment with *zero* privacy.

Each arm that branched off from the main room housed a different department: in-house engineers, accounting, interiors, and the company's conference room. Industrial signs hung artfully from the ceilings, directing guests to the various departments. There were three offices on the back wall of the main room, across from the front reception area, each reserved for the company's executives. Grayson's sat in the very center, nearly twice as big as the two offices surrounding it.

I walked toward his open door, letting Beatrice take the lead as I hung back and tried to get a feel for the work environment. The open floor plan allowed for collaboration, and most of the employees had their heads together as they worked through design problems. A few of them looked up and nodded at me, but most of them stayed busy, drafting and designing.

I wasn't sure what I'd been expecting—maybe more of a prison-like atmosphere, especially after the scene Kelly had pulled in the waiting room. Most everyone looked happy though. That is to say, one was flashing me signs inscribed with "*Abandon all hope, ye who enter here.*"

I smiled at the thought just as Beatrice and I arrived outside Grayson's doorway. Beatrice stepped to the side, and I inhaled a sharp breath. I had a clear view of Grayson sitting behind his large black desk with his phone tucked between his shoulder and ear. His hands worked furiously, jotting down notes while listening to whoever was speaking to him on the phone.

"Just wait here," Beatrice whispered. "He should be done soon." I nodded and she touched my arm gently before taking a seat at her desk a few feet away from his door. Within a moment, she was on a call and I was left to stand there idle as I watched the subject of most of my college-aged fantasies.

He didn't notice me right away—not while he was working—so I stood there admiring him. He was in a traditional black suit, fitted across his shoulders and arms. He'd paired it with a crisp white shirt and a sleek black tie. The soft light from the window hit his cheekbones, accentuating their sharp contours and putting special emphasis on his exquisitely defined jaw. He reached to rub his fingers along his chin, and his eyes narrowed on the sheet of paper on his desk. I wondered what he was studying. So much so, that I dared to take a step closer.

Bad move.

He dropped the drafting pencil, and after one excruciatingly long second, his eyes slid up to me. They were so sharp and blue that they pinned me to my spot, and I was caught between taking another step closer and fleeing for my life. Neither of us moved. I felt like I was stuck in the center of a tightrope, hanging over a canyon with nowhere to go but down.

He spoke into the phone with a deep, authoritative tone while keeping his gaze on me.

"Mitch, I'll have to call you back in a moment. I've got one last interview."

He didn't wait for Mitch to reply. He dropped his phone onto his desk and indicated for me to enter with a flick of his hand. To him, I was an animal he could beckon forward.

I stared down at my feet and rolled my eyes.

"Take a seat, Cameron."

God, I hated the way he said my whole name, dragging it out into something formal and ugly. I'd never felt like Cameron; I was Cammie.

He sighed.

"Do you always take this long to process simple instructions?" he asked, obviously annoyed that I hadn't moved yet.

I stared into his soulless eyes. "You know I'm not intimidated by you."

What a lie.

The left side of his mouth hitched up, defining a dimple that was usually hidden behind layers of resolve and pompousness. Dimples weren't meant for CEOs, even young handsome ones.

"Perhaps we should fix that, Ms. Heart. Shut the door."

The dimple was gone again, replaced with a stern scowl. I huffed and turned to pull the door from its resting place when my eyes locked with Beatrice. My cheeks flushed at the realization that she'd heard my immature outburst, but then she offered me a little thumbs up.

Hmm, maybe I wasn't the only one in the office who wanted to put Grayson Cole in his place.

Once the heavy door was closed, I turned and made my way to one of two matching chairs in front of Grayson's desk. They were mid-century modern in design, which meant they were highly impractical for actual use in an office. The metal was too thin to rest my arms on, so I folded my hands in my lap and stared down at the papers on his desk. Familiar symbols jumped out at me and I knew he was working on a residential project—an impressive one at that.

"Should I be concerned about your appearance?" he asked as his eyes fell to my skinned knees and then back to my face. I guess that was as close as he was going to get to *"Oh, Cammie, are you okay? Please let me tend to your wounds, my love."*

I shook my head and brushed his concerns aside. The bruising and dried blood were the least of my concerns at that moment.

"Well then, I think we should just cut right the chase," he began. "I've taken a look at your resume and I've seen your projects. You're a good designer, much better than most of the people that have come into my office today."

I flicked my gaze up to his face to see if he was being serious. The three lines marring his forehead indicated that he was telling the truth, even if it was a bit painful for him to admit.

"I don't feel like wasting time with the standard interview questions. I've known you for a few years and I think I have a good grasp on what your strengths are, and your weaknesses."

I had to bite my tongue and resist arguing with him. He didn't know a thing about me, and he was delusional if he thought he did.

When I didn't offer a rebuttal, he leaned back in his chair and steepled his fingers beneath his chin.

"Out of all of your studies, which building has stood out as your favorite? And don't limit yourself to just Los Angeles."

I was taken aback by his question, but I didn't have to think long. I'd known the answer for years.

"The Eiffel Tower," I answered with a confident nod.

He arched a dark brow. "Really, Ms. Heart? That answer is almost as trite as listing Frank Lloyd Wright as your favorite architect."

I sat up an inch higher in my chair and narrowed my eyes. "Are you finished, or did you even want to hear my justification?"

The dimple was back and I fidgeted in my seat to keep from staring at it.

"Go ahead," he answered, genuinely curious. "As long as it has nothing to do with it being a symbol of love."

I adjusted my padfolio on my lap and smiled. I loved telling the story. I'd researched the Eiffel Tower endlessly, completely enamored by its rich history.

"During its construction, the Eiffel Tower was considered a colossal waste of money, resources, and space. Most of the French creatives at the time—artists, writers, painters—they all protested its creation. They saw it as a disgusting eyesore of bolted sheet metal."

Grayson nodded, undoubtedly familiar with this part of the story.

"It was never intended to stay past the 1889 Centennial celebrations. It was meant to be demolished shortly after, but when people had a chance to visit it once it was completed, they were taken aback by its immense beauty. Right away, they knew M. Eiffel had created one of the world's greatest structures, and today, it's the world's most visited monument—I don't think that's a coincidence."

His brows rose in interest.

"It's my favorite monument because it serves as a reminder that sometimes it's the architect's job to see things before others can. We're meant to be the visionaries for the communities around us."

Grayson stayed quiet, contemplating my answer for a minute or two before he nodded and leaned forward in his chair.

"You should get this job, Cameron." He stared down at his hands on his desk as he spoke. "You're talented and driven. The only reason I wouldn't give you the position is because it would be a conflict of interest."

I frowned. "A conflict of interest?"

He sighed and adjusted his already perfect tie. It was almost as if he were nervous. *Almost.* "Despite my best efforts to rid myself of it, I've always felt an attraction to you, Cameron. I've ignored that desire mainly because you're too young for me. Now, it's more inappropriate than ever."

My mouth hung open. He couldn't have possibly said those words. My brain must have been processing his speech wrong. Right? *RIGHT?!*

"Excuse me. I'm sorry. *What?"*

He shook his head. "I don't intend on acting on those *feelings.*" He said the word like it was disgusting. "So there's no point in discussing it. I don't have relationships with employees and I won't be having a relationship with you," he said, leaning his elbows onto his desk and effectively cutting off any further discussion. "The job is yours if you want it."

Only Grayson Cole could confidently admit his attraction to someone one moment and then completely move on to work the next.

I thought about asking him to clarify. *How long had he felt an attraction for me? Was it in the past or present? Was he confusing me with someone else?* It seemed unfathomable that a man like him had even noticed me.

And for good reason: let's not forget that he'd completely ignored me up until a few days ago for Christ's sake.

"Cameron?" he asked, clearly irritated with my silence.

Regardless of my desire to press the subject of his feelings, I needed this job. Everything else could wait.

"So, you're hiring me?" I asked.

He narrowed his brows as he considered my question. "It would seem so."

"Yes. Okay," I spoke, surprised by the confidence in my voice. "I accept."

He nodded and stood up, clearly indicating that our 90-second interview was over.

"You'll start in Kelly's old position."

It took me a moment to comprehend his statement. Kelly had been the office's receptionist. She wasn't an architect. *I mean, the woman had just stolen a stapler…and he thought I should replace her?*

"Kelly's position?" I asked, annoyed at how small I felt as he stood over me. I stood from my chair to even the playing field, but he was still a good deal taller than me, despite my high heels.

"There's no better way to learn the company," he countered. "You'll get a feel for how we operate and how we treat our clients."

I leaned forward over the desk so that he'd hear me loud and clear. "I have a master's degree in architecture, Grayson. Hire a monkey to answer your damn phones."

His brows arched in shock at my little outburst and his gaze held mine for three long seconds. Then finally, his hand reached to press the intercom button on his office phone. "Beatrice, hire a temp for Kelly's position and have her here by this afternoon."

I smiled, proud of myself for standing up against him.

"Yes sir," Beatrice spoke through the intercom before Grayson removed his finger from the button, silencing his office once again.

"Go find Kate in HR. She'll give you a new employee packet."

"Thank you, Grayson," I said with a bright smile.

I couldn't believe it. *I was hired.* What my actual position would be? I couldn't tell. At that point, I was just glad I wouldn't be forced to answer phones for nine hours a day.

I gathered my things and checked to make sure nothing had fallen out of my padfolio onto his floor. He stayed behind his desk as I walked toward the door, skipping over the customary handshake. I yearned for him to say something, to go back to describing his feelings about me. I knew that once I left his office, I'd never hear him speak of it again. I'd probably convince myself that I'd made the whole thing up in a week's time.

"And Cameron," he spoke, forcing me to pause as my hand hit the doorknob. I turned my head to look back at him, hope brimming through every pore. "It's not Grayson. It's Mr. Cole. I'm not your friend while you're here."

I bristled at his reprimand. There he was. *The formal prick.* He wanted to put me in my place, but I knew his secret now. You can't just turn attraction off like a light switch. I may have had skinned knees and smudged makeup, but I was the same girl I'd been for the last twenty-two years, which meant—deep down—Grayson was still attracted to me. A small smirk unfolded across my lips as I realized the power that knowledge gave me.

"And what about when I'm not here?" I asked, tilting my head to the side and staring into his blue eyes with more confidence than I'd felt all morning.

He studied me for a moment, unmoving, then he pressed his finger back onto his phone's intercom button. "Beatrice, please escort Ms. Heart out of my office and then get Mitch back on the line."

I laughed at his obvious choice to ignore my question and then turned and saw myself out of his office. *No need for the escort*. Beatrice gave me a knowing glance as I passed by her desk, and I smiled.

As I rode the elevator down to the first floor, I thought of the deal I'd made with myself. I had a very clear outline: concentrate on work, save up, and then fly away to Paris forever. But...maybe, there was room for an amendment to the plan? The end goal would remain the same, but what did it matter if I had a little fun before I left?

After all, I'd just landed my dream job, so it looked like I was onto the newest item on my to-do list:

Grayson Cole.

Chapter Four

I left Cole Designs and took a cab directly to Brooklyn's condo. No passing go. No collecting two hundred dollars. She opened the door for me and stared wide-eyed at my disheveled ensemble before ushering me inside.

"You look like crap-ola," she said, swinging the door open wide. Sisters can get away with saying things like that. Anyone else would have gotten a swift kick to the face.

"I need alcohol. All the alcohol."

Brooklyn laughed and eyed me suspiciously as she pulled down two mugs from a cabinet. "Let's start with coffee. It's not even noon yet."

Could it really still be that early? So much had already happened.

"Okay, but it better be mostly amaretto."

I watched Brooklyn move around her kitchen, admiring her long blonde hair piled up on top of her head in a loose bun. She was usually out and about by this hour, either at the studio, recording an album, or driving around town for meetings. I must have caught her on a slow day because she was still in her pajamas. (Which, by the way, had little crunchy tacos dancing down the pants. The matching shirt said "Jalapeno business". Ha. My sister is witty.)

"Remember when you and your sweet piece of man candy first met?" I asked.

"His name is Jason," she warned over her shoulder. "But sure, what's up?"

"Yeah, Jason, that's what I said. Anyway, I had a morning that kind of tops everything that ever happened between the two of you."

"Wow," she laughed. "That's saying a lot, but y'know whatever."

"No, seriously, you guys are so yesterday," I joked.

Brooklyn narrowed her eyes playfully. "Well. Not really. I mean all of the magazines are still reporting about our—"

"Yeah, we get it. Two pop stars fell in love while riding horses and eating cow pies. Boooring. You guys are like a Lifetime movie where the moral is 'be attractive'."

"You have two seconds to get to the point or I'm kicking you out of my condo," she threatened while pointing toward the door.

"Grab me a donut first," I insisted with a smile that said *"I'm your little sister, please give me donuts."*

She rolled her eyes before turning toward the refrigerator and pulling out some leftover donuts and coffee creamer. I filled up our coffee mugs and took my seat across from her once again so that I could fix my cup: 10 parts cream to one part coffee. (The only way to enjoy a cup, in my opinion.)

I stuffed the powdered donut into my mouth and tried to process where to begin for Brooklyn. I still wasn't sure if I should tell her the truth or keep the interview more private, so instead I shoved another bite of donut into my mouth. The powdered sugar tickled the back of my throat and I started coughing unbearably. Every time I tried to take a breath, it just got worse, and I ended up spitting about 99% of the powdered sugar out onto Brooklyn's kitchen counter.

She flinched back in mock disgust. "Dude! You are an animal. How am I related to you?" But then when I didn't stop coughing, she started to feel bad.

"Are you okay?"

I grabbed for my coffee mug and drank a giant gulp. The liquid finally calmed my cough down enough that I could breath normally again. (*No thanks to Brooklyn pounding on my back like a wild gorilla.*)

Tell her the truth. Just say it. Now.

"Grashsyn admitihehdhe hasfe elingsfhorme," I spoke against the ceramic mug.

Brooklyn laughed and pulled the coffee mug away from my mouth. "Say that again, this time in English."

I stared down at her marble countertops, wishing I could take another bite of donut. *Tell her and then you can eat another bite, you heathen.* "Grayson admitted he's attracted to me." I squeezed my eyes shut. "Or used to be attracted to me. Whatever. I don't know."

Brooklyn gasped with mock surprise before bursting out laughing.

I studied her, trying to get a read. "You knew about it, didn't you? What the hell?"

Had she been holding out on me?

She held up her hands in defense. "No, honestly. I didn't. I just had a hunch."

I wanted to throttle her for details. *How long had she suspected something? Couldn't she tell that I'd been hopelessly pining after him for years?*

She leaned back against the counter and crossed her arms over her chest so that I couldn't see the nosy taco on her shirt anymore.

"I swear it was a recent development on my part. I was going to bring it up with you after your interview, which, I'm guessing went well since you haven't mentioned anything about it yet."

I smiled wide. "Oh, yeah, that. I totally nailed it."

She grinned and came around the kitchen island to wrap me in a hug. "Congrats! I knew you would. When do you start?"

"I have a new hire orientation at 8:00 am Monday morning."

"Perfect," she clapped. "I'm taking you to get a first day outfit, and then you can tell me all about the interview."

• • •

Monday morning I found myself standing in the bathroom on the ground floor of the Sterling Bank Building, studying my appearance in the floor-length mirror. I scanned down my new outfit. The pleated black pants hugged my thighs and accentuated my giraffe-like legs (No, seriously, I'd been teased about it in school. Giraffe Girl. Giraffe legs. Cameraffe. You get the idea.).

My white silk blouse had a black bow that fell against the center of my chest like a soft necklace. My chestnut brown hair fell down my back in artful layers that Brooklyn had helped me blow out earlier that morning.

Would Grayson like this look?

The question popped into my thoughts before I could stop myself, and then an annoying blush creeped up around my cheeks and neck, tinting my skin with a blotchy red glow. *Dammit.*

I fanned my face and took a deep breath, knowing I needed to get a move on if I wanted to be five minutes early for the new hire orientation. I wasn't sure how many of the applicants they'd hired the other day, but I just prayed I wouldn't be the only one.

When the elevator doors swung open on the twentieth floor, I stepped out to join three fresh-faced new hires standing in the lobby. I smiled when I realized that among them was the nice girl, Hannah, who'd chatted with me before my interview the week before.

"You got the job!" she said as she watched me step out of the elevator.

"Yeah," I nodded, choosing not to elaborate any further considering I wasn't sure what job I'd actually landed yet. For all I knew I was part of the junior janitorial squad.

The other two new hires both rattled off their names and I promptly ran through them again in my head so I wouldn't instantly forget them. There was Christoph, a tall boy with a bow tie and clear-framed glasses who seemed to take himself far too seriously. He scanned over my outfit when he shook my hand, nodding agreeably at my designer blouse. The other boy, Nathan, had long brown hair that he swept back into a ponytail. He was the most casually dressed out of all four of us in dark jeans and a wrinkled button-down. All in all, I thought we looked like a cool, well-rounded bunch.

"Is everyone ready?" Beatrice asked, pulling our attention to the doorway behind reception where she stood waiting.

Hannah and I exchanged a quick glance and then I nodded.

"Yup." *Bring on the janitorial duties*.

For the next three hours, the four of us were required to sit in the conference room, filling out tax and insurance forms and listening to the run down on company policies. It was so boring that for one thirty minute stretch I had a vivid day dream about Michael Fassbender, in which he taught me how to drive stick shift and then we bumped uglies in the back of his car.

Finally, after my butt was mostly asleep, Beatrice gave us a tour of the office. The engineering and accounting departments were filled with the standard suspects: picture lots of plaid, wrinkled khakis, and buttons threatening to pop at the seams. The interior design department was a whole different species altogether. The seven women that worked in interiors were each prettier and more polished than the last. The scent of their perfume and hair spray masked the usual office smells as soon as we stepped into their department.

Beatrice lined us up at the front of their small conference area and I felt seven pairs of eyes rake over my outfit and mentally shred it to pieces. *Had this blouse seemed chic earlier? It now felt like I was wrapped in trash I'd pulled out of the back of a Walmart dumpster.* Christoph and Nathan fidgeted awkwardly, unsure of what to do in the face of all that beauty. *Down, boys.*

Just when my self-esteem was at an all time low, one of the interior designers, who had straight front bangs and dainty features, stepped up and smiled.

"Ah, a new batch of architects," she said with a honey-dipped tone as she brushed her strawberry blonde hair over her shoulder. "My name is Serenity." (*No, seriously, that was her name. Like she was some exotic mermaid washed up on land to grace us with her presence.*) "I'll be your point-person for most projects. You won't really need to come into our department much; we work mainly with senior associates."

Serenity paused so she could glance over each of us. Her mouth twisted up into a curious smile when she landed on me.

"Will you be working with us? I wasn't aware we were getting any new interior designers."

My eyes widened and I glanced toward Beatrice for backup. She shook her head.

"Cammie is a new associate designer in the architecture department," Beatrice clarified, for both Serenity and me.

Serenity's smile fell. "Oh, well then. Do you need anything else?" she asked.

For one short moment, they'd wanted to accept me into their weird gynocracy. When Beatrice shook her head again, the glamazon designers smiled smugly and then at once, they turned and went back to work. Clearly they were done discussing their jobs with us.

"They thought you were one of them," Hannah whispered with a hint of amusement as we turned to leave.

I bristled at the thought. I'd rather work with ten burly construction workers then spend my days in a room with seven beautiful women. I'd have a nervous breakdown from the scrutiny and the estrogen after five minutes. *Could you even imagine?*

After the interior design department, Beatrice led us through a few other sections of the office, and then we were on our way back to the main room. We passed by Grayson's office and I glanced inside, hoping to get a quick peek of him at work. I shouldn't have looked. Serenity was sitting on the edge of his desk with a mischievous smile coating her red lips. *Of course... how very cliché of him to like the exotic mermaid chick.* I rolled my eyes and looked away before Grayson had a chance to glance up and find me spying on him.

When we made it back to the conference room, I took a seat next to Hannah and replaced the image of Grayson and Serenity with the image of a dozen strawberry sprinkled donuts. *There, much better.*

"So have you figured out where you're going to live yet?" Hannah asked.

I glanced over. "I hadn't really thought about it," I admitted. It was the truth: I'd slept at Brooklyn's condo the night before, but I only had four days left before I had to move out of my dorm.

"Yeah, same here," she nodded.

Then, it clicked. She was trying to introduce the subject of us being roommates without looking too desperate.

"I know it's kind of weird and you hardly know me," I began, "but we'll both be going to the same place every morning…"

She gave me a weird look. "I'm sorry—are you hitting on me? I'm not a lesbian."

What? *What?*

"Uhh, neither am I. Why would you think that? I thought you were trying to ask me to be your roommate a second ago."

Hannah's eyes widened. "Oh, right. Okay, yeah. Sure, I'll be your roommate. But uh, we're not sharing a room."

I was pretty sure she still thought I was a lesbian. Oh well, it's not like I had other roommate options. I didn't want to stay with Brooklyn and paying for my own place would eat into my Paris budget.

• • •

Later that night I chatted on the phone with Brooklyn while I worked on packing up my dorm room.

"Where should we go for my celebratory dinner this weekend? I want somewhere good. Don't hold out on me, sis," I joked as I shoved another sweater into a cardboard box, thus solving the age-old question: How much crap can Cammie stuff into a single box? Answer: a lot. I was halfway done packing up my tiny dorm room, throwing random articles of clothing into bags and boxes along with various trinkets I'd collected over my college career.

"I'm not sure, but I got Grayson to agree to come out with us," Brooklyn replied.

"You did what?!" I asked, almost dropping my phone to the floor mid-shout. "Why would you do that?"

"Because, Cammie, we're celebrating your new job and he's the reason you have the new job in the first place. He hired you! What's with the dramatic response? I thought it'd be good for you to see him outside of work, y'know, have a chance to talk to him one-on-one."

I groaned.

"Do I want to know how you convinced him?" I asked, propping the phone between my shoulder and my head so that I could fold my favorite Harry Potter sweater. It had a giant "H" knit onto the front and it was supposed to be a replica of the one Mrs. Weasley gave Harry his first year at Hogwarts. It served as a barometer for friend-making: if you got the reference, we could be besties.

"I just asked him nicely, said I'd pick him up, and threatened to end our friendship if he said no. There might have also been a Snapchat of knives. Whatever. I swear his automatic response to anything in life is no, so I just had to convince him to say yes this time."

"Oh God, Brooklyn. You're insane. Listen, I gotta go. Hannah and I are apartment searching tomorrow after work and I've got to finish packing up my dorm."

Brooklyn hummed across the line. "Who is this Hannah? Can you even trust her? You just met her."

"Gah Brook you're such a mom. I wish you and Jason would spawn some baby musicians already so you'd have someone else to worry about all the time."

"Okay...but still, why don't you just move in with me?"

I rolled my eyes. "Two reasons. One, you only have one bedroom and I'm not sleeping between you and Jason. Two, I can't bring home guys to your condo. That's just gross." I left out the third reason: the need to separate my life from hers, but I knew she wouldn't take that answer well.

"Oh! So you're planning on bringing guys home all the time?"

I shrugged, though she couldn't see it. "Not plural. Just one guy."

"I hope you know what you're doing," she replied.

I had no clue.

We said our goodbyes and confirmed dinner for Friday. I dropped my phone onto my nightstand and propped my hands on my hips, wondering how I'd find the time to pack, search for a new apartment, impress my new coworkers, *and* figure out how to seduce Grayson...all in four days.

Chapter Five

Amount saved for Paris: $122
Items I have: a printed travel checklist of all the things I needed to get. *Hey, that counts as being productive.*
Items I need: everything on my printed travel checklist.
French phrases that I know: Bonjour, mon nom est Cammie. Je suis américain et votre accent est sexy… which I think translates into "Hello, my name is Cammie. I'm American and your accent is sexy."

Tuesday morning, I followed Beatrice to my assigned desk for my first real day of work. I carried a small box with me filled with notebooks, my favorite drafting pencil, and a photo of Brooklyn and I when we were kids. It was just enough personalization to ensure that I'd remember which of the array of nearly identical desks was mine.

We passed through the center of the main room and arrived at a cluster of four rectangular desks closest to the back wall of offices. The corner desk was empty and waiting for me. As I neared the desk grouping, I realized that if I leaned back in my chair, I'd have a clear view into Grayson's office, which also meant, that at any given time, he'd have a clear view of me.

"This will be your team, Cammie," Beatrice said with a distracted smile before wandering off and leaving me with my new tablemates. The man sitting across from my new spot smiled up at me. His wild red beard was so outgrown that it nearly covered his neck.

He shot his hand out and smiled wider.

"I'm Peter, the person you'll be staring at for the foreseeable future." His tone was playful and I found myself smiling for the first time since walking into the office that morning.

Sitting next to Peter, diagonal from my desk, was a rail thin man with a terrible comb over—most of his balding head was visible through his stringy black hair. His mustard yellow shirt assaulted my eyes and he didn't even bother glancing up from his work.

"That's Mark," Peter filled in with an apologetic smile.

I nodded and turned my gaze to the final man, and then I paled. It was the rude man from other morning, the one who'd bumped into me on the sidewalk and then kept right on walking as I crawled around to pick up my spilled papers. *What were the odds?*

When he turned to look up at me, I expected some sign of recognition, but instead I was on the receiving end of a bored glance.

"I'm Alan, the senior associate assigned to you. I supervise you, Peter, and Mark. I don't exactly have time to train you, but you have an education, so I expect you to keep up. We're finishing up the final stages of a residential project and then we'll begin designs for a competition the firm will be entering in a few weeks."

After saying his name, he'd turned back to flip through papers on his desk, licking his thumb and using it to pry the papers away from one another.

"What'd you say your name was?" he asked, opening a drawer on his desk and pulling out a straight edge.

"Cammie," I answered, glancing over to Peter to see what he thought of Alan. He shrugged and gave me a half frown.

"Candy, I need you to stop hovering over my desk. Either take your seat or move somewhere else," Alan snapped at me.

I didn't even think. I turned back and corrected him. "My name is Cammie. Not Candy."

Without a word, he picked up his phone and dialed out, continuing to flip through papers.

How could someone be so rude?

"Cammie, how about I show you where the coffeemaker is?" Peter asked, smoothing a hand over his red beard.

He tilted his head toward the kitchen and stood and I followed after him. It's not like I had a choice. I could have either gone with Peter to the kitchen or stared at Mark's comb over while Alan shot me death glares.

In the kitchen, Peter turned on the company's industrial-sized coffeemaker and then he held up two different flavor pouches. "Do you prefer 'French Vanilla' or 'My New Boss Is a Giant Asshole'?"

His joke caught me so off guard that I couldn't contain my laughter. Peter smiled and held up the two flavors. "Just kidding, French Vanilla is really your only choice. I took the last of the 'Donut Shop' flavor earlier this week."

"Thanks. French Vanilla is fine."

He nodded and dropped the pouch in before pressing start.

In that moment I decided Peter was someone I could trust. Also, I just really wanted to tell someone about my incident with Alan.

"I've actually kind of met Alan before. The other day, before my interview, Alan bumped into me down on the sidewalk and I fell and ripped my tights. I had to crawl around to pick up all of my stuff, all while he yelled at me for being in the way. But I don't even think he recognized me this morning."

Peter didn't seem surprised by my confession.

"When I started here last year, Mark wouldn't talk to me and Alan made me nearly cry every day." He paused and lowered his voice for the next part. "A lot of us think he killed a temp once."

"What?! Are you serious?" I asked.

"Well, not exactly. I think the guy just found permanent work elsewhere. He sent me a LinkedIn request last week. The point is, at the time it seemed equally plausible that Alan could have offed him.

"So did it get better?" I asked, just as the machine finished sputtering out the last of my coffee.

"I hate to say it, but not really," Peter said with a sad smile. "The work is great, but Mark still rarely speaks. I'm pretty sure he has some kind of social anxiety disorder or something. And Alan is, well...it's no mistake that his name is so close to "anal". He's meticulous, and rude. So, I just keep my head down and do my work."

I nodded. "Well, now I'm here, so you don't have to keep your head down," I said with a smile. Peter wasn't the type of guy I usually found myself around. His beard was awesome, but probably warned most people away from him. He was tall and had the build of a rugby player, but as I followed him back to our desks, I found myself relieved to have him at my desk cluster on my first day.

However, as soon as we arrived back at our seats, my optimism was squashed.

"First rule, Candy," Alan began, "When you get up and make yourself a cup of coffee, you bring me back a cup as well."

Peter coughed under his breath and I tried to fight back the urge to dump my coffee out onto Alan's hideous green shirt.

Dump it on him. Do it. Do it.

I sighed and shoved down my inner devil. There'd be plenty of time to dump coffee on Alan.

"Right. Okay. I'll get right on that."

And I did. I made him a cup of coffee with grounds I found in the trash, spit in it, and then gave it back to him with the sweetest smile I could muster. I might have to endure him for the next few months, but I would not take his bullshit lying down.

• • •

Alan kept me busy with mundane tasks until lunchtime arrived, at which point he shoved back from his desk and announced he'd be back in twenty minutes. We were expected to be back at our desks when he returned.

"I guess that rules out going somewhere for lunch," I said, glancing toward Peter.

He frowned. "Ah, yeah. I've learned to just bring my lunch. I guess you'll know for tomorrow. Do you want to share mine?"

I smiled and shook my head. "Nah, you go eat. I'm going to try and find my friend."

I tried to find Hannah to see if she needed something to eat as well, but she'd headed out with the rest of her table-mates. Apparently, their senior associate liked to get to know his new team members by treating everyone to lunch on the first day. *How was that for fair?*

Cursing my luck, I ran down to the bottom floor of the building, trying to recall whether or not there was a cafe. When I arrived, I found a room full of vending machines. *Awesome.* I unzipped my coin purse and retrieved enough change to purchase a bag of Cheez-Its and a Nature Valley bar. *That'd keep me full for all of...thirty minutes.*

By the time I made it back up to the office, my lunch break was already half way over. I was prepared to just eat at my desk, but then I noticed that for the first time all day, Grayson's door was open.

I paused a few feet from my desk and leaned back to peer through the slim opening. Grayson was standing in front of his desk talking to a woman. I narrowed my eyes, studying the back of her slender frame, which she'd stuffed into a barely-there bandage dress. She wasn't someone I recognized from our tour through the office, but I couldn't see her face so there was no way to be sure.

"Are you okay?" Peter asked from his desk, clearly confused about my snooping.

I shook my head clear of jealous thoughts and proceeded to my desk.

"Oh, yeah, I'm fine, just finding my way around," I said, dropping my vending machine snacks onto my leftover work from the morning. I wasn't sure if Peter was the type to question my interest in Grayson, so I tried to seem uninterested in my new discovery as I tore through my Cheez-Its.

Who the hell is that woman?

I lasted all of two seconds eating at my desk before my curiosity won out. I had to know who the mystery woman was and I knew exactly how I could find out: Beatrice. She was flipping through a magazine at her desk, quietly taking bites of a salad. *Beatrice was the answer.* She'd know who the woman in his office was, and she'd know to keep quiet about my snooping. *It was girl code 101.*

I dropped my snacks and stood so I could casually stroll over to her desk.

"Hi Beatrice, how's your day going?" I asked with a wide smile.

She glanced up at me with a touch of curiosity.

"Pretty good. What about you?" she asked, flipping past another page of her magazine, this time landing on the "Look at celebrities…they're just like us" section. I caught a glimpse of Brooklyn and Jason taking up nearly half of the page with a picture of them walking on a hike and bike trail. He was pulling a leaf out of her hair, which was apparently newsworthy.

Who was I kidding? I needed to cut to the chase.

"Is Grayson in a meeting right now? I was going to ask him something."

"No, actually," Beatrice replied. "He's with a lunch date."

My hand instinctively tightened on the edge of her desk. *A date?* During a workday? Who does that? As if on cue, I heard a giggle from the inside of Grayson's office. I glanced over to see his shadow loom in the doorway and then his figure cut into view. His mouth tipped into a frown when he saw me standing there but he made no attempt to talk to me. Our eyes met as he reached for the door handle and it wasn't until he slammed it in my face that I forced myself to look away.

"Does he do that often?" I asked, trying to get the image of how incredibly hot he'd just looked out of my head. *Newsflash: he's not looking hot for you. He's on a DATE!*

Beatrice tapped her finger on the magazine as she thought over my question. "Maybe once every few months. Not really that often. And to be honest, the girl he has in there now is a total bitch. Every time she calls to talk to him, she speaks to me like I'm the help until I connect her through."

"Why doesn't he just give her his direct line?" I asked.

Beatrice laughed. "He never gives anyone his direct line."

I nodded. *Good.* Maybe my plan wasn't completely spoiled after all. The girl couldn't mean that much to him if he didn't even give her his extension. I decided she was merely a distraction, but then I heard another one of her giggles and my thin layer of resolve began to crack.

Oh, gross. Who even giggles these days?

I whipped around, grabbed the processed snacks from my desk, and headed to the employee kitchen. There's no way I'd be able to finish my lunch with the sound of their annoying lunch date.

I had two choices: I could give up my little crush on Grayson, just move on, and forget about the idea of being with him, OR I could make sure that I was dressed to kill during our dinner on Friday and put up a real fight.

I liked option two far more. After all, I wasn't a quitter.

Still, I couldn't get over what I'd just seen. It was so smug of him to rub his lunch date right in my face. I decided to give Brooklyn a call so I could vent, but I got her voicemail instead, so I left a heated message, jumping right to the point.

"Why does Grayson have to be so infuriating? He's so smug, like he knows he's torturing me—"

"Sweetie, you do realize you're speaking out loud, right?"

My hand flew to my mouth when I heard someone speak behind me. I hadn't seen anyone when I first walked in, but sure enough, when I turned around slowly, there was a tall blonde woman standing near the back counter. I tried to think if I'd said anything incriminating in the last thirty seconds. *Yes. Literally everything you'd said was incriminating.*

When the woman's light blue eyes met mine, she smiled and continued on with the task she'd been doing while I was leaving Brooklyn a message. She was taking the contents from a box of snacks and stuffing them into a basket inside one of the kitchen's cabinets. There were more grocery bags littering the floor near her feet, and I assumed there was more food inside of those as well.

I narrowed my eyes, trying to figure out who she was. She wasn't dressed in business attire. Instead, she had on a pale pink tracksuit, the kind that J-Lo used to wear a few years back.

"You don't have to stop venting on my account. I'm a pretty good listener and I'd probably agree with you," she said, offering me a warm smile.

"Oh," I said, peering down at my phone and wondering if I should take her up on her offer. Leaving Brooklyn a message hadn't cured my annoyance, so I shrugged and decided to give it go.

"I just really hate my boss…and my boss' boss," I said. Maybe she was a narc, but she'd already heard me shit talking. *What did it matter now?*

I tore into my Cheez-Its while she mulled over my out burst.

"I'll tell you what, Grayson can be a real handful. He was a tough kid to raise and I know he's hard on you employees," she said as she kept right on emptying chips bags into the basket.

I squinted as I worked out her statement. *A tough kid to raise?*

"His dad was in the army. Does he tell you guys that?" she asked, spinning around to look at me. "I suppose not. He's pretty private."

"I'm sorry but, who are you?" I asked with a timid smile.

She threw her head back and laughed before stepping over toward me with her hand stretched out. "I'm Emma Cole, Grayson's mom."

Motherfucktitsfuckass. I am officially a royal idiot.

• • •

Grayson's mom ended up being quite the chatterbox. Even though she should have hated me for what I'd said about her son, we sat in the break room for the rest of my lunch break as she told me bits and pieces of Grayson's childhood.

Apparently, his father was a military man and he was very strict on Grayson and his brother while they were growing up. Grayson was constantly reminded that his actions reflected on his father, so he was expected to stay in line. It was the little things that let Grayson know his father was in charge. Every night at 7:00 pm, dinner was on the table. His father sat at the head of the table, Grayson sat to his right, his brother, Jackson, sat to his left, and his mother sat at the opposite end, across from his father. For eighteen years, save for holidays or a random trip to a restaurant, they ate dinner this way.

Curfew was at 10:00 pm throughout high school, and the one time Grayson pulled in at 10:05, his father had been standing inside the door, ready and waiting to pass down a punishment he saw fit. While no one could argue that he was a stern man, Grayson saw how well he ran his family and how well he operated as an engineer in the army. It was those principles that his father had instilled in him that allowed Grayson to start and run a company the way he had at such a young age.

"Like father, like son," I quipped as I stood to toss my empty bags into the trashcan in the corner of the break room.

"Exactly," his mom agreed.

"Do you come to the office often?" I asked.

She smiled. "Every now and then. Grayson hates that I come here, but if I don't stock these cabinets, no one will."

"Well, I appreciate it," I said. "It looks like I'll be eating my lunch in here from now on."

She smiled and I turned toward the door knowing I was in danger of going over my allotted lunchtime, but before I could leave the kitchen, Mrs. Cole spoke up again.

"Cammie, could I ask you to do a favor for me?"

I paused and turned to look back at her.

"Could you keep an eye on Grayson? Make sure he's taking care of himself, not working until all hours of the night, you know?"

"Mrs. Cole, I don't think Grayson would like me keeping tabs on him. He seems like a pretty independent guy."

She held my gaze as her mouth hitched into a knowing smile. "He does seem that way, but I assure you, Grayson is no different than any man. He needs someone to watch out for him and I'm afraid the women he keeps around don't do a good enough job."

I contemplated her request. I'd be keeping tabs on Grayson whether or not she asked me to. Was there any harm in reporting back to her if he was staying late? I didn't think so.

"I promise that I'll watch out for your son as much as he lets me."

She smiled. "Good."

Chapter Six

Later that afternoon, Grayson announced a company-wide meeting. With mild groans, everyone stopped their work and filtered toward the conference room. By the time I walked through the door there was standing room only. I pressed against the far wall, with Hannah wedged in front of me. Her hair smelled like garlic from her lunch and my stomach grumbled with the reminder that Cheez-Its were *not* enough to tide me over until dinner.

"Listen up," Grayson's voice boomed from the front of the conference room. Everyone paused their conversations and the noise level slowly trickled down to nothing. I shifted in between Hannah and the person beside her so that I could get a clear view of Grayson. *Yup, hot as ever.*

When all eyes were on him, he continued, "We're here to announce the mentor-mentee assignments that will be in effect for the next month or two. Each senior team leader will take on an associate architect. New staff will shadow the team leader, follow them to job sites, and learn how we run our business here at Cole Designs."

The groans from the front of the room indicated that the senior designers were less than enthused about taking on a bunch of newbies. I just crossed my fingers that I didn't end up with Alan. I highly doubted he'd be willing to teach me the lay of the land. In fact, he'd probably leave me at the job site and call it a "learning experience".

Grayson stepped to the side so that Beatrice could have the floor. I watched him as Beatrice started calling out names, pairing up the mentors with mentees. He kept his eyes on Beatrice, never wavering even though I practically begged him to glance in my direction. His hair was still perfect, and his suit looked just as pristine as it had that morning. *So maybe his lunch date hadn't included a happy ending?*

When Beatrice called Alan's name, I held my breath and crossed my fingers behind my back. *Please don't be me. Please don't be me.*

"Hannah Montgomery," Beatrice said. I cringed for her. I wouldn't wish Alan on my worst enemy, least of all my new roommate.

"Cammie Heart," Beatrice spoke, glancing up to try to find me in the crowd. I raised my hand behind Hannah and her eyes flew in my direction. "You'll be paired with Eli."

Eli stood up near the front of the room and I shifted out from behind Hannah to get a good look. OH, HELL YES. Eli looked to be one of the youngest senior associates. He was handsome, with a bright smile and cropped blonde hair that made him look angelic. He'd forgone a suit jacket in favor of rolling his shirt sleeves up to his elbows. The effect made him far less intimidating than Grayson, who was standing a few feet away with his arms crossed, a deadly look permeating his features.

"Actually, Cammie will be with me," Grayson spoke up, cutting Beatrice off as she continued reading from the list.

Whispers broke out immediately and my face flamed. *What the hell was he doing?*

"Um, but you don't usually..." Beatrice began to dispute his outburst, but Grayson held up his hand.

"It's done. Eli is working on the Whitaker Street project and I can't afford any more delays."

My bullshit meter was reading red hot.

After all of the names were called, there was another twenty minutes of humdrum information, which I completely ignored in favor of breaking down Grayson's motives for taking over Eli's role as my mentor. (I couldn't come up with a single one that wasn't part of a freaky fantasy.)

Finally, Grayson announced the end of the meeting. Everyone trailed out, begrudgingly heading back to their work stations. A few pairs of mentor-mentee pairs stopped for a moment to meet formally. Alan didn't even blink in Hannah's direction as he stomped back over to his desk.

"Wow. How did I get lucky enough to land that asshole?" Hannah whispered as we headed out of the conference room.

"Yeah, I was crossing my fingers that neither one of us would get him."

She peered over at me from beneath her lashes. "Well it must've worked, because you ended up with the best option of them all."

We both turned to watch Grayson head back into his office. As I watched him move in his suit, I decided that every man over the age of twenty-one should have to wear tailored pants. The fabric worked wonders for his already rockin' physique.

"Seriously, I can't believe he's your mentor," she said.

"Yeah, I'm not sure how that happened," I admitted, still staring at his closed door.

"Who cares? Figure out if he's single for me. I saw him eating lunch with some girl, but that could have been anything," Hannah said, tilting her head to get a better look at him. "I think he dates around a lot, and he's really only a few years older than me."

I bit down hard on the inside of my mouth to keep from telling her to back off. I wanted to hate her for taking an interest in him, but it's not like I could blame her. Any woman with eyes would do the same.

"That probably won't come up during my training," I pointed out, just as Hannah's table-mates called out for her to join them.

"Whatever. Just ask him. You can mention that you're asking for a friend or something if you're too nervous."

A friend. *Were we friends?* We were roommates, so I guess that made us friends by default?

"Oh, and let's order some takeout later. Nothing like wonton soup to christen our new apartment!" she said, waggling her eyebrows playfully as she backed up toward her desk.

I nodded, letting my gaze slide back to Grayson's door. If I wanted to know why he'd stepped in to be my mentor, why couldn't I just ask him? Beatrice wasn't back at her post yet. He was in his office alone and he'd left the door ajar. Everyone was too busy getting back to their desks to notice me, and even if they did see us talking, they'd just assume it was about him being my mentor, which, technically, it was.

With that thought, I walked directly to Grayson's office, trying to contain my private smile. When I approached his door, I saw him sitting behind his desk, bent over his work and completely unaware of my presence. I tapped my knuckles on the open door, twice. It was a friendly kind of greeting, but when his steely gaze shifted from his work up to me, he didn't appear to want a friendly conversation. No, he clearly would have preferred no conversation whatsoever. I ignored the warning signs and proceeded as planned.

"Looks like you'll be my mentor then," I said with a smile as I took a step into his office. He was never going to invite me in, so either I had to take the initiative or I'd just be stuck in the doorway wishing I was brave enough to enter the dragon's lair.

He adjusted his tie and slid his hand down the material before finally speaking. "We'll start tomorrow. There's a job site I'd like you to see and it's just a few blocks away from here."

Well that was certainly faster than I'd expected.

"Sounds good," I said, trying to think of something else to say that would keep me in his office longer. "Brooklyn told me you were coming to dinner with us."

His left brow perked up. "Did she?"

I nodded and took another hesitant step toward his desk. His eyes shifted down to my feet; he knew what I was doing.

"Yes. She said she had to coerce you."

He leaned back in his chair, running his finger along the edge of his desk. "I'm a busy guy, Cameron. I don't get out too often."

I crossed my arms and settled my weight onto my left leg. "But you'll come out for me?"

He sighed and pointed to the door. "You realize that no one else comes into my office without an invitation. Yet you just wander in here like there's a revolving door with your name on it."

I glanced back at his door, standing wide open. It beckoned me forward, but I imagined that to everyone else, there was a giant red "X" warning them away.

"I like it in here," I admitted, scanning the decor around the room. It was masculine with dark forest green wallpaper and built-in wooden bookcases spanning from floor to ceiling along an entire wall. "Besides, we have a history together."

"I need to get back to my work," he said, his tone gentle enough that I could have probably pulled another five minutes out of our encounter, but I didn't want to annoy him, so I started back up toward the door.

"Tomorrow then," I said.

His blue eyes locked onto my face and he nodded. "Tomorrow. Now shut the door."

"Wait." *Do it, ask him. Do it.* "How was lunch?"

"Cameron." His voice was tired and annoyed. "Get out of my office."

"She was pretty," I said, pushing him even further out of his happy mood.

He narrowed his eyes.

"Yes and we had sex directly where you're standing," he spoke, his words like venomous talons. "Is that what you wanted to know?"

He didn't have to ask me to leave again after that. I turned without a word and slammed his office door shut behind me. The hinges rattled and Beatrice gave me a curious glance as I passed by her desk.

"Nice of you to join us," Alan snapped as I took my seat.

I didn't bother offering an apology for my absence. For all he knew, Grayson was giving me an assignment as my mentor, but my silence must have pissed him off even more.

"Since you have time to bat your eyes at the CEO, I suppose you can stay late and finish drafting those bathrooms I need you to have done by tomorrow," Alan continued with a harsh tone.

Stay late?

Peter shot me an apologetic smile.

I wanted to argue, but I wouldn't give Alan the satisfaction of getting a rise out of me.

"Sounds great," I said with false enthusiasm. The smile felt sour on my face.

Alan grunted and went back to work.

At 5:00 pm, the office started to empty as one by one employees picked up their bags and briefcases and headed for the elevators. I, on the other hand, stayed in my seat, drafting light fixtures for the bathrooms of some high-rise condominium. My hunger was gnawing away at me, but I didn't want to have to ask Alan if I could grab dinner, so I stayed put. My first day on the job had taught me three things: Grayson was an arrogant bastard, Alan was a suckwad, and I needed to shove snacks into every free space around my desk if I had any hope of surviving at Cole Designs.

At 6:00 pm, Grayson left his office with his phone pressed to his ear. Goosebumps bloomed on the back of my neck as he walked behind my desk en route the elevators.

Would he stop and talk to me? I concentrated on the drafting pencil in my hand and pined to listen to the conversation he was having. Had the room been full, I wouldn't have been able to hear him, but we were practically alone—save for Alan—so I could hear every word crystal clear.

"I'm leaving now," he said. "I'll have my car pick you up at your apartment. Don't bother dressing up, we aren't leaving my place tonight."

His words were acid and I had to fight the urge to throw my pencil at the back of his head. There's no way that Grayson was that open with his relationships. He was putting on a show for me. *Right*? He wanted me to know he was unavailable. *Extremely unavailable*. Little did he know, I didn't want him to be *easy* and *available*. I wanted prey.

"You have another twenty of those bathrooms to draft before you leave tonight," Alan reminded me, effectively emptying a bucket of ice water over my head. I inwardly groaned. Alan really knew how to ruin a moment with his drab orders and terrible breath.

Soon, Alan and I were the only two employees left in the office and I knew that in any other situation, I'd have thought he'd asked me to stay late so he could hit on me or something. Maybe another man would have, but not Alan. I had a feeling he was asexual. Like a cactus. Although, to be honest, I was so hungry that if he'd told me I could go home if I let him touch my boob or something, I'd have whipped it out. *I was really hungry and I have great boobs, so whatever*. But this wasn't a soap opera and he was probably not a sex offender, so I had to keep working.

At 7:30 pm, determined to stick it out as long as Alan wanted me to, I texted Brooklyn pleading for some sort of dinner. Alan was in the bathroom, so I figured I had a few minutes to beg for food. Besides, I was in danger of keeling over if I didn't get something to eat soon.

> **Cammie**: SOS. Please send food. Dick boss is making me stay late.
>
> **Brooklyn**: Grayson is making you stay this late on your first day? I'm calling him.
>
> **Cammie**: NO! It's this middle management guy. I'm trying to prove that I can handle the workload.
>
> **Brooklyn**: Nomz on the way.
>
> **Cammie**: THANK YOU! Also, nobody says nomz anymore.

After I sent her a final text, I saw that Hannah had texted me a few minutes earlier as well.

> **Hannah**: Are you going to be home soon? I just ordered pizza.
>
> **Cammie**: No, eat it without me. Alan is making me stay late. :(
>
> **Hannah**: Okay. Whatever. Ask Grayson if he's single!

I deleted her second text immediately. *Whoops, slippery fingers, I guess.*

"I don't think we're paying you to text," Alan said from behind me, scaring the crap out of me.

I nearly tossed my phone at him in an attempt to protect myself.

He rolled his eyes and took his seat beside me once again. I was going to explain that I was just asking my sister for food, like any normal human would, when Alan's office phone rang. The shrill sound ricocheted around the quiet office.

He picked it up after the second ring with a sharp, "Hello."

I couldn't hear the other end of the conversation, but I prayed it wasn't a client needing something done tonight. *How late could he actually make me stay?*

"No. No—we were just leaving." Alan spoke with an edge of fear laced in his voice.

My pencil paused mid-line.

"We wouldn't have stayed later—"

His sentence was cut off and then the sound of dead air replaced the low murmurs from the other end. Alan stood, his chair scraping against the cement floors.

"It's time to go. Grab your things so I can lock up."

He was pissed, more so than he'd been all day.

I grabbed my things and then Alan and I rode the elevator down to the ground floor in silence. The whole time, I imagined what Grayson was doing with the woman he'd been on the phone with when he'd left. *Was it the same woman he'd been with in his office during lunch or was I competing against multiple women?*

I needed to step up my game. Maybe Brooklyn had a pushup bra I could steal. Yeah, that was a good idea.

Step one: blind him with my boobs.

Chapter Seven

I was pouring myself a cup of orange juice Wednesday morning when Hannah stepped into our kitchen. We'd ended up finding a place to rent just a few blocks over from the Sterling Bank Building. It was small, with '70s style shag carpet and appliances that hadn't been used since the Dark Ages, but we could walk to work and the neighborhood was full of hip bars and coffee shops. I just had to survive the potential asbestos in the walls for three months and then I'd be eating crepes in Paris.

"Morning," I said, tipping my cup to her in a little salute before taking a long sip. We'd lived together for a few days but I'd hardly seen her around the apartment; it seemed we weren't on similar schedules. I functioned as a normal human being, while she functioned like some sort of bat.

She grunted and made her way to our coffeemaker. I watched her pour a cup, then she spun around to face me, and her mouth dropped.

"That dress is kind of provocative for work, don't you think?" Hannah asked as her gaze dragged down my outfit.

I glanced down. Sure, the dress was an inch or two shorter than I normally would have picked, but was it really that bad? I'd taken a selfie earlier in my bedroom mirror and sent it to Brooklyn. She'd replied within five seconds with, "That dress was made for you!" Surely Brooklyn would have told me if it was too risqué for work.

"Do you think I should change?" I asked, glancing back up and noticing Hannah's disheveled appearance for the first time. She'd gone out on the town after finishing her pizza the night before and I'd heard her stroll in a little after 3:00 am. The bags under her eyes were showing the effects of her lack of sleep. Still, I was envious of her social life. I'd been too tired after work to do anything but watch Bravo. *Okay, who am I kidding? Even if I wasn't tired, I would have stayed in and watched Bravo. I do have priorities, and they involve reality TV.*

She shrugged. "It's fine. Whatever, let's go."

I frowned and finished off my orange juice, feeling half as confident in my appearance as I had before she'd stepped into the kitchen. I'd put the dress on that morning for Grayson, in a childish attempt to win his attention for the day. He wouldn't confess his love for me because I was wearing a short dress, but maybe he'd let his gaze linger on me for a moment longer than usual. That's all I needed: a chink in the armor.

• • •

"Cameron, may I speak with you for a moment?" Grayson asked as I strolled in front of his door on my way to use the bathroom.

I paused mid-stride and turned toward his office. He was staring pointedly at the hem of my dress and then he dragged his gaze down my bare legs.

"Come in and shut the door."

My stomach flip-flopped at the request. *Oh my god, yes. That was easy. He's going to ask for my maidenly hand in marriage.* I swallowed once, feeling anticipation kick my heart into overdrive.

I'd been hoping for a longing gaze, but an invitation to step into his office with the door closed was much, much better.

Once the heavy door fell closed, Grayson tossed his pen onto some papers and stood, rounding his desk and oozing authority with every step. He crossed his arms and rolled his shoulders back so that his posture was pin straight. I found myself copying him, trying to increase my height in an attempt to match his. I really wished he wasn't wearing a black suit. I could have handled anything better than that black suit.

"Are you familiar with this office's dress code, Ms. Heart?" he asked with narrowed eyes.

I laughed, just once, before I pressed my lips closed. If he wanted to be formal, we could be formal. The cold air conditioning vent I was standing beneath blew chilled air over my bare arms and legs and goosebumps blossomed across my skin. I told myself it was from the temperature and not from Grayson's watchful eyes.

He was still waiting for my reply.

"I'm not sure. Why don't you refresh my memory?" I said with a suggestive tone.

He uncrossed his arms and reached back to press the intercom button. "Beatrice could you see to it that Ms.

Heart gets a new employee handbook. Preferably one with the dress code section printed in bold."

I laughed again, surprised that he'd go through the trouble to alert Beatrice of the situation.

"Right away, sir," Beatrice answered before Grayson lifted his finger from the intercom button, returning the room to silence.

"What time do we leave for the construction site?" I asked.

He shook his head and moved back to his seat, overly eager to put distance between us.

"We aren't going today. Not while you're dressed like that. Wear pants tomorrow and arrive thirty minutes early. We'll go before everyone arrives."

I narrowed my eyes. He was acting like I was wearing lingerie. The dress was a *tad* too short, but this was LA: normal dress code rules didn't apply. Just that morning I'd seen a woman walking her Chihuahua in a bikini top, leggings, and Uggs. *I mean, c'mon.*

When I remained standing on the same patch of distressed concrete, Grayson reclined back in his chair.

"You have work to do," he said, clearly indicating that I should see myself out. "Unless, of course, you'd like to stay late again."

He was dismissing me as quickly as he'd beckoned me. I was hoping for some kind of real conversation, but he'd done nothing but make me feel like an unruly teenager. I turned back toward the door, scrambling for some sort of parting comment. Just as my hand touched the door handle, I smiled slowly, realizing that I had just as much power as he did. I just had to know how to use it. I turned my head and shot him a devious smirk.

"I picked out this dress for you."

He didn't look up at me, but his pen stopped moving and his eyes concentrated on the same spot on his desk.

"So next time you have a lunch date or a girl waiting for you at your apartment, just know that this is my way of begging you to give us both what we want."

The second I finished speaking, Grayson held up his hand with his finger pointed straight at the door. His blue eyes were as sharp as ice. The lines of his jaw muscles shifted beneath his skin. He was *pissed*.

"Get out of my office, Cameron."

He bit out each word like he was in physical pain. I swiveled around and pulled the door open, then let it fall shut after me with a heavy thud. The windows of his office shook in their frames and a few of the architects near the back wall glanced up at me with curious expressions. I ignored their stares and headed back toward my desk with annoyance clouding my vision.

"So nice of you to join us," Alan said as soon as I took my seat. "You're behind on your work, and since you've already been to the kitchen more times than I can count, I don't think you need a lunch break."

I bit down hard on my lower lip and kept my eyes pinned on my work.

"Actually Alan, I've already finished the work you assigned me this morning and I started on my tasks for this afternoon about an hour ago," I said with a honey-dipped tone. "But, is there something else you'd like me to start on?"

He could make me work through lunch—Grayson had a way of completely stealing my appetite anyway—but I was *not* going let Alan think I wasn't taking this job seriously.

Later that afternoon, Beatrice dropped an employee handbook onto my desk with a meek smile. When I flipped it open, the dress code section was highlighted in bright yellow. Peter snickered from his desk, but thankfully Mark and Alan were too busy to notice.

Before I left that night—at 8:30 pm, thanks to Alan's need to ruin my life—I dropped the handbook into a recycling bin and mentally ran through the pants in my wardrobe, trying to think of which one was the most fitted pair. If I had to suffer by looking at Grayson in his tailored suits, he deserved to suffer right along with me.

• • •

"Open up," I said, hammering on Brooklyn's condo door, desperately needing some semblance of normalcy in my life. I hadn't eaten since 10:00 am since Alan had forced me to work through lunch, so I had plans to raid Brooklyn's freezer and fill my stomach with Rocky Road ice cream. *It's healthy because of the nuts…*

The door swung open to reveal a handsome-as-ever Jason Monroe. *Damn.* Sometimes I forgot how lucky my sister was. He wasn't as handsome as Grayson in my opinion, but still, he was worthy of every bit of praise his fans bestowed upon him. I hadn't seen him in a few days, but considering he was barefoot in my sister's condo wearing pajama pants and a t-shirt, it seemed like everything was going pretty well between them. *Two hot rock stars sitting in a tree… K-I-S-S-I-N-G.*

"Cammie! Hey," he said, holding the door wide open for me to step inside.

Jason always made a point to be extra nice to me. It probably had to do with the fact that I'd once sent him a poisoned pineapple in a fruit basket because he'd broken my sister's heart. It wasn't one of my classier moments, but the truth is there wasn't any *actual* poison, just chocolate laxatives. You don't mess with my sister and expect to get away with it. Thankfully, he and Brooklyn worked out their problems, which left me with the awkward task of apologizing for "almost killing him". I mean, c'mon. At the *worst* he would have had to trade his guitar for a roll of toilet paper for a few days. Big deal.

"Whattup J? Move aside, I'm on an ice cream mission," I said, stepping past him and heading directly to the kitchen.

"Oh, no that's okay! Good to see you too, sis," Brooklyn called from the living room. I held up my hand in a lazy wave and then bent down to pull the freezer drawer open. GOLD. Gold, in the form of a pint sized container of Rocky Road, glistening in the freezer light like a diamond in the frost.

I pulled it out, retrieved a spoon, and headed toward the living room, kicking my shoes off as I went.

Brooklyn was sitting on the couch with her guitar resting on her lap. Jason's guitar sat abandoned beside her. They must have been working on their album before I rudely barged in. *Oh well, too late to leave now. I have a pint of ice cream to get through.*

"Sing for me, mon petit fille," I joked, pulling my feet up under my butt so that I could get into a comfortable position.

She raised a brow in my direction before Jason crossed in front of her, picking up his guitar to join her on the couch. Their fans would have killed to be in my position. I had a front row seat to an acoustic session with the two hottest rock stars in the industry. *And all I cared about was ice cream.*

It'd taken a while to get used to the fact that my sister was a pop star, but she'd been famous for a few years now. She had been a solo artist for years, but a few months back, her music label had slotted her for a Grammy performance with Jason Monroe—another notorious solo artist.

I knew from the start that they'd end up falling in love (*I mean, seriously, their babies would look like stylish hipster angels, with combat boots instead of wings*), but it took them a while to figure it out for themselves. Jason was quite the dick in the beginning, but my sister didn't put up with him. *Hmm, come to think of it, maybe she'd have some advice about how to deal with Grayson.* Would Grayson come around like Jason had? *All signs pointed to no.*

I took another bite of ice cream as Jason began to strum on his guitar. I settled in, ready to relax after a long day, but then my phone vibrated in my pocket. *Seriously?* I reached to check it and saw Hannah's name flash across the screen. She'd gone out with the other new hires after work. The three of them had walked toward the elevators at 5:05 pm, their laughter impossible to ignore as Alan informed me that I'd be staying late yet again.

I was slightly jealous that they were already bonding, but it wasn't like I had a choice. Alan was my boss for the time being and I wanted to stay as much on his good side as humanly possible. By the time I left work, the last thing I wanted to do was meet my coworkers at a grungy bar downtown. My feet hurt and my brain hurt. I just wanted to sit on a couch and listen to good music.

I pressed ignore on her call and then watched Brooklyn and Jason play together. They were reworking lyrics they'd just written. Every now and then Brooklyn would tweak a phrase and Jason would scribble it down, adding his own flair. I knew I was taking it for granted, getting to see the two of them collaborating, but to me, it was just a normal night with my sister.

"I'm thinking about quitting my job in architecture to become a pop star like you guys," I said when they set their guitars down to take a break sometime later.

"I'm not a pop star," Jason argued, just as Brooklyn spoke up.

"Cammie, you'd hate it. Besides, you sing like a cat that just swallowed peanut butter."

"Yeah, well, anything would be better than the job I have now. My manager sucks. I just got off work like five minutes ago."

"Are you serious?" Brooklyn asked as she twisted around to check the clock hanging on the wall in the kitchen.

"Want me to come beat him up for you?" Jason asked with a wink.

"Yes," I said without a hint of remorse. I would love for Jason to beat up Alan. Maybe while he was there he could knock some sense into Grayson too.

Brooklyn set her guitar down and cracked her knuckles. "That's it! I'm dropping by to have a little chat with your manager," she said with a tone that I knew she reserved for serious ass-kickings. *Oh jeez.*

I dropped my spoon into my ice cream, cringing. "No. Please don't."

Brooklyn shook her head. "Too late. No one takes advantage of mon petit dejune."

A part of me wanted to tell Brooklyn that she had just called me "her little breakfast", but another part of me wanted to warn Alan. He might be terrible, but hell hath no fury like my pop star sister scorned.

Chapter Eight

Amount saved for Paris: $312
Items I have: a new travel toothbrush I stole from Brooklyn's bathroom
Items I need: everything else
French phrases that I know: S'il vous plait, donnez-moi ce croissant…which I think translates into "Please give me that croissant, if you know what's good for you."

I pulled up in front of the construction site Thursday morning to find nothing more than a concrete foundation and the rough exoskeleton of a future home. From the driver's side window of my car I could spot debris and tools littering the ground. With a sigh, I reached for my worn work boots in the back seat. I knew better than to walk on a construction site in heels. A nail in your foot is not cute. Unfortunately, neither are work boots with slacks. *Grayson, eat your heart out.*

Once my boots were laced up, I checked my phone and confirmed I was at the right address. The sound of crunching gravel caught my attention and I looked up to see a dark gray Tesla turn onto the street from the opposite direction. Like a fish moving through water, the car slid into a parking spot in front of the house and the door popped open to reveal Grayson in dark jeans, a Henley, and work boots. *Welp, my ovaries just exploded.*

He shielded the sun from his eyes and stared up at the house for a moment, probably confirming progress on the build. I sat watching him until he turned and saw me sitting in my car—my twelve-year-old Toyota Corolla, *i.e. sex on wheels*. Not exactly up to par with his car, but I didn't need anything fancy. I'd be leaving the country in three months and I'd sell the car right along with anything else that could fund a day or two abroad.

"Let's go," he hollered when I didn't immediately move to join him.

I rolled my eyes and hopped out of my car, steeling myself for the early morning chill. It didn't come—the morning was muggy and humid. I stripped off my blazer and slung it over my arm as I walked to join him.

He skipped a formal greeting and headed straight into the house; apparently I was expected to trail after him like a dutiful pupil. He immediately started pointing out various aspects of the building, like the support beams and their placement. I knew I was expected to remember them, but I hadn't had my morning coffee yet and the chances of me retaining any of the information were slim to none. Now, the way Grayson's butt looked in his Levi's? *I'd easily pass a test on that.* I could point out and name every section of his derriere.

Usually I would have jumped at the idea of getting a private tour of a build like this, but I was too distracted by Grayson, too busy trying to come up with some way to talk to him.

He pulled me farther into the heart of the house and continued to point out the features of the home. He described how the client had asked for a modern open floor plan. I marveled at the height of the first floor. Grayson had designed sky-high ceilings paired with massive windows to allow for ample amounts of natural light. I knew it'd be a spectacular house once it was finished.

"So, did you have a good night last night?" I asked as we entered what would become the master bedroom.

He paused to glance at me over his shoulder. "I don't think that pertains to the job site, Cameron." His eyes warned me to drop it.

I smiled, already prepared for him to answer like that. "You're right. Let's just stick to nuts and bolts like robots. Beep boop."

Grayson sighed and turned to keep walking. "It was fine," he admitted.

I smiled, though he couldn't see it.

"My night was fine too," I volunteered. "Thanks for asking. I went to a strip club and then I robbed a bank with a bunch of strippers. We didn't take much, since y'know strippers don't tend to have many pockets."

Grayson laughed and shook his head.

"Has anyone told you that you're insufferable?" he asked, continuing to walk ahead of me.

Sure, he said insufferable, but what he really meant was *irresistible.*

After that, he insisted on continuing to talk about the house and I actually listened this time. The design was too amazing to ignore and I loved hearing Grayson walk me through the process with him. It was like getting a glimpse into his creative genius.

I'd assumed we were alone on the job site until we made it to the backdoor of the house and came upon a group of construction workers out on the grass, taking their time getting started for the day. A lanky man who didn't look a day over eighteen was using a circular saw to cut planks of wood into even segments. The rest of the crew was unwrapping breakfast tacos and chatting animatedly until they spotted Grayson walking through the backdoor. They immediately straightened up and paused their conversations, waiting for him to speak. Grayson was both the architect and the general contractor on the project, which gave him nearly full control—a fact that I'm sure made him very, very happy.

I stood to the side as he went over the day's work with them. They were expected to have the kitchen framed by the end of the day so that the siding and roofing process could begin the following day. A few of the guys peered over at me as Grayson spoke, most likely curious about my role. I kept my eyes on Grayson, trying not to let their gazes intimidate me.

When Grayson finished up his instructions, he turned and motioned for me to lead the way back through the empty house.

"Sorry for that. It was probably a little boring," he said, peering over at me as we walked.

I smiled and shook my head. "Nah, it's what I love. Don't worry about it."

He nodded.

"So what exactly did you do last night?" I asked, trying one last time to engage him in a real conversation.

His blue eyes slid to me for a moment and he shook his head. "What's your angle here, Cameron?"

I laughed, holding up my hands in innocence. "Not everything has to be angles and safety factors, Grayson. Can't an employee make small talk with her boss?"

Grayson grunted. "Sure. Except you aren't curious about what I did last night, you're curious about *who* I did last night."

I turned to inspect the kitchen, or what would serve as the future kitchen, so he wouldn't see me blush. My face burned with embarrassment.

"And if I am?" I ventured, still diverting my gaze.

"You're being childish by asking these questions. You think I didn't mean what I said the other day in my office, about us never happening. You're playing a game."

Of course I didn't believe him.

"That doesn't make me childish. That makes me willful," I said, turning to glance at him, residual blush still stinging my cheeks. "And if you remember, this is work, not play."

"I didn't bring you here to have this conversation," he argued, moving ahead so that I had to walk fast to keep up.

I should have dropped the conversation. I'd already pissed him off, but we were back on the street, seconds away from splitting off to our cars and heading in opposite directions. Any chance of having a private conversation with him would be over once we left.

"Do you ever think of me when you're with them? The other women in your life?" I asked, pausing on the grass.

The second the words slipped out, I wanted to reach for them, pull them back in one syllable at a time and replace the question with some vague goodbye. I'd never been as bold as I'd been in the last few days. I usually went after what I wanted, but there was a difference between being confident and being certifiably insane. It's like I wanted him to squirm, to feel uncomfortable in my presence. I needed to jar him out from behind whatever wall he was building for himself.

Something about Grayson pulled out every bit of confidence I had. Maybe it was the fact that I knew he found me attractive or maybe it was the fact that I was leaving soon. Either way, it felt like I had nothing to lose.

He stopped walking mid-step, and glared back at me. We stayed like that for a few seconds, his blue eyes warning me away as best as they could. I stayed rooted to my spot, clenching my fists and waiting for his response.

"No," he said with a sharp shake of his head. "When I was with Nicole last night...in my bed...with her legs wrapped around my neck, I never once thought of you."

I wanted to rear back and punch his stupidly gorgeous face. His demeanor practically begged me to, but instead, I swept up every bit of confidence left inside of me and walked up to him until I was just an inch or two away from his chest. The rounded toes of our work boots pressed together and I jabbed my finger into the center of his ribcage, hard.

"You're such a liar, Grayson," I declared as the tension multiplied around us.

"You know what else I am?" he asked, leaning an inch closer. I stared at his lips as he spoke. "Your boss."

I clenched my jaw, narrowed my eyes on him for another second, and then turned away. He stayed perfectly silent as I walked away from him, heading back toward my car with emotions boiling over inside of me. My heart knocked against my ribcage as I realized there'd be consequences for the game I was playing. He was my boss, and he had major pull in this city. If I pushed him too hard, too fast, my career could be over, but something told me he was enjoying the game just as much as I was.

After all, he didn't have to hire me, and he didn't have to be my mentor. That day, he definitely could have fired me for how I'd behaved...and yet, he didn't.

• • •

Grayson's lover, Nicole, made an appearance in the office for another lunch-time romp later that day. As her size zero frame floated through the main room, I mentally called Grayson every nasty name under the sun. He'd called her on purpose. He wanted me to back down. He greatly underestimated me.

I turned to watch her walk toward Grayson's office. Beatrice caught me staring and did a finger-down-the-throat gag. I smiled and winked.

"Three times in two weeks," Peter spoke up, drawing my attention back to our table. "That's a record."

"What is?" I asked.

"Grayson's lunchtime rendezvous. I've never seen him bring women into the office like this before," Peter said.

I shrugged with feigned indifference and tried to get back to work. The entire time Nicole was behind his closed door, my ears picked up on any subtle noises around the office. I swore I heard her moaning, but no one else stirred so I figured I was imagining it.

Twenty minutes later, as I walked back from the break room with a cup of microwaved soup, the door to Grayson's office opened and Nicole stepped out. Her blonde hair was more tousled than when she'd first walked in. Her red lipstick was smeared beneath her bottom lip and she tried her best to walk casually en route to the elevators, but it was clear what had happened. My stomach rolled with anger and jealousy. *Fuck him, fuck him, fuck him.*

Any appetite I'd had a moment before was now replaced with the need to vomit. I dropped my cup of soup into the trash bin near my desk, knowing that if I held onto it for another second, I'd hurl the entire thing at his door.

"Everything okay?" Peter asked, eyeing my poor soup, now splashed along the inside of my trashcan.

"Peachy!" I answered with a fake smile before turning to Alan. "Alan. I finished my work from this morning. Do you have anything else I can work on?"

Chapter Nine

I didn't see Grayson in the office again the rest of the week, and my confidence in his attraction to me was starting to wane. Everyday, he arrived before I did and either left after I was long gone or while I was otherwise occupied. Who knows? Either way, I was two shots shy of storming into his office just to confirm he was still alive.

On Friday evening, I stood in front of my closet, incredibly annoyed that Grayson had chosen to avoid me since our little fight at the job site. Knowing him, he'd probably try to bail on dinner as well. After all, it was a dinner celebrating my new position at his company—a position he undoubtedly, regretted giving me.

I sighed as I sifted through my cocktail dresses, hoping one would jump out at me and scream, "WEAR ME! I WILL MAKE GRAYSON BEG ON HIS HANDS AND KNEES." Oddly enough, I was left on my own. I guess my clothes weren't feeling particularly chatty that evening.

A gentle knock on my bedroom door distracted me from my dress hunt and I turned to find Hannah standing there with a cup of yogurt in her hand. She peeled off the foil lid and licked it clean as I waved her into my room.

"Heading out?" she asked, eyeing my hair. I'd just finished swooping it into a low knot at the base of my neck.

"Yeah, just a dinner. What about you?" I asked, turning back to my closet. Hannah and I were still working out our boundaries with one another. Living with her was kind of like living alone. She usually got home late after hanging out with friends and I usually got home late from working. In the mornings, we had our walk to work, but she usually liked to check in with her mom then, so really, I was living with a ghost.

That's not to say that I hadn't learned anything about her. I knew that she preferred the thermostat set at freezing temperatures, she had a rule about dishes (namely that she didn't do them), and she preferred to blast rave music at 6:00 am while she was getting ready for the day.

It wasn't all bad: she'd left out some chocolate cake the other day and I'd stolen a bite so small that I'd convinced myself she wouldn't be able to tell. *Hey, sometimes you gotta take what you can get.*

"Oh, you're off to dinner? Fun. I don't have any plans tonight. Well, not unless you count binge watching some episodes of Law and Order."

I frowned at the dresses hanging in front of me. I wanted the dinner to be just Jason, Brooklyn, Grayson, and me, but I also didn't want to leave Hannah alone by herself. We weren't really friends, but this would be a good opportunity to get to know her better.

"Why don't you come with us? It'll be fun," I said with a smile. "It's actually going to be a small group, and Grayson is going."

"Our boss, Grayson?" she asked with raised brows.

I nodded. "He and my sister are old friends."

Her brows raised even more. "Your sister the pop star? Oh my god, will Jason Monroe be there too?"

I forgot how weird it was for other people to hang out with my family. To 99.9% of Americans, Brooklyn Heart and Jason Monroe were the new "it" couple in Hollywood, the stars they saw splashed across magazine covers in disgustingly cutesy poses when they checked out at the grocery store.

"Yes, Jason will be there too," I answered, trying to downplay the whole situation. Maybe this wasn't such a good idea.

"Oh my god! Let me just get dressed really quick."

• • •

Two hours later, as I watched Hannah put her hand on Grayson's shoulder for the third time since our appetizers had arrived, I deeply, deeply regretted inviting her. *Why did I have to care? I should have let her watch SVU reruns until her eyes popped out.* Because of my need to be friendly and polite, I'd all but set myself up to be the fifth wheel in heels.

As soon as we arrived, I knew the evening would be a disaster. The fancy French restaurant placed our group at the best table in the house: a secluded corner with low ambient lighting. *But what good did that do me if I wasn't even sitting beside Grayson?* When we'd arrived at the table and chosen seats, Grayson scooted in beside Jason and then Hannah claimed the chair next to him so fast that I was left wondering if she had some kind of superhuman speed. *No, really.* I'd stood next to the table for a second, watching the four of them take their seats, cozy as fucking bugs in a rug. I'll spare you the terrible details, but for the first thirty minutes of dinner, I had to listen to Hannah monopolizing Grayson's every breath with her stories from college, her stories about growing up, and her favorite things about working at his firm.

Wow, keep telling him it's a coincidence that you both love hazelnut creamer in your coffee. There's hazelnut, and there's vanilla. By that logic, you're also soulmates with smelly Gary from finance.

I peered at Hannah from beneath my lashes just as she subtly hiked her skirt up another inch on her thighs. Grayson was chatting with Jason about investments or something equally as boring, and Hannah was using the opportunity to her advantage. *Why oh why had I invited her?*

"So Grayson, have you ever been down to South America?" Hannah asked, cutting off his conversation with Jason. "Because I went down there with my college's architecture club. Our original mission was to build a school, but instead the kids taught us that you don't need four walls and a dingy old desk, you can learn from anywhere."

"Wait, so did you end up building the school for them?" Brooklyn asked.

Hannah shot her a glare. "No. We lost time because it rained the first day, so everyone decided to spend our last four days touring the ruins down there instead. Anyway, Grayson, the ruins are even better in real life. You absolutely have to take a trip there."

Grayson nodded good-naturedly and I turned back to my food, ill-equipped to deal with the awkwardness of the dinner.

"Cammie, did you enjoy your first week of work?" Jason asked from across the table. Usually, I would have taken a moment to admire him. After all, he was People's Sexiest Man To Ever Be Born…or whatever. But tonight, I wasn't in the mood. Not while Hannah was practically licking her lips, preparing to sink her teeth into Grayson.

"Yeah, it was uh…fine," I said, spinning my ravioli around with my fork. I'd barely managed two bites. Every time I saw Hannah turn her attention to Grayson or—god forbid—emit another one of her giggles, blind-rage replaced my hunger. *If I casually stabbed her hand with my fork so that she'd have to be rushed to the hospital, would that scream "desperate"?* I wasn't sure, so I just filed the idea away in the "maybe" pile.

"Wow, is it that bad working for me, Cammie?" Grayson asked, directing words at me for the first time all night. The fact that he'd used "Cammie" instead of "Cameron" in front of my sister only served to piss me off even more.

"It's not like I'm really working for you. You're locked away in your office all day. I'm left with Alan and his sparkling personality." I practically shivered just saying his name aloud.

"I'll keep a better eye on him," he promised just as Hannah put her hand on his forearm to steal his attention once again. My fork twitched in my hand.

"Grayson!" Hannah all but shouted. "I meant to tell you, I absolutely love the mentor program. I have Alan as a supervisor and he's actually a really great teacher. He showed me the blueprints for the…" At that point her voice completely faded into Charlie Brown-esque "Womp womp womp". I turned to see if I could find solace with Brooklyn and Jason, but they were whispering sweet nothings into each other's ears—or so I assumed—so I was left on my own, rocking the fifth wheel spot like I was born for the role. *Enough.* I dropped my fork onto my plate and pushed my chair out from the table.

"I'm going to go get some air," I said to no one in particular. Brooklyn moved to follow me but I shot her a look to stay put.

A good, solid suck of LA smog was just what I needed. I needed to shake things up. I hated the person I was becoming: this insecure, shell of a girl. I'd been confident in college, outspoken and happy. I didn't care about what other people thought. Now, I couldn't even make it through a dinner without coming undone. I couldn't eat. One minute I'd be fine, and the next, Grayson would make me so angry that I felt completely out of control. *It was all Grayson's fault.*

I toed a rock with my shoe and crossed my arms like a melodramatic teen.

What was I doing wasting my time on Grayson? Why did I feel the need to conquer him? To win him over? Because really, that's what I was after. If I wanted something serious from him, I'd play it cool and take a step back. No. It was about the thrill of the hunt. *But why?* I didn't need the added stress. I just needed three months worth of paychecks so I could get the hell away from LA and find some nice Frenchman to stick between my legs.

Just the idea of leaving LA started to calm me down. I'd start in Paris, of course. I'd yet to see the Eiffel Tower in person and if I was going to jaunt around the world, experiencing life to the fullest, that's where I needed to begin. Maybe I'd stay there for a week or two, eating my fill of croissants and sleeping my way through as many Frenchmen as I dared to try out. *How do you say "Get into my pants" in French?* I'd have to learn. (Or y'know…I could always just default to good ol' body language.)

"Cammie?" a voice spoke from behind me, jarring me from my thoughts. I closed my eyes as I registered the fact that it was Grayson's voice.

He'd followed me out.

I folded my arms even tighter before speaking.

"What can I do for you, Grayson?" I asked, not bothering to turn to look at him. A few minutes ago, I would have been ecstatic that he had cared enough to come out and talk to me, but in that moment, I just wanted to be left alone. I didn't feel any of my confidence. I didn't feel flirty or desirable. I wanted to hit pause on the game.

"I was just wondering what you needed a breather from?" he asked.

You. You. You.

I kept my eyes on the road.

"Nothing." That word held so much power: the power to deny someone your true feelings in a moment of vulnerability. I watched a car drive down the street and tried to concentrate on its movements rather than my feelings. But then Grayson spoke again.

"Cammie."

He said my name like he was begging me to do something. I liked the sound of my name on his lips and when he touched my shoulder so that he could turn me to face him, I didn't resist.

Fine, if he wanted the truth, I'd give it to him.

"Everything. I needed a breather from everything," I answered, keeping my gaze on his navy tie. His ties always laid so perfectly down the center of his shirt, as if they were glued in place. Maybe that's why I wanted Grayson. He was perfect, he had his life together, he was driven and committed—and I was none of those things. At any given moment, I had the desire to fly, to skip out on the rest of dinner and roam the city alone for the remainder of the night.

"Well I can't fix *everything*," he said with a little smile, trying to cheer me up. "Can you be more specific?"

His words were a simple joke, but they reminded me of an argument I'd had with Brooklyn after our parents had just passed away.

I refused to speak to Brooklyn about our parents, refused to see a shrink, refused to go to group therapy. I was practicing the art of avoidance and it was starting to slip into every facet of my life. Brooklyn was doing her best, trying to give me space to heal, but one Saturday night in high school I'd strolled through the front door two hours late, with fresh bruising across my chin. I was drunk from shit vodka that had burned my throat going down and I wasn't in the mood to deal with her.

"Cammie, what do you think you're doing?" she'd yelled as I walked toward my room, ignoring her along the way.

"Oh don't try to be a mom, Brooklyn. Fuck off." Saying those words burned even more than the vodka had. That was a first for us. There's always a first with sisters. The first time you really overstep that line of trust. I remember she flinched at my words, genuinely hurt and taken aback by my cruelty.

"I can't fix everything for us," she whispered. "You can't do this to yourself. You have to get help."

I'd paused and reached up to feel the bruising on my face. I couldn't even remember the incident that had caused it in the first place, but I figured it was probably just drunken clumsiness. Brooklyn stepped up behind me and wrapped her arms around me, so tight and secure around my stomach that it almost hurt.

We stayed like that until I couldn't deny my feelings anymore. I was forced to acknowledge the overwhelming grief that had been locked away deep down inside of me for months. She was forcing me to feel it.

"I'm so sorry," I whispered as hot tears burned a path down my cheeks.

We stayed in the hallway, her chest pressed to my back, and I cried, long and hard. Long enough to realize I had to change.

"Cammie," Grayson said, pulling my attention away from my memories and fast-forwarding my life back to the present.

I swallowed slowly, already knowing what I needed to do.

"Tell Brook that I felt sick and headed home. And make sure that Hannah gets a ride."

"Cammie," he said, reaching out for my hand, but realizing his mistake a moment too soon. His hand fell limp back to his side. "Are you okay?"

I glanced away from him, back down the dark street.

I'll let you know when I know, Grayson.

• • •

I ended up going to my spot. It was the one place that calmed my anxiety. To get there, you had to take a private road that led around the perimeter fence of LAX. If you followed it for long enough, eventually you'd stumble upon a lonely, forgotten cemetery. It seemed like a random place for a graveyard, just off the highway on the side of an airport, but it must have been there long, long before air travel.

I parked up off the road and grabbed a flashlight from my glove compartment. The first time I'd been to the spot, a stoner from my high school had told me that he knew of a place to get high and watch airplanes take off. I'd followed him blindly that night, too naive to realize how dumb I was being, but I didn't regret the mistake afterwards.

The next time I went, I ditched the guy and the pot in favor of going alone. Just me and my flashlight.

It was a forlorn spot, out in the middle of nowhere, surrounded by blackness, but the planes always came right when I needed them. Sometimes I got lucky and I could see four or five landing or taking off all within a few minutes of each other. I'd sit on a lonely grave, lean against a headstone and turn off my flashlight. Sitting there in the dark, I'd imagine it was me leaving on the airplanes. Each time I heard the low rumble of a takeoff, my heart would race and the earth would feel alive beneath me, shaking with the weight of the airliner.

My favorite part of all was the moment when the belly of the plane was directly on top of me, when the howls of the engine were so loud that they silenced everything else.

Chapter Ten

The following week Alan forced me to stay late again on Monday and Tuesday. *What a shocker.* Why had I even found an apartment in the first place? I should have just shoved some clothes in my desk drawers, found a shower, hung a hammock from the ceiling, and stayed glued to my work 24/7. Alan would have *loved* that.

I had a sneaking suspicion that he enjoyed making me stay late just for the hell of it. It's not like the work couldn't wait until the following day. The tasks Alan shoved on my desk everyday at 4:59 pm were menial at best. None of them took much of my attention, which left me with more than enough time to replay Hannah's description of how Friday night had ended for her and Grayson over and over again until I thought my brain would explode. *Oh, we didn't go straight home after dinner. He drove the long way and we talked about everything, about nothing. We were just so comfortable around each other. You know what I mean?* No. I didn't know what she meant, but I knew she'd stolen that line from at least a dozen romantic comedies. *I told him all about my goals for the next few years. He just understands me. Thanks so much for inviting me to dinner. Grayson and I would never have bonded otherwise.* Oh, please tell me more about how you and Grayson bonded. I'd love to hear it. *I know it's early, but I really think he might be "the one".* Barf.

My gut told me she was embellishing the entire experience, and my heart sincerely needed my gut to be right about something for once. Still, every time I saw Hannah near Grayson's office, my hands started to grip my drafting pencil just a *little* tighter.

"You going to be okay by yourself?" Peter asked, standing up from his desk and stretching his arms out above his head. It was Tuesday evening and he was about to bail on me. I couldn't blame him. It was nearing 7:00 pm and if I was finished with my work, I'd be sprinting out of these fluorescent lights as fast as I could. *What does sunlight feel like? I can't recall.*

"Sure, yeah. You go on ahead. I just have a few more things to catch up on." *What a lie.* I had at least another hour or two of work, which meant I'd be working by myself in the quiet office. Oh, wait. The custodial staff would be coming in soon, so at least I'd have them for company.

"Don't work too late," Peter said with a gentle smile as he swung his leather satchel bag over his head and took off for the elevator. I watched him leave, wondering how I'd managed to pick the short straw out of all the new hires. No one else had to work late. Just that day, Hannah had invited me to yet another happy hour. I didn't even bother accepting anymore. I knew I wouldn't get the chance to leave.

• • •

Amount saved for Paris: $800 (it's amazing just how much you can save when you have no social life).

Items I have: travel toothbrush and an international iPhone charger I found on Craigslist.

Items I need: comfortable walking shoes...also sexy heels for going out.

French phrases that I know: Quelle est votre baguette...which roughly translates to "How big is your baguette?", which can serve a purpose inside of a French bakery and also in a French night club...

The next morning, I strolled into the office with a smile on my face, clutching a bag of hot kolaches in front of my chest. I'd had plenty of time to stop at a bakery on the way in to work and I'd had the ingenious idea to ply Alan with baked goods on the off chance he felt like letting me leave at a decent hour that day.

"Cammie get over here. You're late," Alan hollered as soon as I stepped off the elevator.

I glanced down at my thin leather watch. I wasn't late. I was ten minutes early. Most of the desks were still empty except for our little group. Peter, Mark, and Alan were all seated and staring up at me with varying degrees of annoyance: Peter, not annoyed at all. Mark, confused about my presence in general. (*Were we sure that he wasn't an alien?*) Alan, pissed beyond belief for no good reason.

I dropped the bag of kolaches onto my desk with a thud.

"I'm not late," I argued.

"On Wednesdays, we arrive early to work on competition proposals," Alan clarified as if it was the one hundredth time he'd gone over that procedure with me.

"Well, no one told me that," I replied.

Alan ignored my protests and pushed a manila packet onto my desk. For the next hour Alan described the new project we would be working on for the next two months. It was a design competition for a municipal park in northern LA. The city had a vision for the park: they wanted a walking trail to line the perimeter of the land, an amphitheater on one side for a summer theater series, a splash pad for younger children, and a few basketball courts in the heart of the park. It would be a massive undertaking and they were opening the competition up to architecture firms throughout California. Alan, Peter, Mark, and I would be in charge of submitting the proposal for Cole Designs.

My mind began to brim over with ideas as soon as I finished reading over the packet. *This is why I wanted to be an architect.* Community projects like this came around maybe once every ten years, and I was thrilled to get the chance to work on one. Unfortunately, I quickly learned that it wasn't my place to offer input of any kind, save for taking notes while Alan shot out what he thought was design gold. *It wasn't.*

I tried to speak up about my ideas.

"What about a small changing area near the splash pads, so that parents could put their children in swimsuits?"

"That'd be an eyesore," he replied.

"What if we commissioned a mural for the back of the amphitheater stage so that we could showcase some LA artists?"

"No. Graffiti shouldn't be encouraged," he argued.

"What if we design modular booths that can provide options for local prostitutes and drug dealers?"… just kidding. I wasn't brave enough to test Alan's patience with that suggestion.

After being shot down at every turn, I finally just sat quietly in my chair, sketching loose designs and pretending to listen to Alan's crappy ideas.

I was perfecting the crosshatching on an amphitheater sketch when a hand hit the back of my chair.

"How are the designs coming along?" Grayson spoke from behind me, practically scaring me out of my skin. I jumped up off my seat and covered my notepad for fear that he'd realize I wasn't paying attention to the meeting. Then I turned back to look up at him and caught a whiff of his spiced aftershave. His hand was still on my chair and his small smile told me he'd already seen my designs. I blushed and tried to close my notepad as discreetly as possible.

"Great. The park design will have a clean aesthetic," Alan offered with a buttery tone and a smile that showcased his yellowed canine teeth. *Why the hell does a park need a "clean" aesthetic?* It needed to be welcoming and functional.

"Alright. I look forward to seeing some of the mock-ups. And Alan, make sure you're getting input from everyone," Grayson said before pushing off the back of my chair and heading toward his office. His aftershave lingered in the air for a few seconds and I discreetly glanced over my shoulder to watch him. That day he was in a dark gray suit with a white shirt and deep red tie. The whole ensemble was admirably smooth.

"That's enough for today," Alan snapped. "We'll pick this back up again on Friday morning."

I wondered if it was hard for Alan to take orders from someone half his age and twice as successful.

• • •

Later that afternoon, I was watching Grayson walk back from the kitchen when he turned and started to head toward my desk. *Oh shit, he saw me staring. LOOK BUSY, DUFUS.* Every part of my body froze as our eyes locked, and then at once, my heart started pounding and my lungs filled with air.

"Cammie," he spoke when he was a foot from my desk. "We need to head over to that residential project this afternoon. You can drive separately and meet me there at four o'clock. Sharp."

"Oh, um, okay."

Apparently my answer wasn't convincing enough because he didn't move to leave right away.

"Do you remember where it is?" he asked, bending forward to take the pencil out of my hand so that he could jot down the address on a post-it note. Our fingers touched only briefly, but it was enough for me to lose all speech capabilities.

"There's the address in case you need it," he said before heading back to his office. "Oh, and you might want to change your clothes," he said, casting me one last glance over this shoulder. "You'll be getting dirty."

Oh my dear god. I now needed to change my panties too. Thank you, Mr. Bossman.

Obviously, after that little chat my concentration was shot to hell for the rest of the day. Finally, 3:30 rolled around and I told Alan I was leaving for the day. He'd heard Grayson instruct me to meet him at the site, but even still, the look on his face was absolutely priceless. He mumbled under his breath, but he didn't argue as I gathered my stuff and waltzed out of the office, feeling fortunate to get to leave the office when the sun was still up. *Whattup, Vitamin D.*

Once I was free from Alan's overbearing gaze, I grabbed my phone and texted Brooklyn.

> **Cammie**: About to head to a job site with Grayson. Wish me luck.
> **Brooklyn**: I hope you get to meet so many hot construction workers.
> **Cammie**: Aww, thanks sister. I'll be sure to hook-up with as many construction workers as possible.
> **Brooklyn**: That's my girl.
> **Cammie**: Alan made me sharpen all of his drafting pencils today because apparently you need a master's degree to operate a pencil sharpener.
> **Brooklyn**: He is such a tool. Why don't you tell Grayson about him?
> **Cammie**: I don't know. Maybe I will eventually... I just want to prove Alan wrong. I love seeing his face every time I turn in the work he overloaded me with a day early.
> **Brooklyn**: Well, I'm prepared to make good on that threat to poison him. You just say the word.
> **Cammie**: Let's lay off the poison threats. Jeez. We'll both end up in jail.

Brooklyn: That'd be fun. We could wear orange jumpsuits and I could entertain the prisoners like Johnny Cash did.

Cammie: You sing teeny pop ballads…

Brooklyn: Name one prisoner who wouldn't enjoy a good pop song…

Cammie: I don't know any prisoners…

Brooklyn: Exactly. #youlose

I had to race home and throw on a fitted tee and some worn jeans before meeting Grayson at the residential project. I couldn't contain the excitement brimming over as I drove across town. I'd been thinking about the house a lot over the last few days and I was anxious to see how much the build had progressed since I'd last been there.

Dirt-stained trucks lined the street when I arrived at the house. Construction workers were spread out everywhere. There must have been enough men to make up two or three crews, easily. I didn't spot Grayson at first, so I made my way through the house, careful not to step on anything that could pierce the sole of my construction boots.

"Cammie," Grayson called once I arrived in the kitchen.

I turned to see him standing next to two men. When he'd called my name, they all turned to watch me join them.

"Hi," I offered meekly, trying to figure out if I was meant to listen to their conversation or stay on the sidelines.

"This is Cammie, an associate architect at my firm," Grayson told the men. I turned to greet them. There was a hip guy with black dreadlocks and gauges. Next to him stood a lithe man with circular glasses that seemed to teeter precariously on the bridge of his nose.

"Cammie, this is Jim and Patrick. They're helping out with the electrical wiring for the house."

Jim, the guy with dreadlocks, stepped forward and shook my hand.

"It's good to see a woman on site, Cammie. How did you get roped into the architecture field? It's not very glamorous work," he said with a smile.

The men turned to me and waited, and I realized they expected me to actually answer his question. Shit. *Did they have to stare at me so attentively? It's called iPhones, people. Get one and stop paying attention to real life.*

"Oh um, yes. Actually, it's not very interesting," I began, looking around at the construction workers who'd stopped to listen to my answer. I couldn't pick apart anything but their random features: wide lips, frizzy hair, straight noses. My hands shook and I hid them behind my back, trying to hide the evidence of my nerves. "It was actually through a friend of my older sister." I cleared my throat. "He was, uh, he was in graduate school for architecture when I first met him and I overheard him talking about his job. His passion was impossible to ignore." I purposely stared anywhere except at Grayson. "And, um, yeah. Just hearing him talk about architecture is what made me fall in love."

Chapter Eleven

With architecture. With architecture! Hearing him talk made me fall in love with *architecture*! I'd forgotten to add the ending to the sentence. Maybe it was a Freudian slip, or maybe it meant nothing at all. Either way, Grayson would have had to be a fool not to realize that he was the subject of my story. How many friends did Brooklyn have that happened to be architects? One. Grayson Cole.

Did he have a clue how influential he'd been on my life? It felt so embarrassing to admit that I'd molded my entire future off of a conversation I'd overheard when I was in high school. *Who does that?* People who need to be on crazy pills, that's who.

"Well, we're glad to have you, Cammie," Jim said with a warm smile.

I stood there silent as they continued to discuss whatever it was they'd been talking about before I'd arrived. I kept my gaze focused on my feet, trying not to feel like a royal idiot for admitting the truth to Grayson.

A few minutes later, Grayson turned and motioned for me to follow him. I sighed and forced my feet to move. When we were out of sight of the others, Grayson turned and reached for my arm so he could pull me to the side of the hallway.

His hand on my arm, just below the sleeve of my t-shirt, was enough to stop me in my tracks.

"Was that story true?" he asked, staring down at me.

"What story? Oh yeah, the one about Brooklyn's friend Chuck? He's a landscape architect, you probably don't know him."

Evasive sarcasm was my only hope.

He shook his head, staring down at his feet—and then finally he looked up. His icy blue eyes were almost too much to handle.

"I didn't know I was the reason you fell into architecture," he said.

I didn't fall into architecture, I fell into Grayson. The two happened to coincide.

I shrugged, highly aware of the prying ears around us.

"Well, I'm really glad you're here. You'll like this next part," he said as he turned to head down the hallway.

I pressed my lips together, concealing my megawatt smile. When he'd invited me to join him on the job site, it had seemed formal and scripted. But, when it was just the two of us in a deserted hallway, the words were real and their meaning was heavy, tangible... The game was definitely back on. I wanted Grayson Cole.

• • •

When we arrived at a small room near the back of the house, Grayson picked up a sledgehammer off the ground and handed it to me.

"Here ya go," he said with a cheeky smile.

"What? Why do I need this?" I asked just as I caught the full weight of the tool. It was heavier than I thought possible.

"The crew added sheetrock in here yesterday without my approval. The clients want to hang a massive mirror along that side wall so we need to add a layer of plywood before we put up the drywall."

"So you want me to demolish the wall?" I asked, my eyes practically glowing.

He smirked. "Exactly."

He handed me a paper mask to wear so I wouldn't get dust in my lungs and then left me to it. I thought he'd stay with me, but he had other things to attend to around the job site. For a while, the only sounds coming from the room were my hammer slamming through the drywall followed by my heavy breathing against the thin mask.

Even without Grayson's attention, I was enjoying the work. It felt oddly therapeutic to lay my hammer into the wall as hard as I could and then rip away entire sections of drywall in one go. There are only a few times in life when you're given free rein to destroy something.

"Everything good in here?" Grayson asked at the doorway, propping his hands up onto the doorframe.

I nodded, preparing to sink my hammer into the wall again. He smiled at me with a twinkle in his eyes, probably because of how silly I looked with the face mask on. I was mid-swing when I caught sight of his dimple and completely lost track of what I was doing. My hammer made contact with the wall as well as the hidden reinforced beam that lay behind it. The shock of the hit ricocheted through the hammer and up my arm like a bolt of lightning.

"Motherf—"

I dropped the hammer and leaned forward, cradling my arm between my chest and thighs, willing the shock to dwindle away.

Grayson's hand hit the small of my back and I squeezed my eyes shut tighter. My brain wasn't sure which sensation to concentrate on: the fact that my arm was about to fall off or the warmth radiating from his touch. *Meh, you can regrow arms right? Let's focus on Grayson.*

"Damn, I bet that hurt," he murmured, crouching down next to me. "Are you okay?"

I kept my eyes shut and nodded my head once.

"Yes, just embarrassed," I offered through clenched teeth. Everyone knows to check the wall for studs—or random freaking support beams—before you lay a hammer into it. I appreciated the fact that Grayson didn't try to correct me.

"You distracted me." *Good, put the blame on him.*

He laughed under his breath and then he reached to tug my mask down off my mouth.

"Repeat that," he said.

"You distracted me," I repeated, not meeting his eye.

"Ah, sorry about that." He reached for my shoulder and ran his hand gently down my arm. "Let me see your arm."

My mother used to tell me that if I was ever experiencing pain I should touch or pinch another part of my body. It distracts the brain and tricks you into thinking the pain isn't there anymore. When Grayson touched my arm, he didn't just distract my brain, he hijacked it.

113

I let him take my arm in his hands and watched as he slowly lifted it to check for any injuries. He'd never touched me before, save for a random handshake. He had large hands that were worn from manual labor, and I was enamored by the callouses on his palm. He spread his hand over my bicep and I stood stock-still, wishing he'd let his fingers trail to other areas of my body.

He studied me for a moment and then his lips spread into a private smile.

"Looks like we'll have to amputate."

"Ha ha, funny guy."

I pulled my arm back out of his grasp, just in case he was serious about wanting to chop it off.

"Think you're okay?" he asked, eyeing my arm.

I shrugged, the pain already lessening to a dull ache. "I guess I probably just need one of those cookies I saw on the table on the way in."

He laughed and shook his head. "C'mon, I'll show you the drafts for the design while you rest up, slugger."

I followed him through the house and out toward the front porch where a small card table was set up as a makeshift desk. Grayson walked me through the design of the house and even listened to a few of my comments and critiques. He lit up when he was talking about the house and about the family that would live in it once it was complete. As he spoke, I studied his features one at time: his lips as they curved up into a smile, the creases beside his eyes that formed as he pointed to his favorite elements of the design.

As I stood on that porch with him, I knew we were living in some kind of alternate universe. Nothing about the evening felt real, from the way we were dressed to the ease with which we were talking together, laughing and flipping through blueprints. Grayson's guard was down for once and I couldn't help but yearn for just a few more moments, to reach out and pause the evening right there, just like that, forever.

• • •

The next morning I found myself at my desk twenty minutes early. I could hardly sleep thinking of my night with Grayson, how his hand had felt on my bare skin. I'd thrown off my blanket at 6:30 am, gone for a run (which ended up being a slow jog to the coffee and bagel stand at the end of my corner), showered, and gotten ready for work.

I was anxious to see him, to prove to myself that the night wasn't a fantasy, but rather a turning point in our relationship. Finally at 8:00 am, the elevator doors slid open and Grayson stepped out wearing a crisp navy suit. Each step he took in his shiny brown shoes resonated around the room. I smiled wide, excitement brimming over as I tried to think of what I would say to him first. I'd thought about the house design as I was getting ready that morning and I couldn't wait to tell him a few of my ideas.

I leaned back in my chair as he approached and smiled from ear to ear…but as he got closer, I realized he wasn't slowing down. He wasn't even going to glance down at me. He walked briskly by my desk and spoke directly to Beatrice.

"Have Nicole join me for lunch today and hold all my calls until the afternoon."

I swiveled around to watch him step into his office and slam the door closed behind him. I stared at the wood, trying to comprehend how I could have been so off. My favorite pants and the extra coat of mascara I'd applied that morning were an absolute waste. *Had I imagined the night before? Where was the guy that had joked about chopping my arm off?*

When Nicole strolled in at lunch time looking like the cat that ate the canary, I ripped my phone out of my purse and shot a text to Brooklyn.

> **Cammie**: Do you have anyone you can set me up with?
>
> **Brooklyn**: Sure, let me get my rolodex out. Any preference on age or occupation?
>
> **Cammie**: I'd prefer them to have an age and occupation.
>
> **Brooklyn**: Alright, that rules out Larry, the two-toothed hobo on the Q train.
>
> **Cammie**: Your jokes are not appreciated right now.
>
> **Brooklyn**: Sheesh, alright, let's get you laidddddddddd.
>
> **Cammie**: Also, no prostitutes.
>
> **Brooklyn**: Dont worry, we already ruled out Larry.
>
> **Cammie**: ghdkuygl.
>
> **Brooklyn**: I'm not even sure there are any guys in LA that meet your unreasonable standards.
>
> **Cammie**: Grayson brought Nicole in for a lunch booty call today.
>
> **Brooklyn**: That's it. I'm unfriending him on Facebook.
>
> **Cammie**: Wait, what does his relationship status say on there?

I hated that I wanted to know, but I did.

Brooklyn: Single.
Cammie: Good. Now find a non-homeless person to set me up with.
Brooklyn: On it.

Chapter Twelve

My annoyance with Grayson kept growing as the next few days passed and he continued to ignore my presence. I'd work up some courage, make up my mind to storm into his office and tell him off, and then I'd remember that I was a normal person that didn't do things like that to her boss.

On Monday, I strolled into the conference room for a mandatory department meeting and scanned for a seat. The only open chair was beside Grayson, at the very front of the room. I was shocked to see that Hannah hadn't already claimed it, but then I remembered she and Alan had left a few minutes earlier so that she could shadow him at a job site.

Whatever, I could sit by him. *I'm an adult.*

I slid into the open chair and dropped my legal pad onto the table with an audible plop. We didn't even acknowledge each other, and then the meeting began a few minutes later. I scribbled down notes on my legal pad, trying to ignore every time Grayson shifted in his seat or the fact that he was wearing that damned spiced aftershave, as per usual. I wanted to hate that scent, but I couldn't.

Midway through the meeting, when the monotonous drone of the HR representative was too much to bear, I wrote a question for Grayson on the legal pad.

"Why are you ignoring me?"

I tilted the pad so that it encroached on his space and when he cleared his throat, I knew he'd read it. He reached forward and pushed the pad away with a flick of his hand.

I bit down on my bottom lip in anger and then tried again, this time opting for a more *declarative* approach.

I crossed out "ignoring me" and replaced it with *"an asshole"*. Then I underlined the new question five times so that'd he'd definitely see it and know how much I meant it.

Without a thought, he reached for the pad and ripped the top page off, crumpling it in his hand. The noise cut through the conference room, interrupting the HR representative so that his sentence about ethics in the workplace was cut short.

"Are we almost done here?" Grayson snapped with a dark tone.

Everyone shifted in their chairs, trying to become invisible so that Grayson's wrath wouldn't become directed toward them. I grunted under my breath and shifted away from him.

"Sure, uh, we can finish this up another time," the HR representative stuttered, closing his binder as quietly and quickly as possible.

"Great. Let's get back to work," Grayson said shoving his chair back so hard that it hit the wall.

I gathered my stuff and turned toward the door, keeping my eyes focused on the back of the associate architect walking in front of me. I was the second to last person out of the room thanks to my placement at the front of the conference table, but just as I was about to step out, Grayson reached around me and slammed the door shut.

We were alone.

"Do you have any idea how unprofessional you're acting right now?" he asked behind me, his breath hot on my neck.

I didn't turn around.

"Everyone can hear you," I countered, my eyes focused on the solid wood door.

"You seem to be confused about how things will be with us, so I'll clarify it for you. I don't date employees. When I'm at work, I'm focused on my work. You are nothing more than an employee."

I ran my tongue along my bottom lip, trying to calm my anger. It didn't work. Nothing would work. I took a step back so that my heel sunk into the toe of his shoe. He didn't even flinch. One more step brought me against his chest, our hips perfectly aligned. His belt buckle dug into my skin through the fabric of my dress and I reached back to grip the top of his thigh through his suit pants.

Neither one of us moved, but I could see the tendons shifting in his hand as he leaned into the closed door and closer into me. Maybe he didn't realize he was doing it or maybe…maybe he actually wanted to be closer to me.

I took a breath, slid my hand an inch higher on his thigh, and aimed for the truth.

"For whatever reason, you think you're doing the right thing by pushing me away. Maybe you're scared," I said.

He pulled away from me and laughed under his breath like my statement was ludicrous. The sound made my anger brew over, out of my control. I was insane if I thought I could change Grayson. I had been about to tell him that he was wrong, and that I didn't want him to stay away anymore. After he laughed, I decided to change gears.

"Or maybe you really are just an asshole," I said, shoving my elbow back into his ribcage as hard as I could so that he expelled an audible humph. He dropped his hand and hunched over, trying to catch his breath.

I twisted the door handle, pulled open the door, and left him there, feeling good that for once his physical pain was on par with how I was feeling.

• • •

On Tuesday evening, after the last person had left for the day, I slipped off my heels and pulled on my pink fuzzy socks. Alan had given me another two hours of work to complete, but I was going to do it on my own terms. It wasn't as good as getting to leave at a decent hour, but at least the socks were comfortable.

I headed into the kitchen and flipped half of the lights on, knowing I'd need a bit of caffeine to get me through the next few hours. While I waited for the coffeemaker to boot up, I ran through my mental checklist of things I should've told Grayson the day before in the conference room. *He thought I was being unprofessional?* He was having booty calls over lunch for God's sake. *Talk about unprofessional.* He thought it was funny when I tried to have an honest conversation? The next time he spoke to me, I'd show him just how funny I could be.

I slammed the lid of the coffeemaker down a bit too hard and then crossed my arms, waiting for it to brew.

"Cammie?" a voice called from the hallway. I turned toward the kitchen door just in time to see Grayson appear in the doorway, pausing with a solemn expression when he saw me standing there, brewing coffee. I'd thought everyone had already left for the night, but apparently I'd been wrong.

His suit jacket was gone and he'd pulled his tie loose around his neck. He looked younger than normal with his shirt sleeves rolled up to his elbows and his hair slightly ruffled.

"What do you want, Grayson?" I asked, skipping over the pleasantries all together. *He'd thought I was confused about us?* I'd show him just how crystal clear the situation was to me now.

"Why are you still here? You weren't—I mean, you aren't waiting for me are you?" he asked, gently rubbing the back of his neck.

"Oh, fuck off." I rolled my eyes. "Are you serious?"

The coffee sputtered out into my mug and then the machine cut off behind me. I turned and grabbed the steaming mug, wondering if it would be worth it to throw it on him. *Nah, then I'd have to make a whole new cup.*

"I just wasn't sur—"

I cut off his disgustingly charming voice.

"No, contrary to what you may like to think, I'm not stalking you. Alan asked me to stay late again."

Grayson took a hesitant step into the kitchen and ran his hands through his hair. He'd done a lot of that over the last few minutes, fidgeting with his hair and clothes. When he'd first stepped into the office earlier that morning, his hair was perfectly styled; now it was moving toward bedhead territory. I pictured his head on my pillow before I could help it. The sensation that followed wasn't pleasant.

"Does he do any work himself these days or does he just shove it all onto you?" he asked, seemingly concerned.

I shrugged. Alan kept himself busy all day, but I never paid attention to what he was actually doing.

"Who knows? I just keep my head down and do my work."

"Well, you should head home," Grayson said, taking another step toward. I stared down at his pale blue shirt, at the contrast between his tan skin and the rolled sleeves.

"I'm not done," I countered. Grayson might be the CEO of the company, but Alan was the one I had to answer to every day. I doubted Grayson would come to my rescue in the morning when Alan tore into me for leaving before I'd finished all of my work.

"Cammie, I'm telling you to leave," Grayson said, closing the gap between us and taking the mug from my hand. He stared straight at me as he tipped the mug over and poured the steaming coffee down the kitchen sink.

Well then.

His confidence made me smirk. It was just like Grayson to assume that he could pour my coffee out like that.

He took my smirk as a white flag, dropping the mug onto the counter and peering over at me from the corner of his eye.

"Y'know, my rib still hurts from yesterday," he said with a cheeky smile.

"Good. I hope you think of me every time you take a breath." My words were supposed to sound like a threat, but they came out softer, like a plea. I cringed at how desperate I sounded.

Grayson leaned back against the kitchen counter, the dim lighting casting half of his defined features into shadows.

"Oh, I do." He smiled. "But most of the time I think of how much easier my life would be if I fired you."

The way his gaze fell down my neck - toward the patch of skin exposed at the base of my collarbone made me take a slow, calming breath.

We're all alone.

No one would see us.

"And what about the other times? What do you think of then?" I asked with an arched brow. I felt untouchable in the dim kitchen, with the hum of the coffeemaker and the silence that surrounded it.

"Things that a boss should never think of concerning his employee," he said as he studied my lips.

Truth. Real honesty for once. Too bad he still wasn't prepared to act on it.

"Ah, well. I'm sure Nicole is getting restless waiting for you. Tell me, is it fun sleeping with women you don't like? Maybe I'll have to try it out myself…see what all the hype is about."

I stepped to move around him but he reached for my arm and tugged me back so that I was pinned against the counter. My mouth hung open as I tried to keep up. He took a step toward me so that his dress shoes hit my heels. I watched his mouth as his lips parted and his breath slid in and out. Every breath he took made his chest rise and touch mine.

I begged him to kiss me in my head. I wished it with all of my might.

My gaze flickered up to his eyes, but he was still staring at my mouth.

"Why can't you just leave it alone?" he asked, reaching for my hips and gripping them, hard.

"You mean 'why can't I just leave you alone'," I clarified.

He nodded.

"Because I can't. I won't. And I don't think you want to be left alone."

His fingers dug into my side as he bent down, eye level with me.

"You aren't someone to play around with," he said.

I smiled, feeling lightheaded from his touch and the scent of his aftershave. "Ah, that's where you're wrong. All work and no play makes me...restless."

I was teetering on the brink of complete self-esteem annihilation. If he turned away from me then, I wouldn't recover. There are only so many times you can throw yourself at a burning star before you learn that sometimes stars are better left untouched, far away in the sky.

His lips hit my neck, and I closed my eyes.

"Remember that you asked for this," he said, pushing me up onto the counter so that we were eye level once again. As I opened my eyes, our gazes locked, and he didn't wait another second before leaning in and taking a kiss. Our lips crashed together, my eyes fluttered closed, and his hands held my chin on either side, pinning me in place.

It was hopeless.

Trying to catch hold of the frenzied moment was hopeless. I caught snapshots of it, like a dream that escapes you as soon as you blink your eyes awake. *His hands gripping my neck. My legs wrapping around his torso. Our hips pressing together. My fingers dragging down his chest until I found his belt loops and pulled him even closer.*

His lips.

His lips stole the show.

I felt like I was tipping over the edge of the kitchen counter. Falling, falling, falling farther away from something I could control and falling further into Grayson.

"Don't stop," I begged in the quiet kitchen.

As soon as the words were spoken, he pulled back.

The kiss was broken.

In a flash, he stepped away so that I could see his eyes. They were dark, dilated, and wild. He'd been affected just as much as I had. My neck ached from where he'd gripped it too tightly. My lips stung from his kiss. He'd been rough, but I'd liked it.

I held on to the edge of the counter and inhaled sharply, trying to regain my bearings. It helped to focus on the kitchen floor and my pink fuzzy socks falling in and out of view.

That kiss…

That kiss was everything.

After a moment, I let go of the counter, wanting to wrap my arms around Grayson again and keep him close. But when I glanced up, he was already halfway out of the kitchen, already on his way to being gone. His dress shoes smacked the floor with clear intent. When he passed the threshold, he didn't look back. He slammed his hand against the doorframe and left me sitting there all alone.

I'd begged him to kiss me, just once.

At that moment, I learned to be careful what I wished for.

Chapter Thirteen

Amount saved for Paris: $723 (minus the $12.50 I spent at Walgreens for the supplies to make a voodoo doll. Now I just needed to find a DIY guide online.)

Items I have: Keds for walking around the museums and parks.

Items I need: red lipstick and a blue striped top...to fit in with Parisian women.

French phrases that I know: Grayson Cole est une salle de bain géante...which roughly translates to "Grayson Cole is a giant bathroom." (I realize that this isn't a very good insult, but I thought I'd multitask and start memorizing words that will actually help me in Paris.)

I arrived to work early Wednesday morning after having tossed and turned for eight sleepless hours. Grayson had given me permission to leave work the night before (I mean, he went so far as to pour out my coffee), but I hated having Alan's work hanging over my head. I cared about this job. I wanted to prove myself to Alan so that he'd stop giving me crappy assignments. I was a good designer and I just needed to show him that.

I could tell that Grayson was already in his office by the time I set my things down on top of my desk. A thin shaft of light spilled out from beneath his door and I could barely make out the faint sound of his typing. I wanted him to come out and face me, but he never did.

I knew he'd felt something during the kiss. Why else would he have been so angry afterward? No one storms out after a mediocre kiss, I knew that much.

Eventually, I forced myself to focus on the pile of work I'd left behind the night before. A full cup of coffee and freshly sharpened drafting pencils were almost enough to convince me to concentrate on my sketches instead of replaying the previous night in excruciating detail. *Almost.*

I stirred from my work sometime later that morning when I heard Beatrice mention my name on the phone.

"Sure, I'll connect you with Cammie. Let me just put you on hold for a moment," Beatrice said.

I turned toward her desk with an inquisitive brow. *Why was someone calling me on the work line?* Brooklyn was the only person who tried to contact me during work hours and she always used my cell phone.

Beatrice connected the call and I spoke hesitantly, "Hello?"

"Cammie! This is Emma. Emma Cole."

It took me a second to get up to speed. *Why in the world was Grayson's mother calling me?*

"Oh, of course. Hi Mrs. Cole. How are you?"

The question was more of an automatic response than anything. My brain wasn't awake enough to create an actual conversation with Grayson's mom.

"Oh, I'm good, honey. I'm good. Listen, I'm glad I caught you before the day really gets going. Are you too busy to chat for a moment?"

Even if I had ten deadlines to meet, I could spare a few minutes for the mother of my dream man.

"Sure, I can talk," I answered.

"Oh good. Y'know I was calling to see if you've been able to keep an eye out for Grayson like I asked?"

I nearly choked on my own tongue.

"Um, yeah, well, a little bit. He sort of keeps to himself," I said, skipping over the rather obvious encounter from the kitchen the night before.

"Of course, of course. I guessed as much. Anyhoo, are you enjoying your work? Last time I spoke to you, you were a bit overwhelmed with everything."

I glanced up to check my surroundings. Mark had arrived a few minutes earlier, quiet as a mouse, but Peter and Alan's desks were both empty still. I could speak freely if I wanted to.

Was I enjoying my work?

"Y'know, I'm not really sure yet."

"Uh oh." she answered. "Tell me about it. Is my son being too hard on you?"

"No. No. It's nothing like that. It's just a lot more work than I thought it would be," I admitted.

"Well, I'm sure Grayson knows what he's doing. I think these first few weeks will be hard until you get adjusted to the work flow, don't you think?"

I was about to reply when the elevator doors dinged and swung open. I glanced back to check if it was Alan arriving for the day and did a double take when I caught sight of Nicole strolling into the office with her pale blonde hair flowing out around her. *What the hell was she doing here? And before 9:00 am no less? Had Grayson bumped their booty call up to brunch now?*

"Cammie? Are you there?" Emma asked.

I peeled my gaze away from Nicole and turned back to my desk. "Oh, yes. Sorry about that Mrs. Cole. I actually have to be going. I, uh, have to finish up a few things before my manager arrives."

"Oh, that's alright, dear. Thanks for taking the time to chat with me. Tell your sister hello for me when you get the chance, it's been too long since I last saw her!"

I glanced over my shoulder as the scent of Nicole's floral perfume hit me. It stretched across the office, announcing her presence even more than the clap of her high heels on the concrete. Over the last few weeks, every single thing about her had come to annoy me, but most of all it was that floral scent that did me in. I wanted to drown her in it.

"Oh, I will. Bye, Mrs. Cole."

The second the call ended, I watched Nicole step into Grayson's office, securely closing the door behind her. She was probably unbuttoning her blouse at that very moment. *Blech.* Just the idea of them together made me want to vomit.

I had a brief moment where an adult version of Cammie warned me to keep my distance and get back to work. Fortunately, reckless Cammie won out. I couldn't sit idle while he was in there with Nicole. He'd kissed me the night before, *really* kissed me. He'd gripped my neck with both hands like he'd wanted to devour me whole and now he was in there with her?

No. Not happening. I pushed my chair back from my desk and bee lined for his office. After one sharp knock on his door, I opened it before either one of them could decline my entry. Grayson was perched behind his desk, his black suit jacket and tie still perfectly in place. He was leaning forward on his hands, with furrowed brows and a sharp frown. When he saw the door slide open, he swept his gaze from Nicole up to me and squeezed his eyes shut, clearly unhappy to see me barging into his office.

Nicole sat in a chair on the other side of his desk with her hands crossed on top of her lap. The proper pose combined with her white shift dress and strand of pearls screamed, "Junior-League-trust-fund-baby", but when she turned to me, there were mascara stains dotting her cheeks and the whole pristine image was suddenly shattered.

She'd been in there all of thirty seconds and he already made her cry? *The asshole.*

Wait. Why do I care about Nicole?

I glanced back to Grayson with narrowed eyes, prepared to call him out, but he was practically snarling at me by that point.

"Why the hell do you insist on barging into my office, Cammie?" he asked.

My mouth fell open and then I rushed to close it, only to let it fall open again a moment later. I looked like a confused guppy.

"Your mom called me this morning," I finally spoke, hoping the mention of his mom would cool his jets. "She was checking up on you."

Nicole pointed her finger out at me. "What? Why is your mom calling one of your *employees*?" She spat the word out as if she had just accidentally bitten into a non-organic, GMO honeycrisp.

Grayson shrugged, glancing between the two of us. "She likes Cammie, she's a family friend."

"Cammie?" Nicole bristled.

Grayson stared up at me expectantly. "Is that really the only reason you have for interrupting?" he asked incredulously.

I straightened my shoulders and crossed my arms over my chest.

"I just thought you should know that your mom is asking about you. Maybe give her a call every now and then, Grayson."

I purposely used his first name.

"Is this why you're breaking up with me? So you can fuck your jailbait employee?" Nicole blurted out.

Excuse me, we're having a conversation here...wait, did she say they were breaking up? I was back to looking like a confused guppy as she pushed herself onto her feet and leaned over Grayson's desk. I should have excused myself at that point, but I couldn't. It was like watching a train wreck happen in slow motion.

"You'll never find a woman as good as me. You're about to lose the best thing that ever happened to you."

Wow. She was really confident in her ability to quote movie breakup lines.

"Nicole. Calm down," Grayson instructed with annoyance.

She reared back as if he'd slapped her. Her hands flew up in the air and I could tell she was about ten seconds from losing it. *Should I call security?* Nah. Let Grayson defuse the botoxed bombshell.

"Calm down! Calm down?" she yelled. "You string me along for a year and then just break up with me in your fucking office, Grayson? I never met your parents. I never stayed the night at your place. You said you weren't ready for commitment?! Bullshit." Her hands were flying everywhere at this point. "I'm done."

She turned and rushed past me, making sure to subtly swipe me with her purse on the way out. I stared out after her, mostly to ensure that she wasn't going to come back and attack me from behind.

When she was at the elevator bank, furiously typing away on her phone, I finally turned back to Grayson.

For two seconds, we stared at one another, letting the last few minutes settle. Then, finally, I cracked and let the edge of my mouth hitch into a smile. He followed suit, trying to conceal his grin.

"Nice girl. Better watch out though, she's going to start a hate club with that secretary you fired."

Grayson grunted. "She was exaggerating."

I narrowed my eyes, thinking back to my experience with Grayson. "You probably did string her along."

He glanced up and studied me for a moment before nodding. "Probably."

• • •

Around lunchtime, Alan left for a job site with Hannah, leaving Peter and I with thirty minutes of freedom. We decided we deserved some good takeout since most of our lunches consisted of peanut butter and jelly sandwiches supplemented by vending machine granola bars.

"Oohh! What about Thai? I haven't had Thai food in forever," I said, scrolling through Yelp reviews for a restaurant down the street.

"Nah. Not a fan. What about Italian?" Peter asked.

The idea of eating a giant plate of fettucini alfredo was almost too tempting to pass up.

"Yum. I can always eat—"

"Peter I need to speak with you for a few minutes. Are you busy?"

We both turned in unison to see Grayson hovering behind my desk with his arms crossed. Since I'd been hired, he'd never once talked to Peter one-on-one, and the visible shock on Peter's face emphasized that point further.

"Oh, um, sure. I was just going to get lunch with Cammie," he said, offering me a sympathetic frown.

"That's fine. I'll have Beatrice order us something. Cammie can run down and grab herself lunch."

Oh thanks, asshat.

Grayson completely ignored me even as I stared daggers at him, so I scooted my chair back so that he had to jump out of the way before I slammed into his legs. It wasn't a very classy move, but at least he finally met my eye. I almost wavered—those blue eyes were a lot to take in when they were aimed right at me—but I held strong.

"Thanks for stealing my lunch date," I said, grabbing my purse from the back of my chair.

"You'll manage," he said with a cheeky smile. "Besides, it's only fair. You interrupted mine earlier."

• • •

As soon as I sat down at my desk after lunch, Alan began to ramble. "Let's go over the design for the competition. We weren't able to do our usual Wednesday morning meeting, so we'll do it now."

I perked up. Over the last few days, I'd become obsessed with the park design competition. I'd brainstormed a few ideas that I knew Alan would agree with. They would add a lot to the project without increasing the budget. As Alan pulled out the drafting paper we'd used the week before, I jumped into my proposals.

"Alan, I know you weren't in love with some of my ideas last week, but I think I've figured out how we could incorporate a few things without blowing the budget."

I reached for my notebook, where I'd been scribbling down my ideas on the last few pages. The ones I thought Alan should hear were highlighted and circled so that they'd be easy to find.

"I think the changing rooms near the splash pad could fit into budget if we combine them with one of the park's bathrooms. The building material could be sourced from the recycling facility downtown so that the cost would be nominal. Not to mention, using recycled materials would look really good for the city."

Alan slapped his hand down on his desk, jarring me. "Cammie, I think you're confused about your role in this competition. I want you here as more of a silent participant. Maybe you should direct this misguided enthusiasm toward the work I've given you, since you've had so much time to consider this competition design."

My face burned with embarrassment. Peter tried to catch my eye, to ease the pain of being reprimanded in front of all of my table-mates, but I kept my eyes trained on my notebook. I had pages and pages of ideas for the park project. Some of them were wild and much too costly, but a lot of them would enhance the park and fit well with what the design committee had asked for in the first place. Despite all that, if Alan didn't think my ideas were worth mentioning, then fine, I'd stay silent.

I bit my tongue for the rest of the meeting—if you could even call it a meeting. It was mostly Alan blabbering on and on to himself.

What gave him the right to treat me like that? I would have assumed he was a misogynist, but he wasn't any nicer to Peter or Mark either. No, I think he was just a crotchety old man, stuck in the old way of doing things. He thought that his title as a senior associate meant that his word was law. I was all for respecting authority and learning from those with more experience, but Alan wasn't a teacher. He was a dictator without a throne, and I was sick of putting up with him.

By the time our *"meeting"* was over, I'd decided to do something wild. No, actually, something insane. The decision would jeopardize my relationship with Alan, my career at Cole Designs, and potentially my future in the architecture world.

Despite all that, if Alan didn't want my help with the proposal, then I really only had one choice. I'd just break the rules and enter the competition on my own.

The Design

Chapter Fourteen

"Hurry!" I yelled back at Hannah as I took the stairs two at a time.

"Oh my god! I can't believe you're actually getting to leave work on time. This is the best. We should go grab dinner for once," Hannah said as I pushed through the doors of the Sterling Bank Building. Alan had a meeting with Grayson just before 5:00 pm, which meant he hadn't had time to assign me extra work before the day ended. As soon as the clock struck five, I'd bolted out of the office with Hannah in tow.

"Yes! Let's go, we deserve it," I said.

We ended up finding a little bistro on the way home from the office. It was packed to the brim—as all good restaurants are in LA—but we managed to find two seats at the bar.

"Y'know I lied to Grayson the other day," Hannah said with a little smile as we perused the menu. "Alan is the worst."

I laughed. "Um, duh. I'm glad we can agree on that now. I thought Alan had hypnotized you for a while."

She laughed and I went back to browsing the menu. The restaurant had everything from pasta to hamburgers so I knew I'd have a hard time picking just one entree. I glanced over to see if Hannah was having the same problem, but she was fidgeting on her seat and glancing around the restaurant. Either she was nervous about something or really hungry.

"You okay?" I asked with a chuckle.

Her eyes lit up. Clearly, she'd been waiting for me to ask.

"You'll never guess what happened at work today," she said, dropping her menu and glancing over at me with dreamy eyes. She looked like she'd just been struck by Cupid's arrow.

"What?" I asked while simultaneously wondering if I was hungry enough for an appetizer or not.

"Grayson invited me to go to happy hour with him," she said, her voice brimming over with excitement.

I slapped my menu onto the bar.

What?

"Excuse me?"

That lying bastard.

• • •

I barged into Grayson's office on Thursday morning like a bat out of hell. I pushed his door open so hard that it slammed back against the wall and shook the books on his shelf. Everyone in the office would have been able to hear the racket, but no one was in yet. I'd purposely arrived early to kill Grayson in peace.

"Looks like I chose the perfect day to install a new deadbolt on that door," he remarked, keeping his focus down on his work.

I ignored him and shoved the door closed behind me.

"You realize that I'm trying to work, right?" he asked,

I scowled, crossed my arms, and waited for him to acknowledge me.

"The least you could do is bring me a cup of coffee when you interrupt me."

"I'm not your secretary," I snapped.

He rolled his eyes and pressed the intercom on his phone.

"Beatrice?" he asked. Silence.

She hadn't arrived yet, which meant he was on his own with the coffee. He stared up at me expectantly, but I arched a brow and held my ground.

It was his move.

With an annoyed groan, he pushed his chair back and stood, his full height threatening my confidence for a moment.

"God. Fine, I'll go get your damn coffee," I hissed, turning on my heels and heading toward the kitchen. I ran through every ingredient that I could sprinkle into a mug inconspicuously enough so that Grayson wouldn't notice. *Did we keep cayenne pepper stocked in the cabinets?*

"Get out of my way, Cammie," Grayson hissed as soon as I opened the kitchen cabinet to reach for a mug. He moved up right behind me and reached over my head to get to the cabinet.

"I said I'd make it!" I snapped.

Grayson laughed. "I'm not drinking your spit. Now, move."

I hadn't had the confidence to tell him how I felt a moment before, but now his attitude made it all too easy.

"So, which of your two faces are you wearing today, Grayson?" I snapped, spinning around and pressing my hands onto his chest to push him away from the counter. "All of that bullshit about not dating employees and then you invite Hannah to get drinks with you? What the hell is that?"

"What are you talking about? And can you keep your voice down?" he hissed.

He slammed the cabinet door closed and moved around me to turn on the fancy espresso machine.

I hated that he was ignoring my outburst so he that he could continue on making his damn coffee.

"Let me speak slower for you," I dragged out. "You. Invited. Hannah. To. Drinks."

He narrowed his eyes, but didn't speak.

"I understood the whole Nicole thing, but seriously, *Hannah*? Is this all just a game to you?" I asked.

Grayson slammed his mug onto the kitchen counter, practically shattering the ceramic in the process, and then he grabbed my arm just above the elbow and dragged me out of the kitchen. His grip was tighter than necessary and his fingers pinched the back of my arm so that I had no choice but to follow him. He pulled me after him as he walked to the side stairwell near the kitchen, an exit hardly anyone ever used.

As soon as the heavy metal door closed behind us, he let go of my arm. We were standing on a small concrete platform with stairs leading to the floors above and below us. Out of the thirty-odd floors in the entire building, there wasn't a single person using the stairwell. It was as private as we could get inside the building.

"I didn't invite Hannah anywhere. Are you clinically insane?"

I reached up to slap him, but he caught my wrist two inches away from his cheek.

"What in the world did I ever see in you?" I asked, yanking my wrist away from him.

He growled and turned back toward the door, rubbing the back of his neck to calm his nerves, no doubt.

"There's an office happy hour Monday night. Everyone's invited. Hannah must have overheard the conversation and embellished it. I don't know what to tell you, but you're acting like a child."

He didn't invite Hannah?

I'm acting like a child?

I was still trying to connect the dots when Grayson moved toward me, so quickly that one second he was a few feet away from me on the platform and the next he was pressed against me, pushing me back against the wall and caging me in against the cold concrete.

"I'm not dating any employees." His breath hit my neck. "I'm not *fucking* any employees. But if I were…it wouldn't be Hannah."

His lips touched my skin just beneath my ear, a sensitive spot that interrupted my breathing and forced me to squeeze my eyes closed.

We paused there for a moment, on the precipice of something more. Just as I fluttered my eyes opened, prepared for him to walk away, his mouth collided with mine. The force of the kiss would have slammed my head into the wall had his free hand not reached up to cushion the blow. I gripped his arms, residual anger still burning inside of me. Then his hands found the hem of my skirt and my anger dissolved in an instant, replaced with an emotion equally as compelling: lust.

I gripped his arms tighter, but that didn't warn him away. His hand slipped beneath my skirt until he was touching the bare skin of my upper thigh.

We were in the middle of an office building at the start of a busy work day. There might not have been anyone in the stairwell yet, but there would be soon. Grayson didn't seem to care about that fact. His tongue slid past my lips as his hand pushed my skirt up higher. I was about to pull away, to warn him about us getting caught, when his finger skimmed the edge of my panties.

My grip tightened on his arms, but there was no way to warn him of the consequences. My warnings couldn't develop past fleeting thoughts. There was only Grayson. Grayson's mouth as he gently bit down on my lower lip. Grayson's hand as he gripped my hair, keeping me pressed back against the wall. Grayson's finger as he stroked the hem of my panties.

Instinctively, my leg wrapped up around his waist, easing his access. He moaned against my lips and then pulled back to watch me. For a moment, I kept my eyes squeezed shut, gripping onto the sensation of his touch, but then I opened them and my world lit on fire.

Grayson was touching me, *stroking me*, in a stairwell in the middle of our office building. At any moment someone could walk out and spot us with my leg tangled around him and his hand hidden deep beneath layers of clothing.

"Someone is going to walk out and see us," I spoke through soft moans. I hardly got the sentence out before pleasure rattled my spine. I let my gaze settle on his stare and focused there as his touch grew harder and harder to ignore. He was enamored with me, with my body pressed against his.

He bent low, circled his finger again, and then whispered in my ear. "Let them."

That's not right. That's not professional. I should have argued with him, but my mouth wouldn't move. The words wouldn't even form in my thoughts because, the truth was, as my body shook from an earth-shattering orgasm, I knew that I'd *liked* being with Grayson in a public place. The desire to be with him at that exact moment, where anyone could have interrupted us—it spiked my veins with adrenaline in a way that made it so easy to lose control.

And he knew it.

• • •

Grayson walked back in first, leaving me with one last kiss on the lips. I straightened my clothes, leaned against the wall, and caught my breath in that stairwell for what felt like hours before finally stepping back into the office.

"Morning, Cammie," Peter offered with a small smile as I took my seat at my desk. I wondered if he could tell how shook up I was. *Is there any redness from where Grayson's hands gripped my neck a few minutes earlier?*

"Hey," I murmured, taking my seat and forcing myself to look down at my desk rather than peeking back at Grayson's office.

"Did you hear about the office happy hour on Monday? I think we're meeting at O' Keefe's right after work," he said.

I blushed and nodded, keeping my head down so he couldn't see my cheeks. "I'll be there."

• • •

"Do you have a sexy top I can wear for a work happy hour?" I asked as I scanned through Brooklyn's clothing later that night.

"Why would you want a sexy top for a work happy hour? Have I raised you to get ahead by using your body? You aren't secretly humping Alan are you?" Brooklyn asked, coming up to stand alongside me and help me hunt for a top.

"Ew. No. I just want something that makes me feel good. Like a nice blouse I could wear underneath a blazer."

She didn't need to know that the top was meant specifically for Grayson.

"Guys! The stir-fry is almost done," Jason yelled from the kitchen.

"Sounds good, babe!" Brooklyn replied.

Oh, blech.

"Tell me again how you managed to land a cute rock star who also happens to cook?" I asked Brooklyn. Just then, I spotted a slinky cream top with crisscrossed spaghetti straps. The back was low cut, but the front was fairly conservative. It was perfect considering I'd have a blazer on in the office all day.

"You can thank LuAnne for the cooking part. She made sure to teach him a few recipes before he left Montana."

LuAnne was Jason's housekeeper back at his ranch in the Middle of Nowhere, Montana. She kept everything in order for Jason while he was in LA with Brooklyn. Technically, LA was where Jason called home, but I knew he and Brooklyn both longed to go back to Montana. The ranch was where the two of them first fell in love. The ranch had served as a catalyst for their relationship and their collaboration as musicians.

"How about this top?" I asked, pulling out the one I'd spotted and letting it fall against me so that Brooklyn could see how it'd look when I put it on.

"It's perfect," she said with a clap. "Now, c'mon. Let's go eat."

I took the blouse out into the living room with me so that I wouldn't forget it. Once it was draped along the back of the couch, I followed Brooklyn into the kitchen and cracked up when I spotted Jason. His apron was completely covered in what looked to be soy sauce, and there was definitely a small piece of broccoli stuck in his hair. *Clearly, LuAnne was not finished teaching him the art of cooking.*

Brooklyn knocked the piece of broccoli off before reaching on her tiptoes to kiss his cheek.

"When do you think you'll go back to Montana?" I asked them. "I'm sure LuLu misses you guys."

Jason paused cooking and shot Brooklyn a sharp glance.

"You haven't told her, Brooklyn?" he asked.

I turned in time to see my sister trying to mouth something to him.

"Told me what?" I asked, glancing between the two of them. "What are you guys keeping from me?"

Brooklyn sighed and shot me a "please don't kill me" smile as she clasped her hands in front of her chest.

"We are actually heading back in two weeks." Her puppy dog eyes weren't enough to cover up that shocker.

"Are you serious? For how long?"

Jason left the stove to join Brooklyn. He wrapped his arm around her waist and brought her in close.

"Not for too long, Cammie. It's just that Brooklyn goes on tour in a few months and we have to have the album finalized before she leaves. Montana is the best place for us to focus on our music."

Jason. Beautiful rock star Jason with broccoli in his hair. I couldn't be mad at him.

My sister? Now, *she* I could be mad at.

"How could you not have told me before now?"

She blanched. "We just finalized the details earlier this week. I know you have so much going on right now and I didn't want to add anything to your plate before I knew what was happening."

For a second I thought about arguing with her or maybe forcing her to stay with me in LA, but then I realized that I couldn't truly be mad at her. I had this giant secret brewing behind the scenes. A secret that was MUCH worse than her going to write in Montana with her boyfriend.

Brooklyn had no clue that I wanted to go to Paris and if I had any hope of her continuing to speak to me after I hopped on that international flight, then I knew I needed to cut her some slack about heading to Montana. *Y'know, lead by example and all that.*

"You know what? Fine, you can go," I said before pointing to where I'd set her blouse down. "But, I'm keeping that shirt."

Chapter Fifteen

It was impossible to concentrate at work on Monday. I'd had an entire weekend to recreate, dissect, downplay, and fantasize about what had happened between Grayson and I in the stairwell. I hadn't spoken with him since that day, but happy hour was just a few short hours away and we'd definitely face each other then. I could hardly wait.

I worked through lunch, ensuring that every single task Alan put on my desk would be completed by 4:59 pm at the latest. I didn't have time to worry about Grayson's whereabouts in the office if I hoped to leave work on time. I even caught the scent of his aftershave a few times but I resisted the temptation to turn around. Instead, I kept my face down and pressed on, finalizing sketches and handing them off to Alan with lightning speed.

As the office clock struck 4:50 pm, I initialed the final sketches Alan had requested for the day and smiled. *All done.* I straightened up my desk, packed up my things, and signed out of my computer. My excitement was starting to brim over and I knew that Peter could tell. He'd shot me curious glances all day, but I just shrugged them off, feigning random cheerfulness. *Was it a crime to love your job?*

"All done?" Peter asked with a bemused smile.

I stuck my tongue out at him. "Some of us know how to get our work done," I joked.

Alan perked up and glanced over at my desk. I expected a "good job" or at least a nod in my direction. Instead, he raised his brow and reached for a crate beneath his desk.

"I'm glad you finished. These sketches you completed a few days ago are all off. The measurements you used weren't correct. I need you to redo them and have them ready for me in the morning."

He dropped the crate onto my desk with a thud and my mouth dropped.

No. No, he couldn't possibly do that to me.

"You gave me the measurements I was supposed to use. I double checked each sketch," I argued, reaching for the paper at the very top of the stack, more than sure of myself.

Alan rolled his eyes. "Yes, but the measurements changed. We just got word from the engineering team. So change it. The new stats are written on a post-it note in there."

He motioned to the crate and then turned back to his work, leaving me to my own personal hell. I stared in disbelief at the sketches that would keep me at the office well past the end of happy hour. I should have known Alan would find some way to screw up my plans. After all, making me miserable was his number one goal in life.

"Can't she do them tomorrow, Alan? We have that work happy hour at five," Peter spoke up.

I shot him an appreciative smile.

"Happy hour? Are you kidding me, Peter? These sketches take precedence over getting drunk. You of all people should realize that."

Peter chewed on his bottom lip, fighting with himself over whether to speak up or drop the subject all together. I decided to step in before he took the fall for me.

"It's fine. I'll get them done, Alan."

And I would. I cared about this job and I cared about impressing Alan too much to worry about some happy hour. *So what if Hannah would get a chance to hangout with Grayson while I was tethered to my desk? So what if they would laugh and have a good time while I worked on dumb sketches that didn't even matter?*

So what?

That's the mantra I kept repeating to myself as I watched Peter and the rest of the architects pack up for the day. Hannah and her table-mates chatted as they stood and collected their things. I caught a glimpse of her outfit before she left: a tight black dress she'd hidden beneath a loose jacket all day.

I sighed as I turned back to my work, spreading the sketches out in front of me so I could count how many more I had to go through.

"Want me to stay with you? We could hammer them out pretty quickly together," Peter offered with a timid smile that told me he really hoped I would say no.

"Nah, you go on ahead. Have a beer for me," I said with the biggest smile I could muster.

• • •

My phone buzzed on my desk just as I'd finished up the first half of the sketches.

Hannah: OMG. Having so much fun! Where are you? We just did an office shot!

Before I could stop it, the image of Grayson taking a body shot off Hannah played out in my mind with HD clarity.

Was he there with her? He wasn't in his office but I hadn't seen him leave either.

My phone buzzed again and I glanced down to see another text from Hannah. This time she'd attached a selfie of her holding up a shot to her mouth, ready to down it.

"Fuck," I murmured under my breath.

I glanced back down to my pile of sketches. I had so much work left to do, but all I wanted to do was leave.

Alan's phone rang, jarring my attention toward his desk. I hated the fact that he'd stayed late with me. If he wasn't there, I'd have already left and just come back to the office at the butt crack of dawn to finish the sketches.

"What do you want, Suzie?" he yelled into the phone.

Good to know he's pleasant to everyone in his life...

"Are you kidding? You expect me to help you with the kids whenever it's convenient for you?"

I stayed stock-still as he continued yelling at the person on the other end of the line.

"No," he argued. "You claimed full custody so you could keep them from me. I'm not going to help you out now."

Oh jeez. Alan was nothing but a shrewd asshole to me, but from what it sounded like, he was dealing with quite a lot at home. I should have known something was going on with him. No one is as rude as he was for no reason.

"Dammit, Suzie. Fine. I'm on my way."

He slammed his phone back onto his desk and shoved his chair back.

I peered hesitantly up at him, confused about how to proceed.

"Do you, um, do you want me to finish up that stuff for you too?" I asked, pointing to the papers on his desk.

He squeezed his eyes shut and shook his head.

"No. It's fine. Just head home."

He sounded completely defeated and I hated it. It was easy to deal with asshole Alan. I could silently curse him in my head and move on with my life, but this sad, depressed version of Alan? It was unchartered territory.

"Okay, well. Goodnight," I said, offering him a timid smile.

He ignored me, already en route to the elevators.

As soon as he was gone, I reached for my phone and shot Hannah a text.

Cammie: I'm on my way! Save me a shot!

I stood up and slipped my nude heels back on, then pulled off my blazer. On the way down in the elevator, I touched up my makeup and let my hair down from a clip so that it framed my face and brushed against my bare back.

I couldn't wait to see Grayson's face when I walked into the bar.

• • •

Just as I'd suspected, Pat O' Keefe's was just a few blocks away from Cole Designs. Its location paired with their happy hour specials (which were long gone by the time I got there at 8:00 pm) drew in a young urbanite crowd. I was making my way along the bar when a group of rowdy men wearing football jerseys sitting atop bar stools threw their arms up and erupted in cheers. The largest guy of them all nearly knocked my head off while he was celebrating but I ducked out of way just in time.

"Oh shit!" the man said, spinning around to face me. His brows instantly rose in interest. "Ah! I'm sorry about that. Let me buy you a drink," he said, reaching out for my hand. His friends all catcalled and it was clear that they were all three sheets to the wind. I smiled good-naturedly and kept right on walking. I'd already lost enough time with Grayson as it was.

As I made my way farther into the bar, I finally spotted Peter's wild red hair near a row of dartboards in the back. He was in a sea of architects from our firm. Thirty to forty people were crammed together. Drinks were sloshing and laughter drowned out the rock music playing in the background. My blouse—sans blazer—warranted a few lingering gazes as I stepped up to the group, but I brushed it off. *They're shoulders people, everyone has them.*

"CAMMIE!" Hannah yelled over the crowd.

I turned to find her with the other new hires, Christoph and Nathan, who I'd hardly managed to speak to since starting the job. When I joined the group they both squinted as if trying to place me. *Oh my god, they didn't even remember me.*

"Cammie," I said, holding my hand to my chest, reminding them of my name. They both visibly relaxed when I saved them from awkwardly having to pretend to know me.

"Let's take a shot," Hannah said, reaching out for my hand so she could drag me closer to the bar.

A shot sounded like a terrible idea, but I didn't want to be a party pooper, especially since it was a miracle that I was at happy hour to begin with. I let Hannah drag me through the crowd and I trailed after her, all the while spinning my head to find Grayson. He was there somewhere. He said he would be. I wanted to ask Hannah about it, but saying his name to her seemed like a bad omen. Especially since she'd lied—or *"embellished"*—the fact that he'd invited her here.

"Dude, you missed all the action. Some guy from the accounting department took seven shots in a row and then threw up everywhere."

Wow. Sounds wonderful.

"Huh, that's crazy," I said, unable to hide the boredom in my voice.

"Yeah. And turns out Grayson is a no-show. So lame!"

I snapped my head back to her. "What? I thought you said he invited you?" I asked with a gentle tone. It was as close as I was going to get to calling her out on her lie. I mean, I did still have to live with the girl, after all.

She shrugged off my question and turned to slap her hand down onto the bar.

"Bartender! We've been waiting forever!" she snapped.

I cringed and shot an apologetic smile to everyone casting us annoyed glances.

"Bartender!" she yelled again.

I took a step away from her so that people wouldn't associate us as friends, but she didn't even notice.

"You want a straight whiskey shot or something else? We can get one of those buttery nipple things?" she asked, slurring her words more and more by the second.

I glanced around the bar to confirm Grayson's absence, but she was right. He wasn't there.

"You know what? I don't feel that great. Why don't you keep hanging out with the other guys? I'm going to head back to the apartment."

"What? BOOOOO. You suck," she said, reaching out to push me. She probably meant it to be a light, playful move, but I lost my footing and bumped into the waiter walking behind me, spilling one of his cocktails in the process. Red liquid spilled over the edge of his tray and soaked his white shirt.

"Oh no! I'm so sorry!" I exclaimed before turning back to Hannah to see if she saw the damage she'd just caused.

No. She was already bending over the bar, stealing another shot and flirting with the bartender.

I rolled my eyes, apologized to the server again, left the bartender a hefty tip, and then walked out of the bar.

Grayson wasn't at happy hour. I hadn't talked to him all day and I was now officially experiencing withdrawal symptoms: shaking (probably due to the fact that I had no blazer on and it was chilly outside), fatigue (sure, maybe I was tired because I woke up early), and irritability (probably owing to drunk Hannah more than anything).

As I walked home, I imagined the various reasons why Grayson had skipped the happy hour. Maybe he was busy with a client or doing something else for work...or maybe he was back with Nicole?

Yuck. Yuck. Yuck.

I couldn't help but imagine the entire scene in full detail. She had probably arrived at his apartment wearing some kind of skimpy outfit and then forced him to let her in. She'd probably found a way to convince him to let her stay and then they'd had raucous makeup sex all over his what-I-assumed-to-be-badass apartment.

I stabbed my keycard into my apartment building and pulled the door open. The metal handle hit the concrete wall with a dull thud, but I didn't care. The concrete was the least of my worries.

I'd gone to happy hour for Grayson—just like I'd done so many things for Grayson over the last few weeks—and he hadn't even been there.

Why wasn't he there?

"Cammie?"

Chapter Sixteen

Grayson stood a few yards down the hallway, half cast in shadows. He was blocking my apartment, leaning back with his hands tucked into his suit pants and his foot propped against the door. The single overhead light was enough to make out the pieces of him that I found irresistible: the strong jaw, the defined cheekbones, the dark brows, and the James Dean attitude.

He'd been waiting for me.

"You missed happy hour," I said, pulling out my key ring to unlock the door. My hands shook with nerves, but I doubted he could see that in the dim lighting.

"Did you walk home by yourself?" he asked. A polite person would have given me space to unlock the door, but he crowded me, making it so I had to brush against him to reach the lock.

"I'm home. Does it matter how I got here?" I asked, turning the key in the lock.

"Where's Hannah?" he asked.

I turned to glance up at him and froze when I realized how close we were to one another. If he bent down an inch or if I stood on my toes, our mouths would meet and my heart would splinter into two parts: one that belonged to me and one that would always belong to Grayson.

"Back at the bar," I answered, turning my knob.

"Good."

Grayson pressed one hand to my lower back and used his other hand to push open my apartment door. I didn't have time to think as he ushered me past the threshold, into my dark apartment.

"What are you doing here?" I asked.

My question was met with the sound of my door locking back into place. *Clearly he intended on staying.* I stepped into the living room, trying to create a safety zone between the two of us.

I shook my head and turned to face him.

"Wait, how do you know where I live?"

He was inspecting my apartment, turning in a slow circle as he pulled his suit jacket off and tossed it onto the arm of my couch.

"Well you can go if you're just going to be weird and quiet," I said after he'd ignored my question.

He turned to me and smirked. His dark eyes captivated me, shaking my confidence. When I continued to speak, my voice was shaky and softer than it'd been a moment before.

"I'm tired, Grayson. And stupid Alan gave me extra work so I have to wake up at like four in the morning…"

My sentence trailed off as Grayson stepped forward and reached for my hands. He gripped them between his palms and pulled me back toward the hallway that branched off to the two bedrooms.

"You asked me what I was doing here," he said.

I nodded, mute. My eyes focused on his lips as he spoke, maybe because they were at eye level or maybe because I knew they were the key to my demise.

"Do you want to know?" he asked with an arched brow.

I tried to nod, but Grayson was quicker. He gripped my chin and raised it up just before he bent and stole a kiss. I closed my eyes and inhaled the moment as my fingers dug into his biceps. His lips were feather soft but his kiss was rough, full of desire and impatience for things to come.

My body moved instinctively, pressing against him and pushing him in the direction of my doorway. His hands drifted up into my hair, twisting the strands between his fingers and using them to tilt my head to the side so that he could deepen our kiss.

We backed up into my bedroom together slowly, clumsily. I jabbed him with my elbow. Our knees crashed together as we tried to sync our steps. He tripped over a pair of my heels in the hallway, and I laughed, carefully stepping over them before we fell through my open bedroom door.

He kicked the bedroom door closed behind us and we were finally, blissfully alone in my room. Thin shafts of light streamed in from the window beside my bed, and Grayson didn't bother with turning on the light switch.

"Do you want this?" he asked, reaching for the hem of my blouse, already working it up over my stomach before I could reply.

My mouth dropped.

Who the hell was this person and how was I supposed to keep up?

"I…think so," I answered, proud of the truth.

I wanted to do this. God, I wanted to do *anything* with this man. But to say I was scared of the aftermath was an understatement. It was impossible to lose myself in the moment as he gently tugged my blouse over my head. My mind worked overtime, firing off question after question.

Why did he suddenly want me?

Was he drunk?

What would happen tomorrow when he was back to wanting nothing to do with me?

"Relax," he whispered as my silk blouse brushed against my cheeks on its way over my head. The cool air conditioning hit my bare skin and I couldn't stand it. I couldn't stand there as he undressed me. We had to be on an even playing field. I reached for the top button of his shirt and slowly worked each button loose until I could slide my hands inside, over his hard chest, and push the shirt to the ground.

"How many men have you been with?" he asked, twisting me around and pulling me back to press our bodies together. His pecs brushed the top of my shoulder blades. His arms encircled me. He bent to take my earlobe between his teeth as his palms slid down the front of my stomach, down over my belly button. My muscles tensed with nerves, but his hand continued its descent as my head fell back against his shoulder.

"How many?" he asked again. His lips tickled my earlobe as he spoke.

"A few," I answered, truthfully. I hadn't counted. Maybe five or six, but he didn't need to know the exact number.

"Were you in love with any of them?" he asked, keeping one hand on the base of my stomach as his other hand trailed up the center of my chest, over the lace of my bra and around the edge of each cup.

"Not always."

My eyes fluttered closed for a moment.

"And what about you? Do I even want to know?" I asked.

His right hand unbuttoned the top of my pants as his left hand slid the strap of my bra down over my shoulder. I let his touch roam over my skin, trying to ignore the sound of my heavy breath in the silent room. His right hand slid further down my stomach, inside the waistband of my pants and then past the hem of my panties. I squeezed my eyes closed harder and gripped the front of his thighs as my heart rioted inside of my chest.

"Enough," he answered, emphasizing the final syllable by sliding a finger inside of me.

I bit down on my bottom lip to keep from crying out. It was all too much, a complete sensory overload. My mind was screaming, *"Why me? Why now?"* and my heart was yelling, *"Shut up and enjoy the ride."*

I'd never experienced someone like him. I'd fumbled around with guys in college, boys who were curious and just as nervous as I'd been. Grayson was confidence personified as he unhooked my bra and tossed it the ground, taking control of the situation in a way that left me breathless.

"Did you mean it the other day when you said you just wanted to play around?" he asked, throwing my words back to me. I'd uttered them in a moment of confidence, and now I was going to have to back them up. Either that, or ask him to stop. For a moment, I stood there, thinking over my options.

Then I let a slow smile unfold across my lips.

"We want the same thing, Grayson," I said before stepping out of his grasp and spinning around to face him. I was already naked from the waist up, but I could take it a step further, showing him just how serious I was.

I backed up to the edge of my bed and met his sharp blue eyes as I hooked my fingers around the hem of my pants and underwear. I shimmied my hips as I slid the material down and then let it drop to the floor.

Neither one of us spoke as he stood, scanning my bare skin in the moonlight streaming through my window. That exposure that comes with allowing someone to see all of you never gets easier to handle, but I stood still, letting him get his fill until he wanted more.

He moved fast, stepping forward and pushing me back until I fell onto the rumpled blankets on my bed.

My hand reached forward for the pocket of his suit pants and I used my grip on the silky fabric to tug him forward so that his weight fell onto me. For a few delicious seconds I felt suffocated by him, by his weight and presence crushing me against my soft blankets.

He stared down at me with a newfound desire just before he bent to steal another kiss. From that moment on, I was a puppet under Grayson's strings. Each part of my body reacted so willingly to his touch. I tried to keep up, to tease him like he teased me, but he wasn't having it. Our lips fought, pressed together so hard that his breath was my breath, his lips were my lips.

The rest of our clothes hit the floor and my sanity slipped away with them.

I clawed the sheets as he slid into me. He was over me, his gaze holding mine. My eyes started to water but he couldn't tell in the moonlight. It was just the two of us, giving in to the one thing we'd wanted from the very beginning.

"How long have you wanted this?" he whispered into my ear as his hips rolled with mine.

I felt his cheek against my lips as I pulled him down to me.

When I answered, my eyes were closed and my heart was trying desperately to stay whole, in one piece and out of Grayson's grasp.

"Always."

• • •

I woke up sometime later to the sound of my apartment door slamming shut. A drunk Hannah stumbled in, giggling as she made her way through the apartment. A loud thud, shuffling feet, and more giggles hinted at the fact that she'd probably just tripped over the same pair of high heels that Grayson had only a few hours earlier.

I turned my head to see Grayson staring up at the ceiling, awake as well. Chances were, he was contemplating the very things that were running through my own mind. We'd just had sex. Rock-your-mama's-socks-off sex, but now we had to repackage our relationship as best as possible.

I kept repeating the same phrases over and over again in my head: *This changes nothing. You did what you wanted to do. Now move on. This changes nothing. You did what you wanted to do. Now move on.*

"You need to distract Hannah while I leave," he said, pushing off the bed. I stayed still for a moment, studying the contours of his body before he found his pants and pulled them on in one deft motion.

I didn't want to be sad that he was leaving. I would have left too if I were him. What were we going to do? Snuggle up together and fall sleep, then wake up and make breakfast together? That scenario didn't fit into our reality, so I pushed the pang of sadness aside and tried to make the best of the situation.

"Can't you just go out the window like they do in the movies?" I asked with a cheeky smile.

He shot me a deathly glance that was more charming than threatening, but I still pushed myself up off my bed.

"It's up to you. Do you want your roommate knowing that I was here?" he asked, reaching for his shirt and slipping it back on. There were far more wrinkles in it now that it'd made its debut on my bedroom floor. Even with the wrinkles, when he had his shirt and suit pants back on, he looked far more like the CEO of Cole Designs and far less like the man who'd waited for me outside of my apartment earlier that night.

I found my robe behind my closet door and pulled it on before heading toward my door. I reached for the knob and glanced back. Grayson was standing there encased in moonlight, watching me watch him. There was so much to say and yet neither of us spoke a word.

I opened the door a smidgen and pushed through, praying that Hannah wasn't standing on the other side.

She wasn't. She was in our shared bathroom at the end of the hallway, brushing her teeth and leaning heavily on the counter.

"Hannah! You're home!" My acting was mediocre at best, but at least she was probably too drunk to notice.

"Hey roomie," she said, not bothering to pull her toothbrush out of her mouth. Toothpaste sprayed across the mirror and Hannah erupted in a fit of giggles. *Yeah, hilarious.*

"Here, let me help you with that," I said, stepping into the bathroom and pulling the door closed behind me so that Grayson could sneak out without being seen.

Hannah kept right on brushing her teeth as I barricaded the door closed as casually as possible. I listened as she spit out details of her night—at least I thought that's what she was saying over the sound of the electric tooth brush—but my hearing was actually tuned to the front door as I waited for the audible click.

"You missed so much!" she exclaimed, leaning over the sink and using toilet paper to wipe away her eye makeup. It wasn't working very well, but she didn't seem to mind. "You and Grayson were both missing! Grayson, ugh. I wish he had showed up. I really wanted to have a drink with him." I nodded while my cheeks flamed red. *Would she still be raving about Grayson if she knew what had just taken place?*

"He was supposed to be there. He would have looked so fucking hot in one of those suits he always wears." She continued droning on about him, but my emotions were too raw to handle a drunk version of Hannah raving about Grayson. My Grayson. I left her to finish up in the bathroom and stepped back out into the hallway with a tinge of hope still burning. Maybe he hadn't left. Maybe he was still in my room.

When I got to the doorway of my room and found it empty, I breathed in the taste of disappointment. My eyes swept over the dark space to take in the crumpled bed sheets, my clothes scattered across the floor, the condom wrapper left on my nightstand. Grayson had ripped it open with his mouth in the heat of the moment. Those things were the only evidence that Grayson had been there at all and yet they weren't enough to sustain me.

This changes nothing. You did what you wanted to do. Now move on.

I stepped inside and closed the door behind me, wondering what I was supposed to do. *Go to sleep? Wake up and go through the motions?*

This changes nothing. You did what you wanted to do. Now move on.

I moved to my bed and breathed in the remnants of Grayson's cologne and aftershave. I crawled onto the very center of the sheets, where his scent was the strongest, and wrapped my bedding around myself. With every inhale, I breathed in his aftershave, and with every exhale, I reminded myself that nothing was different.

Now move on.

Chapter Seventeen

Despite my best efforts to get rid of her, Hannah stood next to me in the office's kitchen Tuesday morning, sipping her coffee and getting on my last nerve.

"I can't wait until I see Grayson," she said, leaning against the counter with a dreamy look in her eyes. "I'm going to find out why he didn't show up to the bar last night."

"Great idea," I replied with an edge of sarcasm that she didn't catch.

"It's probably better that he didn't come," she continued. "I was so trashed by the end of the night. Every time I turned around, another guy was offering me a shot. And, I mean, I didn't want to be rude, so I just took them. But, oh my gosh, that Peter guy was there—your table-mate with the crazy beard? He doesn't take a hint, does he? I swear he tried to talk to me like fifty times."

Hmm, yeah, great. Sure, tell me more. I continued to feign interest as I poured my third cup of coffee for the day.

My first two cups hadn't cut it, and I was hoping that by some miracle this one would be laced with crack or something so that I could actually focus on my work.

The copious amounts of coffee were owed to the fact that I'd had to arrive early—*too early*—to finish the sketches for Alan and I was already running on fumes. (And yes, the sketches were done. No thanks to Grayson keeping me up late the night before.)

"Hey guys."

I looked up from my mug to see a Peter smiling in the doorway.

"Hey Peter." I offered him a small nod.

"Oh god. It's him again," Hannah whispered under her breath.

I had to clench my fist to keep from punching her in the boob. Peter was ten times the person she'd ever be.

"We have a team meeting in ten in the conference room. They want all the architecture staff in there," he announced, tapping his hand on the doorframe twice and then heading off down the hall.

I stared back down at my coffee, attempting to keep my cool. There was a 50/50 chance that Grayson would be leading the meeting, which meant I'd be forced to see him for the first time since last night, in a room full of my coworkers. I guess it was as good an opportunity as any to gauge his reaction to me. If he ignored me all together, I'd know we were back at square one, that last night really hadn't changed a thing.

"Well there's my chance to confront Grayson," Hannah said with a confident smile.

I took a sip of my coffee to avoid saying something I'd regret and then trailed after Hannah toward the conference room. With every step, my anxiety grew and my stomach tightened. Why was I so nervous? Grayson had come over to *my* apartment. He'd sought *me* out and *he'd* made the first move.

I was mid-thought when I stepped into the conference room and was met by a room full of my yawning coworkers. They each tried to subtly hide their fatigue behind mugs of coffee, but no one wanted to be in a meeting this early after a late night of happy hour-ing, least of all me.

My gaze automatically sought out Grayson, and when I saw him, I paused mid-step. He was stationed at the front of the room, donning a black suit that molded to him like he'd been dipped into the fabric that very morning. His tie was a bright blue hue and although his gaze wasn't directed toward me, I knew the color would complement his eyes perfectly. It was almost painful to look at him—as if I was staring into the sun, knowing I was damaging my eyes in the process, yet unable look away. This was the moment I'd dreaded all morning; and now it was upon me and it was every bit as hard as I imagined it would be. I knew what every single inch of him looked like beneath that suit. *That jacket. That shirt.* They did nothing to disguise the man that lay beneath, a man made for a singular purpose: breaking my heart apart piece by piece.

A part of me wanted to disguise myself, to step to the back of the room and hide behind my fellow coworkers. It was easy to watch him when he was talking to someone else. There was no harm in appreciating him from afar, so I let the other architects fill in the space in front of me as I fell back against the conference room wall. Each person that filled in the space before me felt like another layer of protection between him and me.

Movement near the front of the room drew my attention toward Hannah. I'd lost her when we'd entered the conference room and now I knew why. I'd gone for a post in the back, somewhere safe and discreet. Hannah, on the other hand, was trying to get as close to Grayson as possible, working her way through the crowd until she was nearly breathing the same air as him.

"Is Hannah your roommate?" Peter asked beside me. I hadn't even realized he'd snuck in after me, but I suppose I had been a bit distracted by other things.

I glanced back toward Hannah, who was checking her reflection in a small compact mirror.

I laughed. "Yup, that's my roomie."

"She was pretty trashed last night," he said, making a drinking motion with his thumb and pinky finger. "Kind of a bold move at her first office happy hour."

I smiled. "No kidding. In her defense, I'd be drinking too if Alan was my mentor."

"I ended up calling a cab for her. She wasn't looking so good at the end there."

I glanced back toward Hannah. She was staring up at Grayson adoringly, inching closer toward him by the second. He didn't even notice her presence as he kept right on speaking with another associate.

"Thanks for doing that," I muttered. "She actually said something about you trying to hit on her." I slid him a playful smile so he'd know that I was on his side.

He chuckled and shook his head. "Oh god. Please tell me you have more faith in me than that. I was probably trying to tell her that the cab was ready to take her home."

I shot him a wink and was about to reply when Grayson interrupted me.

"Good morning, everyone," Grayson's voice boomed from the front of the room. My heart skidded to a stop as I glanced up at him. *That voice had whispered in my ear just a few hours earlier.* "I won't be keeping you long, so listen up. I want to update everyone on the current projects we have lined up. We've had quite a few jobs come in during the last week so I'll assign each team a new client before we leave and I need you to establish contact with them by the end of the day. Meetings with the engineering and interior teams should be set up for sometime next week."

Every person in the room was staring at him and memorizing his words or jotting them down quickly in their notebooks. His voice was rich and sharp—too confident to be ignored. Twenty-four hours ago I didn't know what that voice sounded like in my bedroom. I didn't know what it was like to hear him whisper dirty things into my ear as his hands slid across my skin. Now I knew his voice all too well and I couldn't escape the memories bombarding me from every angle.

That's what happens when you sleep with your boss, genius.

As if he could read my thoughts, Grayson's eyes finally found me, huddled against the side wall with my arms crossed.

I held my breath, trying to steel myself for the worst possible reaction. His speech faltered for a moment and then the side of his mouth hitched up almost imperceptibly, but I saw it and it was all I needed to know.

Things *were* different. *Last night changed everything.*

The meeting didn't last more than ten minutes after that, and before I trailed out, Grayson called my name.

I stopped in the doorway and turned toward him, aware that there were still twenty or so employees milling around the room, and at least half of them had paused their conversation to see what he wanted to talk to me about.

I walked toward him and paused a safe distance away. "Yes, Mr. Cole?"

He smirked at my formality.

"Would you mind reading this and passing it along to Alan?" he asked, holding out a small post-it note. Alan had walked out of the room not two seconds before. I knew this because I'd been trying to avoid walking near him in an attempt to save us both the trouble of small talk. Grayson could have easily given Alan the post-it note himself.

I took the post-it from his hand, careful to avoid physical contact, and then walked out of the conference room without another word. Midway back to my desk, I glanced down at the note. He hadn't taken the time to fold it or conceal the message. The words were there, plain to read: *Meet me at Lawry's Deli for lunch.*

When I glanced back to the conference room, Grayson was already chatting with a few senior associates.

Did he really intend on having me pass the note along to Alan?

My gut told me no, which meant my lunch break was about to get a lot more interesting.

• • •

At half past noon, I walked into the deli during their lunch rush. Lively music blasted through the speakers overhead and employees with bright bandanas wrapped around their foreheads were whipping up sandwiches behind the deli counter at lightning speed. Every few seconds, an employee would ring the bell next to the cash register and then shout a name.

"Carol! Order up!"

Another ding of the bell.

"Sandy! Your order is ready!"

Ding!

Their sandwiches must have been pretty good considering how many people were in line to get one. Just as the bell on the counter rang again, accompanied by another shouted name, I felt a hand wrap around my waist until pausing on the inside of my hip bone.

"You didn't deliver the note," Grayson teased, bending down to whisper in my ear.

The deli was only a few blocks from our office; I'd walked there in less than ten minutes so it wasn't out of the question to think a coworker was there enjoying a sandwich as well.

"Grayson," I hissed, turning out of his grasp and scanning the room for any familiar faces.

He chuckled and shook his head, pocketing his hands in a display of earnestness.

"There. Better?" he asked with a smirk.

I pressed my lips together to conceal my smile and nodded.

My entire body was humming with nervous energy, taking in the noisy deli, the delicious smells, and the fact that Grayson Cole was standing directly behind me with his hip touching mine.

"Are you hungry?" he asked, gazing over the menu that was written in chalk above the counter.

My stomach was wound so tightly I doubted I'd be able to eat a thing.

"Not really. I had a lot of coffee this morning."

I turned to look up at him, to try and decipher what he was thinking. *Was this really a casual lunch together? Or did he have more devious plans?* Something told me not to let my guard down. My downfall would come if I got too comfortable, too used to his attention being aimed at me. I felt like I was at the top of a roller coaster: I knew that sharp drop was coming, the plunge to the ground. So I took a breath and held on to the high as hard as I could.

"Did you drive here?" I asked.

He pointed to his sports car out front, its gunmetal gray paint gleaming in the sunlight. The lines were sharp and sexy—a dangerous car for doing dangerous deeds.

"Let's go," I said, walking toward the door without waiting for a response.

I had a wild idea and I knew I'd lose traction if I paused for even a moment.

He followed me out and unlocked his car. The locks popped up and I swung the passenger door open so I could slide down onto the cool black leather.

"Where to?" Grayson asked as the car roared to life.

I turned toward the window and spoke with feigned confidence. "Somewhere close and secluded."

A second later we were blazing down the boulevard, weaving in between cars and gunning it through yellow lights. My body pressed back against the leather as he pushed the gas pedal down harder. I studied the veins on his hands as he gripped the steering wheel with utter control.

We didn't drive for long, a few minutes at most and then we were pulling off the road into the parking lot of an abandoned warehouse.

"Unbuckle your belt," Grayson demanded as he swung the car into a spot behind the building.

Adrenaline was getting the better of me. I didn't hesitate and as soon as I was free, he killed the engine and I slid over onto his lap. My high heels fell off in the transition and my head hit the roof with a thud. The space was too tight, but we worked together so that I could straddle his hips comfortably. *This is happening.* He was already working to push the hem of my skirt up to my waist. The thin fabric ripped, echoing our actions throughout the interior of the car.

"Grayson," I whispered as his hand hit the inside of my thigh.

Last night wasn't the end.

I couldn't move in the confined space. If I leaned back, I'd honk the horn, so I leaned against him, letting my head fall to his shoulder and my lips press against his neck. My breath faltered as his fingers slid higher, our devious actions starting to become harder to fathom.

"Unzip my pants, Cammie," Grayson demanded with a rough voice.

Our bodies were sealed together, so I had to slide my hand down between us, feeling my own soft curves against his hard chest. My hand skimmed over my breast and my back arched in response. Grayson groaned beneath me, clearly enjoying the way I pressed down against him as my back arched further.

"Now, Cammie," Grayson urged, digging his fingers into the back of my thigh in a painful show of power.

I bit down on my lip, stifling a cry.

His zipper was easy to find and even easier to slide down.

"Pull your panties to the side," he said as he drew his fingers to his mouth, wetting them with his tongue while he waited for me to follow his instructions.

I did what he asked, feeling the cool air against my sensitive skin. And then he was there, dipping his fingers inside of me and dragging me down further into my fantasy.

"Let yourself slide down," he begged into my ear as my eyes rolled back.

This was it. This was the top of the ride. The ascent was over and the impending plunge would ruin me for life. I knew all of that, and still there wasn't a moment of hesitation as I gripped his shoulders and let my thighs relax. He watched me with rapt attention as I slid down millimeter by millimeter.

"Fuck," he moaned as I felt his fingers press against my sweetest spot.

"This is crazy," I gasped, letting my head fall back.

His free hand wrapped around my neck as he kissed down to my collarbone.

"I want you to come like this," he demanded, taking the reins back into his own hands.

I stared up at the ceiling and begged for more. We thrived off the intensity of the moment, the exhilaration of tugged hair and clawed arms and kissed lips. His rhythm stole my resolve again and again until the windows fogged up, I'd accidentally honked the horn twice, and I'd bruised my elbow on the car console more times than I could count.

The entire experience was dark and frenzied and utterly heartbreaking.

The ride back to the office was quiet and tense. I did my best to conceal the damage to my clothes and hair; but it was a windy day so I hoped no one would pay attention to a little sex hair.

When we arrived back at the Sterling Bank Building, Grayson pulled up at the corner of the block, away from prying eyes.

"Should I go up—" I asked at the same time he spoke.

"We should probably go up separately."

I nodded, fumbling with the obnoxiously fancy door handle. There were at least thirty knobs and whistles on the damn door and I was left pressing anything that could possibly get me out. He chuckled and leaned over, popping the door open for me.

"Wait," I said, suddenly growing curious about something. "What made you give me that note this morning in the conference room?"

"Do I have to give a reason?" he smirked.

I laughed. "Yes."

"I liked the way you looked," he replied with a cheeky smile.

"No," I shook my head. "There's more to it than that."

He sighed and looked out the window for a moment before meeting my eye with a look of steely resolve.

He shrugged, trying to downplay the sincerity of the moment and then he finally answered, "You've always been someone who *interests* me."

I smiled. "Ah, now that makes sense. I am a very interesting girl." I winked and he shook his head, pretending to be annoyed with my joke.

"I'll see you up there in a just a minute," he promised before placing a kiss on my cheek.

It was such a gentle move—a chaste kiss on the cheek wasn't Grayson's style—and yet it was enough to send me walking away from his car with a smile, wondering what in the world would come next.

• • •

Fifteen minutes later, Grayson stepped out of the elevator with two brown paper bags. I leaned back in my desk and squinted to read the black writing on the side of the bags, but I didn't get the chance to make out the logo before he dropped one of them onto my desk.

"Thanks for doing that errand for me during lunch," he spoke with a formal, impersonal tone. "I figured you didn't have time to eat. "

Like mine the night before, his acting was mediocre at best, but Peter and Mark were both busy on the phone and Alan was too preoccupied to care that Grayson was giving me lunch. Still, it made me smile all the same.

"Thanks. That errand worked up my appetite," I said.

He nodded and turned toward his office while I examined the brown paper bag.

"Lawry's Deli" was printed in black cursive and when I opened the top of the bag, there was a note scribbled on one of the deli's napkins.

"I ordered you my favorite sandwich. Hope you like it. PS You left your jacket in my car. I think I already know a way that you could earn it back. - G"

Chapter Eighteen

I was at my desk on Wednesday morning, brainstorming ideas for my secret design submission, when my work phone rang so unexpectedly that I almost jumped out of my skin.

I stared down at it with wide eyes. Someone was calling my work phone. The last person that had called my work phone was Grayson's mom. So, chances were Grayson's mom would be on the other end of the line.

The phone rang again and Alan's beady little eyes sliced over to me.

"Are you going to answer that phone or let the client get your voicemail? Jesus Christ."

"Oh, right."

I reached for the receiver and crossed my fingers beneath my desk. *Please don't be Grayson's mom. Please don't be Grayson's mom.* I liked her, but the only update I actually had for her was that I was currently doing the horizontal tango with her son.

"Hello?" I asked hesitantly.

"There you are slutasaurus rex. You didn't answer your cell phone so I thought I'd try you at work."

Brooklyn. Oh, thank God.

"Is that annoying boss beside you right now? Is that why you aren't talking?" Brooklyn asked when I didn't respond.

I peered over at Alan from beneath my lashes and slyly lowered the receiver volume a few notches.

"Oh hello, Mr. Duncan," I spoke on a whim. *Mr. Duncan?* I didn't know a single person with the last name Duncan.

Brooklyn laughed.

"Cough once if you want me to kill him. Cough twice if you want me to get Jason to kill him."

"I'm not sure about either of those options, Mr. Duncan," I droned, peering over again to see if Alan could hear her.

"Sorry, those are your only choices. Oh, wait, hold on." I heard Jason mumbling in the background and then Brooklyn dropped the phone into a box of tin foil—or so I assumed since it felt like my ears were were going to fall off from the loud scraping sounds.

"What are you doing? Jeez, that's so loud."

"Oh, sorry. I'm doing the dishes. Jason wanted me to ask you about going to get a drink tonight. Could you come after work?"

I glanced down at my pile of work and sighed. The work would be waiting for me tomorrow. I deserved a night of fun and I hadn't seen Brooklyn in a few days.

"Yeah, just send me the details."

I hung up the phone as inconspicuously as possible. Alan cleared this throat.

"Was that a personal call, Cammie?" he asked with a shrewd glance.

I had a brief moment of panic before composing myself. "Yes. It was my gynecologist. He wanted to discuss my latest pap smear. Do you want to know how the cells on my cervix are doing?"

Alan visibly blanched, as most guys tend to do at the mention of the dreaded pap.

"No. That's all right. Just get back to work."

"Okay, but I can't stay late tonight. I have another pap smear after work."

He grumbled and nodded, scooting a half inch away from me.

Well that was easy.

How many pap smears could one person conceivably get in one month? Fifteen, twenty? "Damnit, inconclusive again! Well Alan, it looks like it's just pap smears through June."

• • •

Later that afternoon, I asked Beatrice if Grayson was available. His office door was closed and he was probably deep into his design work, but I hadn't seen him all day. I just needed a few minutes, just to assure myself that whatever was happening between us wasn't over yet. A vision of our lunch the day before flashed through my mind and I blushed.

"Oh, let me see," she answered, picking up her phone and buzzing through to him.

"Mr. Cole do you have a moment?"

I couldn't hear what he asked on the other end, but she looked up at me and replied, "Cammie."

I twisted my hands together, knowing I wouldn't handle his rejection well, but then Beatrice hung up and waved me forward.

"Go on back," she said with a smile before turning back to her work.

I stepped forward and turned the knob, aware of my pulse thumping wildly as I pushed the door open. Grayson was behind his desk, encased in the light streaming through the window behind him. His lips were twisted into a smirk that did nothing but pull me in closer.

I made sure the door was secured behind me, twisting the lock so that the audible click punctuated Grayson's steps toward me.

"I was just about to ask you to come in," Grayson said as he approached me. One hand wrapped around my waist, pulling me closer, and the other tilted my head so that he could dip down to steal a quick kiss.

Was he going to touch me in his office, where anyone could hear us?

His confidence took me by surprise, but I let him pull me closer until our hips met and I could wrap my hands around his neck.

"I haven't seen you all day and I wasn't sure how busy you were," I spoke as our eyes met.

He smiled and bent to kiss me again before replying, "Very busy."

I hummed against his chest and inhaled the scent I'd come to love. His suit was softer than I expected and I could feel his toned arms beneath, keeping me pinned against him.

"I'm busy too. The CEO here is a real tyrant," I said with a cheeky smile.

He chuckled and let me go, taking a step back to lean against his desk. His eyes slid down my body and I felt far too exposed in my fitted pants and jacket.

"I'm going to get drinks with Brooklyn and Jason tonight," I blurted out. I wanted him to come, but we were in that gray area that accompanies situations like ours. I couldn't just come out and tell him that I wanted to see him later because that'd be too obvious. I had to make it seem casual so that I could try to hold my cards close for as long as possible.

He nodded and crossed his arms. "What time?"

"Six."

Ask if you can join. Ask if you can join.

"Should be fun. Jason's a good guy."

He wasn't going to make this easy.

I nodded and took a minuscule step closer.

"Why don't you come with us?"

I wondered if he heard how shaky my voice sounded.

He smiled. "I'd like that."

I bit down on the side of my bottom lip, elated that he hadn't turned me down.

"Does Brooklyn know about us?" he asked.

I swallowed. "No. Should she?"

He shrugged. "I just wanted to make sure I played it right."

I took a minute to mull over our options and then I came to the conclusion that telling Brooklyn about us this early would be a bad idea. Surely she'd have her own opinions about us, but I was still trying to figure out where we stood on my own. I didn't need her influencing anything yet.

"So, it'll just be a *friendly* happy hour," I said with suggestive smile.

He reached out and dipped his finger into the waist of my pants so that he could pull me toward him. I had no choice but to comply or I'd have tripped forward over my feet.

"What if I can't fake it later?" he asked, letting his hands drift up to my bare neck.

I closed my eyes and tried to come up with a response. Voices from the office drifted through the door and goosebumps blossomed beneath his touch. His left hand trailed up around my chin and brushed a few tendrils of hair behind my ear.

"Maybe we should kiss right now and get it out of our system," I suggested selfishly.

He laughed. "Somehow I don't think a kiss would do it."

I opened my eyes and took a step backward.

"You're right, I'd better just get back to work," I said.

Grayson laughed and reached out for me again, twisting us around so that the back of my thighs pressed against his desk. He pinned me there, held my neck, and dipped me backward.

I twined my fingers together around his neck to keep from falling back as he kissed me and slipped his hand beneath the hem of my blouse. My stomach quivered as he skimmed over my bare stomach, blazing a trail of desire as he went.

"Grayson!" The intercom speakers blared through the room and I jumped away from him. "You have a meeting with Walters in fifteen minutes. If you leave now, it'll take you about ten minutes to get to his office."

The intercom cut off but my face still heated as if Beatrice had actually walked in and caught us in the act.

The Design

"Oh God, that kiss was a terrible, terrible idea," I said, pushing him off me so that I could straighten my blouse and pants.

He laughed and shook his head, already en route to a small bathroom to the side of his office.

"I like playing with fire," he said, meeting my eye in the mirror. "And I don't have any intention of stopping."

I watched him straighten his tie and suit jacket in the mirror. Every single one of his features was sharp and ready to deliver a killer presentation. His pants however were sporting a noticeable bulge, one he needed to attend to if he hoped to walk through the office without causing a scene. I smiled at the knowledge that I'd been the cause of it.

"You have my number, right?" Grayson asked, reaching down to splash some water on his face and then dabbing it dry with a hand towel.

"I stole it from Brooklyn's phone a while back," I admitted.

And by "a while back", I mean when I was eighteen.

"Good," he said, coming out of the bathroom and collecting a few papers from his desk. "Text me the info for drinks. I'll be there."

• • •

"Have a good meeting with Grayson?" Hannah asked as I refilled my coffee in the kitchen an hour later. Since leaving Grayson's office I'd been *very* productive: I'd managed to check an email, pick up the phone only to forget who I was meant to be calling, and then sip two cups of coffee while recreating our various make outs in my head.

I glanced up at Hannah with a confused glance.

"Uh, yeah, I guess the meeting was good." I was hoping I sounded nonchalant, but the words came out more defensive than I'd intended.

She narrowed her eyes. "You know he doesn't have meetings like that with anyone else. You must be pretty special."

"I think you're reading too much into it," I shrugged. "It's boring mentor-mentee stuff, just like your meetings with Alan."

Hannah stepped closer so that she could reach for a mug of her own. The fact that I had to quickly duck so that the cabinet door wouldn't whack me in the face didn't faze her.

"Well it seems funny, because I tried to schedule a meeting with him yesterday and Beatrice said he wasn't available for a few days, yet you just waltz right up to his office and he lets you in. Strange, right?"

I set my mug down on the counter, crossed my arms, and turned to Hannah.

"What are you getting at, Hannah? Just say what you want to say."

Her stern expression broke into a smile, a deviously placative smile. "What?" She laughed. "I was just wondering if there was anything you wanted to tell me. Y'know, as roomies."

I shivered at the way she said *roomie*. We'd only lived together for a few weeks, and I hadn't seen this side of her. I thought her attraction for Grayson was a silly crush, but as she stared at me from over her coffee mug, I had a feeling I'd underestimated her obsession with him.

I'd definitely be locking my door from now on.

I offered her a fake smile. "I don't think you have anything to worry about. Grayson is my sister's friend and that's probably why he doesn't mind meeting with me. He doesn't want to piss her off," I laughed. My entire demeanor seemed glaringly transparent to me, but I hoped Hannah couldn't tell.

She tilted her head and watched me for another few seconds before a small, genuine smile unfolded across her lips.

"That's right," she nodded. "I forgot how close they were."

I inwardly sighed. "Oh, yeah, like family," I continued, embellishing the details. "They've known each other for years and she'd kill him if he was rude to me— listen, I gotta get back to work. Alan has been on my case all day."

She nodded as if she understood. "Oh, I bet. I'll see you later," she called after me, sounding far more chipper than she had a few moments before.

As I left the kitchen, I made a mental note to play it safer with Grayson while we were at work. If Hannah suspected something, there was a good chance that she wasn't alone. There definitely couldn't be any more late night sneaking around in our apartment. I couldn't put the blame on my sister if Hannah found Grayson standing in our kitchen in his skivvies.

Chapter Nineteen

Amount saved for Paris: $1382 (minus the $98.99 I spent at the small boutique I passed on the way to drinks. The mannequin in the window was wearing a pair of ankle boots I needed for Paris. *Needed.*).
Items I have: #ankleboots.
Items I need: An outfit to wear with my new awesome #ankleboots.
French phrases that I know: Mon père est Liam Neeson, alors ne me prend pas…which translates to "My dad is Liam Neeson, so don't take me!" I figure it's a pretty important phrase to have in my arsenal.

Brooklyn picked a swanky bar for our happy hour. I could practically feel my wallet shrinking as I walked through the frosted glass entryway. The bar was on the bottom floor of a high-end LA hotel and there were two separate sides.

Normal people were filtered in on the left, and celebrities, moguls, and rock stars entered in on the right. I belonged on the left side without a doubt, but Jason and Brooklyn were far from normal. They weren't even in the normal VIP section. She'd texted me to let me know that they were in some kind of secluded VIP area—even fancier and more badass than the normal one. *Ah, the life of a rock star.*

"Ma'am, can I help you?" a bouncer asked as I tried to enter the special VIP section. I'd had no problem making it past the first round of bouncers. I had that skinny model look going on, mostly because asshole Alan never left me enough time to eat actual meals (*and when I did manage to sneak away, I spent the time boning my boss in the driver's seat of his swanky car*). I'd also unbuttoned the top two buttons of my blouse after leaving work just for some added incentive.

"Sure," I replied. "I'm here to see my sister, Brooklyn Heart."

The bouncer scoffed and gestured to his buddy next to him like *"Get a load of this crazy fangirl."*

The bouncer pointed behind me, toward the exit. "Yeah, *okay*. You need to head back to the front. If it makes you feel any better, you made it farther than most."

I huffed and then redialed Brooklyn's number for the thirtieth time.

"Oh, weird, maybe she changed her number," the other bouncer mimicked in a girlish tone, before punching his buddy playfully.

"That's the funniest thing you could come up with?" I asked them with a harsh glare right before I hit redial *again*.

By some miracle, she finally answered.

"Are you here?!" Brooklyn asked.

"Yeah, butthead. Come let me in. These bouncers don't believe that I'm VIP-worthy. They even think my 'Cameron Heart' driver's license is fake—I don't even know how to get a fake ID."

"Assholes. Hold on, I'll be right there."

I hung up and crossed my arms, trying to come up with the best possible thing to say as soon as Brooklyn showed up. If it were the mid 90s, I would have thrown out a classic "Whasssuppp suckers!" but that didn't feel cool enough for the current decade.

"Cammie!" Brooklyn sang as she pushed through the thick black curtain that concealed the VIP-VIP section from the rest of the club. She looked beautiful in a fitted sky blue dress and matching heels. Her long blonde hair swished back and forth as she walked closer and her lips were split into a giant smile aimed right at me. Every club-goer within a ten-foot radius completely freaked out when they caught a glimpse of her. Cell phones were whipped out and flashes started to blind me as they tried to snap a quick picture of her. Brooklyn was completely unfazed by the attention; I would have had a nervous meltdown.

"Boys," Brooklyn began as she placed her hand on one of the bouncer's shoulders. "This is my sister, Cammie. She shall pass, so quit giving her the Gandalf treatment."

The bouncers looked back at me with wide, shocked expressions. As I walked past them, I settled for a self-righteous smile because I didn't think *"That's right, motherfuckers,"* would have gone over well. I mean, altogether the bouncers weighed the amount of a small army tank; there was no reason to taunt them.

As soon as I crossed through the red rope, Brooklyn wrapped me up in a massive hug.

"She shall pass? Since when do you watch Lord of the Rings?" I asked.

"Jason and I may have been procrastinating on our album all week. Besides, Orlando Bloom is hot. Speaking of looking good, Sis," she said, holding me at arm's length. "Is that a new work outfit?"

I laughed and glanced down at my fitted cream blouse and navy blue skirt. "You bought it for me. You should know."

"I have such good taste," she winked. "Let's go wet your whistle."

She pulled me after her, deep into the center of the VIP section. The lights were low and the music was seductive and dark, with heavy bass reverberating around the room. It felt like I was stepping into an underground lair, especially when I caught sight of one of the bartenders sporting bright neon pink hair.

A massive black bar with a mirrored tile backsplash spread out against an entire wall of the room. We'd just made it to the far edge to order a drink, when I caught a whiff of what I swore was Grayson's aftershave. *It had to be.*

I turned to scan the bar, trying to find him. I hadn't seen him since he'd left for his meeting earlier and I wasn't convinced that he'd actually show up for drinks. Yet, there he was, standing next to Jason and another man I didn't recognize. The three men were all leaning against the bar, chatting and sipping their drinks.

Jason was facing away from me, but I could still see his leather jacket and worn jeans. Grayson was still in his tailored suit from earlier. Jason's hair was ruffled and wild, but Grayson's coal black hair was slicked back away from his face—ever the perfect businessman. They were so similar, yet polar opposites in many ways.

"Cammie!" Brooklyn said, snapping her fingers in front of my face. I assumed she'd been calling my name for the last few seconds while I'd been admiring the guys.

"Sorry. What's up?"

She eyed me curiously. "What do you want to drink?"

"Just whatever you're having," I said before glancing back over her shoulder. The boys had spotted us at the bar and three pair of eyes locked on me as I glanced over. Jason waved animatedly. The blonde stranger next to him smiled, and Grayson held up his glass in a silent salute, a private smirk already there, waiting for me.

I loved seeing him outside of work, in a dark room with people too busy to care if he and I wandered off together. My mind worked overtime to create scenarios where we could sneak away from the group. Maybe I could ask him to mentor me on the project we were working on and then he could mentor me in the bar's restroom.

Yeah, that sounded pretty good.

"Here ya go," Brooklyn said, holding out a small colorful drink for me. An orange slice was perched on the rim and when I took a sip to test it out, my tongue practically danced with excitement.

"This is amazing!" I said, clinking my glass with hers.

She laughed and started to head toward the guys. "It is, but it has a ton of alcohol in it, so be careful."

We wove through the young Hollywood crowd with our drinks and I tried to stay as close to Brooklyn as possible. In the two minutes it took us to reach the guys, I saw three movie stars, two famous singers, and a notorious heiress who'd leaked her own sex tape not three weeks before. They all looked like they'd been partying for hours and it was hardly 6:00 pm.

"Cammie's here!" Brooklyn called out as we joined the group.

"Finally!" Jason cheered, holding out his drink so that he and I could do a little cheers.

"Whattup, J-money," I quipped.

"Not much Cam-dog, lookin' good," Jason joked back.

Brooklyn made a show of rolling her eyes, pretending to be annoyed. "Can't you guys go back to hating each other? The rapper names need to go."

I winked at Jason. "She's just jellin'."

Grayson laughed and stepped forward, reaching a hand out as if to formally shake mine.

"Good to see you, Cameron," he said with a wicked grin.

I took his hand and narrowed my eyes, trying to keep up with our act. Our hands bobbed up and down for much longer than necessary, but his hand was strong and I didn't feel like pulling away.

"Seriously?! He still calls you Cameron? God Gray, you sound like a high school principal," Brooklyn complained as she tried to pry apart our hands.

Great, now I'll have enough fantasy scenarios to last a lifetime.

"Maybe your sister likes how I act around her, Brooklyn," Grayson quipped with enough hidden meaning to make me blush.

"Alright enough, you two," I said, letting go of Grayson's hand and glancing toward the fifth person in our group: the blonde man.

"Oh, sorry for that embarrassing introduction. I'm Cammie," I said with a polite smile.

Jason reached a hand around the blonde guy's shoulders and tugged him closer.

"Duh, why didn't we introduce you guys first? You're the reason we're here in the first place!"

"Oh my gosh!" Brooklyn said. "We're terrible at this."

I frowned, confused. *Terrible at what?*

"Cammie, this is Stuart, my accountant," Jason continued. "We invited him today so that you guys could meet."

Oh, Jesus.

Combined, Brooklyn and Jason had the subtlety of a screeching banshee. They basically sounded like they were my pimps. I smiled awkwardly at Stuart and shook his hand quickly, realizing that I'd majorly messed up. I'd completely forgotten about asking Brooklyn to set me up with someone. I guess I thought she'd never actually get around to it.

Welp, she *had* gotten around to it and now I was in for the most awkward happy hour of my life. It almost sounded like the punch line of a bad joke: so my sister, her rockstar boyfriend, the boss I'm secretly sleeping with, and an accountant walk into a bar...

Oy vey. Fortunately, Stuart seemed equally annoyed with the way Jason had introduced him. He stepped forward and straightened his shoulders, trying to smooth out the awkward transition. All in all, he was pretty good looking. He had clean cut blonde hair, a strong jaw, and cute, black-framed glasses.

"As Jason said, I'm his accountant," Stuart said with a proud smile as he assessed me, much the same way I'd just done to him.

Wow, an accountant. Be still my quivering loins...

"Cool. So you like numbers?" I asked, trying to make polite conversation.

Stuart smiled and adjusted his glasses, but he could reply, Grayson cut in, "So Stu, do y—"

"Uh, I actually prefer Stuart," he replied.

"Stuart." Grayson punctuated the end of his name with a touch of annoyance. "Do you think you can handle a girl like Cammie?" He asked the question with an innocent smile as he tipped his drink in my direction. Both of his dimples were on display, which meant that poor Stuart basically didn't even exist to me anymore.

"Grayson! Jeez, cool it. Nobody likes a cranky fifth wheel," Brooklyn chimed in.

I suppressed a snort and Grayson held up his hands in protest. "It was a joke. I just happen to know firsthand that Cammie can be quite feisty when she wants to be."

At once, Brooklyn, Stuart, and I replied.

"What?!" I asked.

"And how would you know?" Brooklyn glared.

Stuart smiled. "I'm sure I can manage."

Jason cut the tension by passing us a round of shots, which I pretended to take, but instead placed on the table behind me. I needed to have all of my cylinders firing during this hangout if I hoped to make it through. Having Stuart, Grayson, and Brooklyn in one room was a recipe for disaster.

"So Grayson, how do you know Cammie?" Stuart said, inching toward me in a clearly territorial move. His hand fell against the table behind me, so he wasn't exactly touching me, but the message was loud and clear.

"She's a friend," Grayson answered, taking a slow sip of his drink while his eyes locked with mine. *A friend?* I quirked an eyebrow and smiled, knowing he'd be able to tell what I was thinking.

"Also Cammie works at Grayson's architecture firm," Brooklyn clarified with a peculiar glare in Grayson's direction.

He grinned. "That too."

"Oh, really? I'd imagine it's pretty awkward seeing your boss out at a bar," Stuart said, turning to me for backup.

Grayson's blue gaze focused on me. "Interesting. What about you, Cammie? Do you feel awkward with me here?"

I was going to slowly and torturously murder him later. Like kill him using finger nail clippers so that it took one hundred hours. He deserved it. Also, sorry for the imagery, that's disgusting.

I shrugged. "I've been to worse happy hours."

The group laughed good-naturedly and I thought for a second that the situation might work out...and then Stuart decided to ruin the moment. He turned toward me and stepped closer so that we were cut off from the rest of the group.

Oh no he didn't.

"So tell me about yourself, Cammie," he said with a gentle smile.

Was I supposed to list off my horoscope or something?

"Oh, um, well," I kept on mumbling as I tried to peer around him and catch Grayson's eye.

Stuart moved with me and blocked my path, obviously aware of what I was doing.

"Have you always lived in LA?" he asked, filling in the silence for me.

I sighed and took a sip of my drink. If he wanted to talk, I'd talk to him. It wouldn't hurt to be nice. I answered Stuart with bland details as he asked me question after question. All the while, I also tried to hear what Jason was talking about with Grayson.

"Are you seeing anyone right now?" Jason asked.

ACCOUNTANT, PLEASE BE QUIET SO I CAN HEAR GRAYSON'S REPLY.

"Oh, yeah, I've just been—" I heard the first part of Grayson's answer before Stuart's voice cut in.

"I've just always had a knack for numbers," Stuart said. "Ever since I was a kid. I remember doing the 'million dollar' project in school and using it to buy a fictional laundromat. I was the only one to spend the money on a business that would make money in return!"

Oh my god, so he's not just a boring adult, he's been boring since he was a kid.

I leaned closer to where Jason and Grayson were chatting, trying to hear their conversation.

"Did you hear about the match-up for Sunday's game?" Grayson asked.

No. *Noooooooo.* I'd missed his answer. *C'mon!*

"That's so great, Stuart," Brooklyn said, cutting in before I made a complete fool of myself. "Cammie always had a knack for drawing. When she was little she'd carry around a sketchpad with her everywhere," Brooklyn said, basically carrying the conversation for me.

"How neat. I always wish that I could draw, but I never learned how," Stuart said, trying to catch my gaze. "Even my stick figures are terrible!"

I couldn't stand it any longer. I didn't want to talk to Stuart and who knew when I'd get another chance to be in a bar with Grayson. I excused myself for a bathroom break then sought out the first bartender I could find.

"Can I do the thing where I send a drink to a guy and you give him a napkin that has a sexy message on it?"

The bartender scanned me once, feet to chest.

"I'll do whatever you want me to do," he said, taking a step closer.

I held up my hand. "Jeez, alright. My eyes are up here."

He chuckled and pulled out a pad of paper. "Who do you want me to send a drink to?"

I pointed Grayson out for him and he nodded.

"And what drink?"

Oh damn, I'd forgotten to check what Grayson was drinking. Did it matter?

"Is there some kind of sexy drink you usually send?"

His laughed. "None that a guy would drink."

I groaned. "Whatever, just give him a drink with this note. I don't care what it is." I took a pen out of my purse and jotted down the sexiest thing I could think of. Three simple words that hinted at so much more.

Come find me.

Chapter Twenty

I stood in a dark hallway of the bar waiting for Grayson. Black and gold filigreed paper masked the walls. Ornate gold light fixtures hung from the ceiling and five doors dotted the hallway, each leading into small private bathrooms. I blocked the last door at the end of the hallway. People trailed in and out of the other rooms, seemingly unconcerned with my presence. I watched two girls stumble out from behind a closed door, giggling and supporting one another as best as possible. One of them fell against the wall, her blonde hair spilling down around her face as her friend tried to keep her from slipping down onto the black marbled floor.

I was watching them, when Grayson turned the corner and came into view at the end of the dark hallway. Dark sleek hair. Sharp, defined jaw. Straight nose, strong brows, and a predatory look aimed right at me.

I wiped my sweaty palms on the front of my skirt and then slid them up, crossing and uncrossing them for lack of a better pose. The lounge's seductive music seemed to pick up, the beat of a kick drum matching each of Grayson's steps as he approached me.

His narrowed eyes proved he was more than prepared to take me up on the challenge I'd penned for him. When he was a few feet away he pulled his hands out of his pockets and unbuttoned his suit jacket.

He passed by the drunk girls without so much as a side glance and then his gaze met mine. As he stepped closer, I realized the full extent of what I'd begun by sending him that note.

"Skipping out on your blind date already?" Grayson asked. At once he wrapped a hand around my neck and used his other to turn the door handle behind me so that we fell back into the small bathroom. "That's not very ladylike."

We stumbled, entwined together. I closed the door behind us and he locked it.

Click.

The audible confirmation of what we were about to do.

He walked me back to the edge of the black sink and I glanced around the room. For a bathroom, it was covertly sexy. It's like they *wanted* couples to sneak away into them. The black marble floor and decorative wallpaper continued into the room, but the lighting was even dimmer, casting a romantic yellow haze over the two of us.

We were right up against the sink when Grayson spun me around to face the mirror. I was sandwiched between the countertop and Grayson, and when I glanced up into the antique mirror, I caught sight of us together for the first time. Grayson was right: I didn't seem very ladylike. My dark brown hair fell around my shoulders. My blouse was pulled tight over my chest, revealing a sliver of my pink lacy bra. My eyeliner and mascara had smudged around my eyes, giving me a mysterious, dangerous glow. *My darker side was showing.*

Grayson's height made it so the top of my head fell just beneath his chin.

"Do you realize how much of a tease you are? Walking around my office every day?"

I managed to shake my head no, mesmerized by his words.

"Every time I see you, I want to spread your legs just like this."

His left dress shoe hit my designer heel and then he kicked it out so that my knees buckled. His hand reached out to hold me up as I secured my footing with my feet spread much wider than they'd been just a second before.

I shot him an annoyed glance and he squeezed my hip as reassurance. The smirk he wore proved he enjoyed sweeping my feet out from under me, literally and figuratively.

"They'll be able to hear us in the hallway," he said, pushing my pencil skirt up around my hips.

I bit my lip and gripped the counter even tighter. I watched my knuckles turn white as he shimmied my panties down past my hips. I had to pull my feet back together so that the lace could slide down, but the second they were gone I moved back to how he'd placed me a moment before. The low groan he emitted told me I'd done the right thing.

A new, seductive song kicked on in the lounge as he unbuckled his belt.

I swallowed slowly, nerves starting to get the better of me as his palm slid up the back of my thigh. He left goosebumps as his touch trailed higher and I tried my hardest to watch it all happen in the mirror. It was hard though to confront your deepest desires head on. I'd never done anything like this, and never with someone like Grayson.

"Can you see my hand in the mirror, Cammie?" he asked as he touched the center of my thighs.

The mirror cut off just a few inches above my hips so I pressed up onto my tiptoes and nodded.

I could see it all.

"Keeping watching," he said as he brushed a finger over my skin.

My knees threatened to buckle.

The music grew louder.

My moans matched his.

I squeezed my eyes closed and he told me to open them, to watch.

My stomach pressed against cold marble.

His hands dug into my hips as he held me in place.

Someone rapped on the bathroom door, and we completely ignored them.

He pressed into me with one hard thrust and I nearly lost my footing.

He held onto me tighter, keeping me in place.

We moved with the music. My heart matched the beat.

I pushed my hips back to meet his and his eyes rolled closed.

When I cried out some time later, Grayson bit down on my earlobe and whispered, "I found you just like your note asked...but now I think I'm going to keep you here all for myself."

• • •

"Are you kidding me right now?! ARE YOU FREAKING KIDDING ME!?" Brooklyn yelled.

I took a step back, holding my hands up in defense. If I hadn't been two drinks in, I would have been looking for some kind of escape route. Alas, I had to face Brooklyn's fury head on.

"You need to calm down. It is not that big of a deal," I said—obviously the *best* thing to say to an angry person.

We'd gone back to Brooklyn's apartment after happy hour. Jason had stepped out a few minutes earlier to get us ice cream, per my request, and some more wine, per Brooklyn's request. We didn't have long to talk before he returned, but she'd asked me where I'd gone in the middle of happy hour and I'd decided to tell her the truth.

Now I was regretting it.

"Not a big deal! Not a big deal? You're sleeping with Grayson Cole. Grayson! In the middle of a bar bathroom."

I rolled my eyes. "If you don't stop yelling, I'm locking you in the bathroom until you calm down."

She paced around the center of her kitchen island, oscillating between calm and crazy. Every few seconds she'd reach for something on the counter—a knife, an empty bottle of wine, some chocolate—then stop mid-grab, realizing that none of those things would help our situation. *Unless, of course, she wanted to stab me.* Which would really put a damper on our sistership.

I met her halfway around her fifth lap of the kitchen island and gripped her shoulders so she couldn't move.

"Okay." I said, trying to meet her eye. "Okay. I'm really, really sorry. I really regret having sex with Grayson and will try and purge all of the sexy images from my mind." By the end of my heartfelt apology, I had a dopy smile on my face.

She pointed at that smile and groaned. "You're not sorry! Jeez, Cammie. That's so reckless...and fine, yes, it's actually quite hot, so I can't really get mad at for you about that, but still! I'm mad at you for ditching Stuart like that."

"C'mon, did you hear him? His childhood dream was to own a laundromat for Christ's sake," I moaned.

"It doesn't matter, Cammie. You should have told me to cancel on Stuart or something."

"I didn't know you were even going to bring him! And don't worry about him, he has that Clark Kent look. He'll be fine. But dear god, he needs to get a new job. I've never met a sexy accountant. No one wants a guy to balance their budgets."

The door opened at that moment and a smiling, naive Jason walked in holding two paper grocery bags.

"Cammie, they were out of that gelato stuff that you like, so I grabbed a bunch of other stuff," he explained, dropping the bags onto the counter and rifling through the contents. He pulled out a pint of ice cream and held it up for my examination.

"Oh, that looks awes—"

"Cammie doesn't deserve ice cream. She DEFINITELY doesn't deserve Triple Chocolate Fudge ice cream," Brooklyn interrupted with a snotty glance.

Jason frowned, slowly dropping the pint onto the counter.

"Brooklyn doesn't know what she's talking about," I replied. "She forgets that I'm an adult, and as such, I can stick my spoon in any pint of ice cream that I wish."

I flipped my sister off—because that's what adults do—and then walked out of her apartment with the ice cream in hand. It was one of the finest exits I've ever pulled off, and there was a bonus: I had a pint of ice cream to eat as I walked home.

It was a fifteen minute walk—ten if I was really stepping on it—so I dipped into the Chinese restaurant next to Brooklyn's condo, stole some chopsticks, and ate my ice cream as best as I could using a sort of "flick it into my mouth and hope my aim is right" technique.

As if I wasn't juggling enough things with my hands already, I dialed Grayson's number when I was halfway home.

He answered right away.

"How's Brooklyn's?" he asked, skipping right past the formal hello.

"I'm not at her place. I'm walking back to mine," I said, flicking some ice cream toward my mouth and missing by a long shot. I turned behind me to see where it landed, only to find a trail of melting ice cream on the sidewalk. *Whoopsies*.

"You're walking home? It's eleven at night."

"Don't worry, I have ice cream and chopsticks," I said, only half joking.

He groaned and I could visualize him doing that thing where he tugged his hair as if exasperated by my existence in general.

"Could you come pick me up and take me to your place?" I asked, digging my chopsticks into the melting slush.

I could hear rustling clothes in the background, the buckling of a belt, and then keys sliding off of a table.

"Where are you?" he asked.

I rattled off the cross streets and then hung up so I could eat my ice cream in peace.

Brooklyn's condo was in a very ritzy part of Los Angeles, so I wasn't worried about sitting alone on a stoop at night, but when Grayson pulled up—looking like Batman in his dark gray sports car, I might add—he didn't seem to agree with me.

He hopped out of the car, leaving the engine quietly purring, and walked around to meet me. He had on a pair of worn jeans and a white undershirt. I'd never seen him so dressed down and one of my chopsticks drooped midway to my mouth when he stepped closer. *Hello, Grayson Cole.*

"Thanks for coming to my rescue," I smiled up at him.

He ignored me, taking in my appearance and the chopsticks in my hands.

"I shouldn't have let you go home with Brooklyn," he said, reaching for the chopsticks so that he could toss them into a garbage bin near by. I didn't argue; I'd already downed most of the pint and my stomach was starting to protest the random contents I'd consumed in the past twelve hours.

He turned to help me back up, secured my hands in his, and lead me to the car. I could have walked by myself, I wasn't drunk or anything, but it felt good to have him there to support me nonetheless.

I was chatty during the drive, anxious to see where he lived and giddy that I would get to rifle through his things, maybe even learn a thing or two about him that he hadn't yet revealed to me. (I was betting he had a weird CD collection. Closet One Direction fan, maybe?) But, if I'd been paying attention to his route, I would have realized that he wasn't directing us to his place, he was taking me back to mine.

My apartment building was deserted when we pulled up. Grayson killed the engine and I sat for a moment, studying the entrance as I grasped for an appropriate thing to say. I'd asked him to take me to his place and he'd driven me back home. *Wasn't that a bad thing?* It definitely felt like a rejection.

"Thanks for picking me up," I said, turning toward him for a brief moment before reaching for the door handle—which I could now operate on my own, thank you very much.

"Next time call me *before* you start walking around alone at night," he said, reaching to slide his hand beneath my hair and up around my neck. The warmth of his palm sent shivers down my spine and I paused for a moment, wanting to stay in his presence for another few seconds.

"I'll see you at work tomorrow," he said, before reaching over and offering me a chaste kiss on the cheek.

I thought of how contradictory Grayson could be as I took the elevator to my apartment. He'd bend me over the sink in a bar bathroom, but then he'd kiss me so gently, like a porcelain doll he was scared to drop. The two things seemed mutually exclusive to me.

"Oh, hey," Hannah said from her spot on the couch when I pushed through the apartment door. She was wearing pajamas and flipping through channels on the TV with a bored expression.

"Hey," I said with a slight nod. The awkward tension was palpable as I made my way past her.

"Fun night?" she asked.

I paused mid-step, realizing how suggestive her curt tone was. There was so much meaning wrapped in that question and when I turned to look back at her, she was wearing a small "gotcha" smirk.

Had she seen Grayson's car outside?

"Yup. Great night," I replied as I opened my bedroom door and then closed and locked it behind me.

Chapter Twenty-One

Brooklyn: Your birthday is tomorrow. Your birthday is tomorrow. You are the best little sister ever because your birthday is tomorrow. Faalllalalala.

Cammie: Wow. Was that supposed to be a song? I thought you were a Grammy award winning singer-songwriter?

Brooklyn: I'll admit, it's not my best work. BUT I'M SO EXCITED. What do you want to do? Spa day? Dinner? A little party? It's a shame you have to work.

Cammie: Most people have to work on Tuesdays, Brook.

I mulled over the possibilities she'd listed, but none of her suggestions sounded fun. We'd just done happy hour the week before and I was too stir crazy to sit through a spa day. If anything, I needed to lock myself in my room and concentrate on my secret proposal for the design competition. The deadline was fast-approaching, but I knew Brooklyn would never let me get away with not celebrating my birthday.

Brooklyn: Well that's boring.
Cammie: Tell me about it. What if we just go to dinner this weekend? Just you and me? I'm pretty busy this week.
Brooklyn: Boo. I leave for Montana on Sunday!

My chest tightened at the realization that she'd be leaving so soon, but then I reminded myself that her departure was a good thing. This is what I wanted. Some distance was healthy. After all, it's the whole reason I was going to Paris.

Cammie: So it will be a little farewell dinner combined with my birthday. See you Saturday!

I hadn't told Brooklyn about Paris yet and it was probably a good thing she'd be on the other side of the country when she found out because she wasn't going to take the news well. Maybe I'd call her once I'd already landed in Paris—y'know the whole "beg for forgiveness rather than ask for permission" method.

● ● ●

Around lunchtime on Monday, while most of the office was off grabbing food, I tapped on Grayson's office door.
"Come in," he called.

"Are you free for a few minutes?" I asked as I held onto the door, hovering between stepping into his office and staying on the other side of the door, the safe side.

He smiled up at me and dropped his drafting pencil onto his desk.

"I'll take that as a yes," I quipped, stepping in and closing the door behind me.

"Are you hungry?" he asked, glancing at the clock on the wall next to me. "Should I order lunch?"

I shook my head. "I had a late breakfast."

I took a seat on one of the chairs in front of his desk. A week ago, the seating arrangement would have made me nervous, like I was on the chopping block, but a lot had changed in the last seven days.

"I never asked—are you going to see Stu again?" he asked, his eyes twinkling with charm.

I scrunched my nose. "Who?"

Grayson barked out a laugh, tipping back in his desk chair.

"Are you serious?"

I cracked a small smile. "Only slightly. "

He smirked. "Do you want to come by my place after work tonight? Maybe grab some takeout?"

He was basically asking me if I wanted to see the Holy Grail. Normally, there was no way I'd normally turn down the offer...but I had to really focus on my competition proposal if I wanted to have something decent to turn in the following week. I'd forced myself to work on it all weekend, but I was nowhere near being done.

To delay having to turn down his offer, I stood and walked around the desk. He sat still, eyeing me with curiosity as I slid my hands down over his chest. His suit was crisp, but the fabric was thin enough for me to feel the muscles that lay hidden beneath. When his breathing picked up, I finally replied.

"I can't. I have to get some work done."

He craned his head back to place a kiss beneath my neck. "You mean the work that I'm paying you to do?"

I laughed.

"Mmhmm," I murmured half-heartedly as he continued to kiss along my neck.

"That's taken care of. You are now officially free after work. Here's the address." He reached forward out of my grasp to jot down his address on a small post-it note.

I took it from him, but I knew I wouldn't be stopping by.

"Sorry, but this work is unrelated to you, so I'll just see you tomorrow morning," I said, walking around his desk and waving the post-it note in the air with pride.

"I'm not used to being told no, Heart," he said as I reached the door.

I turned the handle without looking back. There's no way I would have been able to turn him down with those stern baby blues boring into me. I reminded myself that I'd have plenty of time to spend with Grayson in between finishing up my competition submission and leaving for Paris.

There it was.

That punch to the gut that seemed to accompany my departure to Paris in the recent days. It was becoming increasingly impossible to ignore and I knew exactly where it was stemming from: the closer Grayson and I became, the more Paris seemed like a bad idea.

But I couldn't let myself stray from the original plan. Paris was happening.

I needed it to happen.

• • •

True to my word, I went home after work and locked myself in my room. I spread out my favorite architecture textbooks from college, my sketchpad, my straight edge, three drafting pencils, and my computer with AutoCAD pulled up so that I could start taking my designs from paper to computer.

I'd done projects like the park proposal when I was still in college. The difference was I'd had an entire semester to work on those projects. For this, I had one week left.

I skipped dinner and tried to ignore Hannah's incessant knocking on my bedroom door.

"What are you doing in there?" she asked.

"Nothing. I don't feel well."

"What do you have? A sore throat? Fever? You'd better not get me sick," she demanded.

Aw, what a thoughtful roommate I had.

She wanted to know what I was doing in my room but it's not like I could invite her in. I was breaking *at least* three company rules by submitting my own proposal behind Alan's back, and I didn't trust Hannah as far as I could throw her. So, I feigned sickness and waited until I saw her shadow move from beneath the door before I continued working.

Chapter Twenty-Two

"Happy birthday to you. Happy birthday to you. Happy birthday—uhh, Cara— Colleen—Cameron..."

To their credit, my coworkers did their best to add my name at the end of the song. I'd only worked with them a few short weeks and there were quite a few architects to keep track of at the firm. Thankfully, Peter all but yelled my name so that people would catch on.

"...Happy birthday to you!" they finished before I leaned over the tray of cupcakes and blew out the few candles I'd seen Beatrice scrounge around for in the break room earlier that morning. My coworkers did their best to wait a respectful time—all of thirty seconds—before taking a cupcake and fleeing the break room like their lives depended on it. I didn't blame them. Getting a break from the desk was nice, but having to make small talk with coworkers quickly negated the benefits of free cake.

I watched them all trail out and frowned as I realized Grayson still hadn't shown his face. He was in his office working away, completely ignoring my birthday.

"Happy birthday, Cammie," Beatrice said, leaning against the counter beside me.

I mustered a small smile. "Thanks for getting me cupcakes. Vanilla is my favorite."

She nodded and finished chewing a bite. Pink sprinkles dotted the edge of her mouth but she licked them up before I could mention it.

"You're welcome," she said with a smile.

I scanned the room, surprised by how little I knew about my coworkers. If I wasn't planning on leaving the company soon maybe I would have made more of an effort to make a name for myself at Cole Designs, but it felt like there was no point in making friends if I'd just be leaving them behind in a few weeks.

So what was I doing with Grayson?

"He doesn't ever show up to these things," Beatrice said, pulling me out of my reverie.

I furrowed my brows. "Who?"

She turned toward me, dropping her voice so that it wasn't overheard. "Grayson. He never comes to these things. It would have looked suspicious if he'd come."

I studied her expression for another moment, trying to extract more information, but she was already taking another bite of cupcake, apparently finished giving me secret intel about my not-boyfriend-maybe-hookup-buddy-and-also-kind-of-a-friend. Clearly, we were still working on our Facebook status.

He doesn't show up to these things? So what? When Beatrice had announced to everyone via mass email that we'd be having a small party for me in the break room during lunch, I'd expected Grayson to show up. I'd purposely gotten up from my desk slowly so that I could walk with him to the break room, but his door never opened.

The party was starting to die down, so I put my hand on Beatrice's arm, thanked her one more time, and then slid two cupcakes onto a styrofoam plate to take back to my desk.

Unfortunately, my path was blocked by Hannah on the way out of the break room.

"Good to see that you're feeling better, Cammie," she said, eyeing my two cupcakes. "Is that dessert for two, or are you just feeling extra hungry?" she asked with clear disdain.

I smiled and tipped my head. "Starving. Excuse me," I said, brushing past her so that my shoulder bumped into hers—accidentally, *I swear*.

Grayson's door was cracked open when I walked back into the main office. I scanned around the room. Alan and Mark were at lunch. Peter and the rest of the young associates were still enjoying cupcakes and trying to extend their break for as long as possible. Everyone else was wrapped up in their work or chatting with their coworkers. I decided my path was as clear as possible.

I didn't bother knocking. His door was open, which I took as clear sign to enter.

"You missed my birthday," I said as I stepped into Grayson's office.

He was standing up, pacing back and forth while holding his cell phone up to his ear. When I spoke, he turned toward me and glanced mournfully at the cupcakes on my plate.

He mouthed "sorry" as he crossed the room and closed the door behind me.

"Hey Mitch. Could I call you back in ten? Something's come up."

Mitch must have agreed because Grayson hung up and then reached for the cupcakes in my hand.

"You missed my birthday party in the kitchen," I repeated.

He dropped the plate of cupcakes onto a small bar cart near the door and scooped me up.

"But you brought me a cupcake," he said bending to steal a quick kiss.

I shook my head. "Wrong. Those are both for me."

He laughed and leaned back to inspect my expression.

"Let me take you out tonight to make up for it," he said, hope brimming in his gaze. I could practically see the gears turning in his mind as he tried to come up with the exact right place to take me.

I squeezed his biceps reassuringly and stepped out of his grasp. I should have turned him down since my design submission wasn't even close to be being complete, but it was my birthday and everyone deserves to take a break on their birthday.

"Fine. Let's go somewhere, but I already know of the perfect place. Pick me up around 8:00 pm and bring some snacks," I said with a wink before taking *both* of my cupcakes back to my desk.

Like I'd bring him a cupcake...

I was still mulling over the absurd thought when I noticed that my desk drawer was cracked open a few inches. An open desk drawer isn't usually suspicious, but I remembered tidying up my desk just before lunch and I'd closed all of my drawers.

I set my cupcakes on my desk, glanced over my shoulder, and then pulled the drawer open all the way.

Inside, resting on a stack of pencils, there was a small card tied to a crystal paperweight in the shape of the Eiffel Tower. It was an exact replica of the real tower: someone had taken the time to painstakingly carve out every detail. Even in the shadows of my drawer, the crystal twinkled and I knew it'd be even more gorgeous in the light of day.

I flipped over the small card tied at the base of the tower to read what it said.

"Happy Birthday, Cameron. You deserve to have the real Eiffel Tower, but this will have to do for now. The French Government didn't seem interested in selling me the real thing. Love, G."

• • •

"And this is perfectly legal? To wander around back here at night?" Grayson asked as we pulled up to my spot at the cemetery behind LAX.

"Is anything perfectly legal?" I asked, turning to glance back at him after I'd opened my door.

He hadn't made a move to get out.

"Going to sit there all night, Cole? Scared of ghosts?" I quipped, trying to get him to meet my eye.

"I'm not a big fan of cemeteries," he admitted before reluctantly opening his door.

I hopped out and rounded the front of the car with my flashlight illuminating the ground in front of me.

"Are you serious? Grayson Cole is actually scared of something?" I asked, aiming the light at where he still sat in the safety of his car.

"I'm scared of a lot of things," he assured me as he made his way out to join me. "Hurricanes, hippos, a zombie popping up out of one of these graves." He reached for my hand and we started walking farther into the cemetery.

"Hippos? Seriously?"

He stopped walking and turned toward me, holding the flashlight up under his chin like he was getting ready to tell a scary story.

"Hippos are exceptionally dangerous. They attack more humans per year than any other animal. I think." He added the last part with a little smile.

I laughed and tugged him forward, leading him along the path I normally traversed.

"Well, I promise there won't be undead hippos popping up out of these graves. I come here a lot and have yet to be attacked."

He laughed and I squeezed his hand for reassurance.

We walked in silence for a few yards until we arrived at a familiar clearing. I turned to flash my light onto one of the gravestones that had a row of fake flowers lining the ground around its base.

"Georgina Heart. 1893-1960," Grayson read aloud. "Your great-grandmother?"

I smiled and shook my head. "No. I just like to pretend that I'm related to her. I brought those flowers out here last year. I have no clue how they've managed to stay there this long."

"How do you know you aren't related to her?" Grayson asked.

I took a seat in front of the gravestone, the bed of fake flowers offering a bit of support between my lower back and the aged concrete.

"I don't," I answered simply, feeling the ground start to shake. It was subtle, but I knew what it meant.

"Hurry! Sit!" I said, reaching for his hand and pulling him toward the ground.

I thought he'd be more hoity-toity about his suits— dirt didn't mix well with Italian wool—but he didn't seem to care. He nudged me over to get a bit of the gravestone for himself and then pulled my hand onto his lap.

"This is very romantic, Cammie. What's next on the birthday tour, jury duty?" he joked, still unsure of what we were doing at the cemetery.

"Be quiet and listen!" I said, holding my hand up to silence him.

He dropped a brow and stared at me with curiosity before I reached to turn off both of our flashlights. His features were impossible to make out in the darkness. We were left with one fewer sense as the earth started to shake harder.

The low rumble from the runway was impossible to miss.

"Oh! Are you serious? I didn't even think we were close to the airport anymore," Grayson said, sounding like a giddy child.

The rumble grew louder and louder, the ground shook harder, and the engines howled as we clutched each other's hands.

"It's coming," I warned.

The plane picked up speed as the engines roared to full throttle. We were encased in darkness and then I spotted the first light from the plane. In a flash, a dozen more lights appeared in the sky, lit across the belly and the wings of the plane. I stared, mesmerized as it flew directly above us for one brief second. It was louder than ever, stealing every bit of sound from around us.

Grayson and I clutched each other's hands as our necks craned to keep careful watch of the plane's ascent.

And then, just like that, it was gone, and the cemetery was silent once again.

Grayson loved the spot just as much as I did.

We watched three more planes take off before he took me by the hand and led me back to his car. He pulled me onto the backseat without a word. We peeled off each other's clothes without the aid of the flashlights. We fumbled in the darkness, but it was better without the light. Having to seek each other out from memory meant that there was hardly a patch of skin that went untouched.

He stretched out as best as he could on top of the smooth leather and then he pulled me down on top of him. Our mouths met as his fingers tangled in my hair. I gripped his arms and succumbed to my desire for him.

I loved Grayson in the backseat of that car.

I loved the way he touched me. I loved the way that time dripped when we were together.

You see, I knew that being with Grayson wasn't permanent. I knew that in a few weeks I'd be gone, sitting on one of the planes we'd just watched taking off. I'd have nothing but the memories of him to cling onto, and for that, I loved him fiercely, wholeheartedly, and without abandon. Nothing makes you love someone like the shadow of an impending goodbye.

Chapter Twenty-Three

Amount saved for Paris: $2103 (minus $5.32 I used to buy bubblewrap so that I could protect the Eiffel Tower paperweight en route to Paris).

Items I have: updated Passport and picture. Goodbye thirteen-year-old brace-face portrait.

Items I need: a Paris Metro map so I can start to learn my way around the arrondissements.

French phrases that I know: Pas de l'enfer. Je ne veux pas un colocataire...which translates to "Hell no. I don't want a roommate." It seemed like necessary knowledge, considering Hannah and I spoke the same language but still mixed like oil and water.

The next morning I woke up early to work on my designs for the competition before going in to work. I was nearing the final stages, but the entries were due by next Monday. I knew Brooklyn and Grayson would probably keep me occupied over the weekend, which meant I really only had three more days to get it done.

Thankfully, Hannah wasn't awake when I padded into our kitchen to make my first cup of coffee for the day. I stood in the quiet space, waiting for our Keurig to boot up and reminiscing about the night before. It'd definitely been one of the best birthdays I'd ever had, all thanks to Grayson.

Once I had my coffee in hand, I locked myself back in my room and surveyed my progress. My park designs were scattered across my desk in piles that I swore I could differentiate, though your guess was probably as good as mine. I cleared a small space so I could set down my coffee and then booted up my laptop and sat down. The crystal Eiffel Tower paperweight caught my attention on the windowsill. It was beautiful in the early morning light, and seeing it there reminded me again of the night before. I smiled and took a sip of coffee and then paused, alarm bells ringing. Grayson's post-it note was missing. I'd stuck it next to the paperweight and had meant to put the address in my phone since my desk was currently a war zone, but I hadn't had time to do it the day before.

Immediately I stood and started to rifle through the papers on my desk, organizing them as I went. I glanced beneath every single one, even making sure the post-it note hadn't stuck to the back of any of them. I checked behind my desk and on the carpet beneath it. Nothing. It was nowhere to be found.

In the end, I had a very neat desk and no post-it note. I checked my purse and the rest of my room, but I didn't find it anywhere. I cursed myself for not putting it in my phone earlier. Losing something within forty-eight hours was a new low, even for me.

I sighed and made a mental note to ask Grayson for the address again. *Was that embarrassing to have to ask him for it twice?* Oh well, I didn't have a choice.

I spent the rest of the morning working on my designs and trying to come up with a casual way to ask Grayson about his address again.

It seemed silly to want his address so badly. Eventually he'd take me to his apartment and then I'd know it by default. But what if he didn't take me and I left for Paris without his address? How could I send him postcards or letters?

In a way, it felt like one more way that I was slowly losing Grayson at the same time I was starting to find him.

• • •

Saturday morning, my whore of a big sister had to leave for Montana (*before we even got the chance to have a going away dinner for her*) and I was crying at the airport like a sad sack. I knew she had to work on her album with Jason. I knew that bad weather in Montana meant that they needed to fly out earlier, and yet I couldn't pull it together.

"I will be back in a few weeks! What's wrong? Are you sad you don't get to see Cowboy Derek?"

I sniffed and wiped the snot dripping from my nose like a faucet.

"No! God! I'm not crying because of Cowboy Derek!"

Cowboy Derek was a ranch hand who worked for Jason up in Montana.

"So then you're this sad that I'm leaving for a few weeks?" she asked, clearly confused.

The waterworks kicked up another notch.

I could handle being away from Brooklyn for a few weeks, but she didn't realize that it was actually the last time we'd see each other in who knows how long. I'd be in Paris by the time she arrived back in LA.

"I'm… I'm…" I couldn't get a word out without crumbling into a blubbering mess once again.

Jason exchanged a wary glance with Brooklyn, one that hinted at the fact that they both thought I was going a little insane. I had to pull my shit together. I was a twenty-three year old adult woman. *Lion hear me roar, right?* I took a deep breath, wiped my eyes, and nodded.

"Okay. You can go. I'll be okay," I said, feeling very confident and wise.

Brooklyn smiled, her twinkling blue eyes meeting mine. "Okay, well I need you to let go of my suitcase then."

I glanced down. My hands were still clutching her suitcase for dear life. *Whoops.*

"Oh. Yeah, right."

I reluctantly loosened my grip on the bag and she pulled it to her side.

"And I need my wallet," she said, holding her palm out flat.

"Your what?" I pointed to Brooklyn and met Jason's gaze with one of those "*get a load of this girl*" glances.

"Cammie…"

"Fine!"

I pulled her dumb designer wallet out of my back pocket and gave it to her.

Jason shook his head and glanced down at his watch. I knew I was making them late, but they were flying privately and besides, I didn't care. I'd miss them so much that even this exchange, while embarrassing, was better than letting them go.

"Do you have anything else?" Brooklyn asked.

I thought about lying and telling her no, but the inevitable would happen anyway. Jason and Brooklyn were leaving and stuffing my pockets full of their crap wouldn't make them stay. Although, it seemed to always work in the movies, so, maybe I was doing it wrong.

With a sigh, I unloaded Jason's cell phone from my back pocket, Brooklyn's laptop charger from my purse, her I.D. from my bra, and then I pointed to Jason's luggage.

"There's a toy gun in your front pocket," I admitted sheepishly.

"Cammie!" they both exclaimed like scolding parents. *Yeah, whatever.* I'd rather have Jason detained than have them fly across the country to Montana.

"I'm sorry!"

Jason unzipped his front pocket and a little blue water gun rolled out.

He laughed. "You even filled it up."

I shrugged. "I didn't want the tabloids reporting that Jason Monroe is shooting blanks."

He walked toward me and wrapped me up in a bear hug. I gripped his shirt and closed my eyes. In the past few weeks Jason had become a big brother to me. He put up with my shenanigans and treated my sister like a princess. I couldn't have asked for a better man for her.

"I'll take care of your sister and you can always come visit us in a few weeks," he whispered to me before stepping back and placing the toy gun in my hand.

"Later, J-money," I said with a sad smile.

"Adios, C-stacks."

That only left my sister. I knew she could tell something was off. She stood a few feet away from me, frowning and trying to read between the lines. We'd done this same goodbye not two months earlier and I hadn't shed a single tear. I'm sure I was adding undue guilt onto her conscience with my waterworks. She needed to work on her music and I needed to stand on my own two feet. This was *not* that big of a deal. I smiled and held my arms open like a mom greeting her child after school.

"Get over here, you monster," I said with as much jokiness as I could muster.

She smiled and bent down to give me hug.

"I love you so much, my little pop star princess," I said.

She laughed against my shoulder and squeezed me even tighter.

"I love you too."

We hugged until I thought I was going to breakdown again, and then I stepped back and held her at arm's length. She told me she'd call me as soon as she landed and then I watched her and Jason walk into the private airport together. I stayed where I was until their plane took off thirty minutes later. Then, instead of calling a cab, I started to walk back to my apartment. I had no clue how long the walk would take; maybe I'd call a cab when my feet got tired, but it felt cathartic to walk through the city. It gave me a sense of purpose that I would lose the moment I got back to my apartment and realized that Brooklyn was really gone and I was one step closer to my own departure.

It wasn't until I got home some hours later—after stopping for a latte and people-watching at the cafe—that I realized I still had Brooklyn's guitar pic. I'd slipped it into my back pocket earlier, fully intending to give it back to her along with the rest of her things, but now I was selfishly glad I'd forgotten about it. The apartment was quiet with no signs of Hannah, so I went to my room, lay down, and stared at that guitar pic like it would come alive and tell me whether or not I was making the right decision to leave for Paris.

A while later, my phone buzzed next to me on the bed and I reached for it, assuming it was Brooklyn telling me she'd arrived safely in Montana.

"Hello," I answered, hating the way my voice cracked midway through the word. Brooklyn would know I was still crying.

"Heart?" Grayson's deep voice spoke into the phone. "What's wrong?"

Chapter Twenty-Four

Grayson knocked on my door twenty minutes later.

I'd done everything I could to assure him that I was fine on the phone, but he insisted on stopping by. Hannah still wasn't home and I figured if we just stayed in my room and I put some music on, she'd be none the wiser.

I pulled open my apartment door to see Grayson standing on my doorstep in jeans and an old MIT t-shirt. I knew from stalking him that he'd gone there for his master's degree before starting up his own architecture firm. His arms were piled high with various items. Just on the surface I could see two bottles of wine, a bag of Snickers, and a DVD case with Will Farrell's face on it.

"I've come with reinforcements," he said, stepping into my apartment as I pulled the door open wide for him.

"10-4. Quick, take it all back to my room. I'll grab some spoons and wine glasses."

Five minutes later, we were sitting on the floor of my room with a Pandora playlist turned up to max volume.

Grayson was opening the wine and I was shoveling ice cream into my mouth like there was no tomorrow.

"So Brooklyn left today, huh?" he asked, peering up at me as he worked the cork out of the wine bottle.

I smiled, despite my shitty day. "Yes, Brooklyn left today and that's why my eyes are puffy."

He frowned.

"But I'm glad you're here now," I added, leaning up onto my knees to give him a kiss.

"You could have called me earlier y'know, when you were sad about her leaving."

"Grayson Cole, therapist?" I joked, because I was awkward during sentimental moments like this.

He shrugged, a red tinge dotting his tanned cheeks for the first time that I could ever recall. Grayson was being earnest and I was falling deeper into something that I wouldn't for the life of me call love.

"I have a plan," I said, trying to shake myself back into safe, neutral territory. "Let's get drunk on wine, eat this tub of ice cream, and then make prank phone calls."

His brow dropped in confusion. "Prank calls?"

I grinned. "Yes. Like we did in high school."

He shook his head. "I never did that in high school."

I feigned shock just as his cell phone started ringing in his back pocket.

"Were you too busy going to dweeb conventions?" I asked with a wink.

He pulled his phone out of his pocket and shot me smile. "Actually, yes. I was in math club and part of a robotics team. We went to state my senior year."

"Oh my gosh, you *were* a nerd!" I laughed, playfully nudging his arm.

"Hold on, I need to take this really quickly," he said, swiping his finger across his phone to answer the call.

I reached over to turn down the music and then listened by the door to see if Hannah had come home. All was quiet still.

"Yeah, I'll look at it right now—ok—yeah, I'll email you back in a second."

I turned back to see Grayson glancing around my room until his eyes landed on my desk—which happened to be newly cleaned. If he'd come over a day earlier, the desk would have been piled high with designs for a competition I was hiding from him. Luckily, all of the information was tucked away in a manila envelope, ready to ship to the design committee's address first thing on Monday morning.

"Do you mind if I check a design on your computer really quick? Mitch said he just shot over an Adobe file and I can't look at it on my phone."

I shrugged. "Go right ahead, but if it's cool, then I get to look at it too."

He laughed as I booted up my computer for him. Maybe other people would have minded that their boyfriends were working on the weekends, but I understood his love for his job. He had a hundred people counting on him and if he needed to check an email for a second, I'd manage just fine with ice cream and wine.

"It's for that residential project you helped me with. Do you remember that house a few weeks ago?" he asked.

"Yes! I loved that house."

He logged onto his email, pulled up the design, and walked me through the changes Mitch had sent over.

Sitting on his lap as he worked at my computer ended up being the most fun date I'd had in a while. (I guess I couldn't make fun of him for being nerd. Talk about pot calling the kettle black.)

When he was done sending Mitch a reply, I handed him his glass of wine and pulled out my cell phone.

"Now, it's my turn to teach you something," I said as he swiveled in my desk chair to face me.

He quirked a brow in interest and pulled me down to sit on his lap.

"What are you going to teach me?" he asked, kissing my shoulder.

"The art of a prank call."

The Design

Chapter Twenty-Five

On Monday morning I had two missions to complete:
1. Arrive early for a design meeting with Alan, Mark, and Peter to finalize our company's design submission.
2. Arrive twenty minutes before that meeting so I could complete my own submission.

That morning, I'd put on a black silk blouse and black slacks in an attempt to look and feel like a badass ninja, but as I took the elevator up to the twentieth floor, my confidence began to wane.

Two weeks ago, one week ago, hell, even twenty-four hours ago, the idea of submitting my own design had seemed like a good idea. Then I'd learned of the last requirement I needed to include with my design proposal. It was a requirement I hadn't prepared for, and one I couldn't quite justify in my mind. Each submission had to be accompanied with a signed letter from the CEO of the company, confirming the design entry and validating the work. Since the CEO of my company was Grayson...that meant, I needed *his* signature. Or at least one that looked like his.

I'd tried to think of some way around it. At first, I thought of creating my own fake architecture firm so that I could leave Grayson and Cole Designs out of it completely, but I knew that wouldn't work. If I truly wanted to proceed with my submission, I'd have to break into his office, find a piece of letterhead, and forge his signature. The thought didn't sit well with me for obvious reasons. I would have never even begun to design a submission if I'd have known I'd have to drag Grayson into it.

As the elevator continued to rise, I thought of all the ways that I was playing with fire. Submitting my own design and stealing company letterhead were both in violation of company policy. Those two things were bad enough, but paled in comparison to the idea of betraying Grayson.

Was it truly that important for me to submit my own designs? I'd completed them and I knew they were really good. Why couldn't that be enough?

I couldn't fully explain it. A part of me needed to submit my own design just so I could prove to Alan that I was capable of great work. Another part of me felt like I was rebelling against every "Alan" I'd had to deal with in the architecture world. In college, I'd been forced to watch my male classmates receive internships and design awards, not because of their talent, but because they were part of the boys club. Misogynistic males ruled the design world and I was sick of sitting on the sidelines.

When the elevator doors opened, I glanced down at the manila envelope in my hands. It held all the keys to a great design, and it was stamped, labeled, and ready to be sealed once I had the letterhead to add to it. I cringed at the idea of having to trash my design, especially when I knew I had a real chance of winning. On the other hand, if I chose to proceed I'd be jeopardizing everything Grayson and I had built in the last few weeks.

I stepped into the office and stood for a moment, surveying the dark room. No one was there yet. My meeting with my table-mates wasn't due to start for another twenty minutes, but Alan would probably arrive five minutes early, so I had to get a move on if I still wanted to find a piece of letterhead.

I set my things down on my desk and did a quick run-through of the office, just to ensure there were no accountants or interior designers trying to get an early start to the day.

The office was empty and I wasn't sure how I felt about it. If someone had been there, my decision would have been made up for me. Instead, I was alone with my options and still unsure of what I wanted to do.

Either way, time was running out. If I wanted to proceed with the next part of my plan, I needed to do it now.

My hands shook as my conscience warred with me to stop.

If you break into his office, you'll ruin his trust in you.
If you break into his office, he'll never forgive you.

I couldn't give up yet, though. My design was good and I wanted someone to recognize that. I moved toward Grayson's door, slowly, and without real intent. *I can still turn back at any time.* Once I stood in front of it, I glanced over my shoulder and tried the door handle.

Unlocked.

I sighed; one less thing I'd have to feel guilty about. *Was I technically even breaking in if the door was unlocked?*

"YES!" *my conscience screamed at me.*

But maybe it was a sign that I was meant to proceed?

My heart rate picked up as I slipped past his door. *This is wrong. I'm a bad person.* I tried my best to ignore the nagging thoughts in the back of my mind.

I walked straight to his desk and pushed his heavy leather chair out of the way. His mahogany desk was annoyingly clean, which meant there were no stray pieces of letterhead waiting for me there.

My gut told me that I was doing the wrong thing. Grayson meant more to me than this dumb submission. *Right?* But, at the same time, just because I got a piece of his letterhead, didn't mean that I *had* to go through with the plan. *I can still stop at any time.* I'd get the piece of his letterhead and then decide.

I checked my watch and then turned to his desk drawers. The top left drawer was completely filled with office supplies: pens, pencils, paperclips, and a stapler. I moved to the drawer beneath it but it was locked and so was the drawer at the very bottom. I cursed under my breath and shot to the other side of the desk. I could feel a cold sweat trickle down my neck and I knew my time was running out. If Alan decided to show up ten minutes early, instead of five, he'd catch me red-handed.

Grayson's top right desk drawer was unlocked, but it was full of junk: stray business cars and rubber bands. I rifled through its contents to no avail.

Shit. Shit. Shit. If I didn't find a piece of his letterhead, the committee wouldn't accept my design submission and I'd have snooped around his things in vain. I had to find at least one piece.

I tried to pull open the second drawer on the right, to find that it was locked. The rest of the drawers were all locked as well, which meant I had to revert to plan B. I reached for the bobby pin I'd set down on top of his desk and finagled it into the small gap in the lock. Five seconds passed and it didn't budge. Ten seconds. Twenty. Thirty. I rotated the bobby pin in every direction and tried to shove it into the hole as far back as I possibly could. Nothing helped. Maybe lock-picking wasn't quite as easy as it looked in the movies.

I shoved my bobby pin back into my hair and mulled over every idea I could think of. *Maybe he kept his stationery somewhere else?* No. It would definitely be in one of his desk drawers. I sighed and pulled open the top right drawer again, looking for anything that could help me.

I shoved aside the highlighters and drafting pencils, and then my fingers touched cold metal.

A key.

Without hesitation, I pulled it out and tried it on the drawer I'd just attempted to break into.

It worked. The drawer slid open, and inside, waiting for me in a neat pile, was Grayson's stationery. I squealed as I pushed aside two boxes of business cards so that I could reach the pristine stack of letterhead at the back of the drawer. The Cole Design logo was printed at the very top and beneath that, "Grayson Cole, CEO" was embossed in bold black lettering.

I reached for one, then thought ahead and grabbed two. With my luck, I'd accidentally rip the first one or spill coffee on it and have to repeat the whole process over again.

I'd done it. I had the letterhead and I could submit my design. I pushed the drawer closed again and it locked into place just as the phone on Grayson's desk started to ring. The shrill sound made me jump out of my skin as it ricocheted off his office walls. It rang again, the piercing sound seeming to grow even louder. Without thinking, I reached out for the phone, and pressed the first button I could find.

The ringing stopped and I stood frozen, unsure of what to do. *Why had I touched it at all?* I should have just let it ring!

A second later, his voicemail began playing on speakerphone and Grayson's voice surrounded me.

"Hi, you've reached Grayson Cole. I'm not in the office at the moment so leave your name and number and I'll give you a call when I get in. Thanks."

Hearing his voice made me feel a sharp pang of guilt for what I was doing. *Grayson trusted me and how did I repay him?* By breaking into his office and stealing company property.

What was I doing? I had to get out of his office. I couldn't go through with the plan. I couldn't forge his signature.

As I started to move, his voicemail cut off and then the person who'd called started to leave a message.

"Hey Grayson. It's Mitch. I have some things to discuss about—"

I scrambled to end the message. I couldn't listen to one of his client's messages. I didn't need anything else to feel guilty about. I reached for the phone and pressed down on the same button as before, hoping to cut off the voicemail. I needed to get out of there, but Mitch's message wouldn't go away. I kept pressing buttons, cursing under my breath, until finally, Mitch's voice cut off.

Get out. Get out. Get out. I repeated the phrase over and over again as I replaced his key and rolled his chair back to where it had been positioned before I'd moved it in the first place.

"First saved message," the voicemail began.

"No! Crap!" I stammered.

"Hey, Grayson. This is Frank from Whitmoor Apartments."

I reached to stop the message from playing, but paused with my hand midway over the desk.

Whitman was *my* building.

"We were able to install that security system you asked for on unit #450."

My unit.

I could feel the color drain from my face as Frank continued on.

"I'll shoot the bill over to your email and I'll include an invoice for that portion of the rent you requested."

What the hell?

I reached for the phone and slammed my hand down onto every button until the message cut off. Truthfully, I wanted to rip the phone from the desk and chuck it across the room, but I refrained. Instead, I stood there in a daze, trying to replay the last few seconds in my mind. *Maybe I hadn't heard what I thought I'd heard.*

No, I definitely had.

Why in the world was my landlord calling Grayson? How did he even know who Grayson was?

As calmly as possible, I clutched the two pieces of Grayson's letterhead in my palm and left his office. I glanced back once, ensuring everything was in its correct place, and then paused when my gaze landed on his phone.

In the matter of two minutes, my world had flipped upside down.

What the hell was Grayson doing installing a security system in my apartment without asking me? And what was Frank saying about my rent? Hannah and I split the rent 50/50 each month.

None of it made sense and there was no time to try and decipher it. Alan, Mark, or Peter could walk in at any moment and I didn't want them to see me standing in his office.

I had a layer of sweat on the back of my neck, my heart was hammering against my ribcage, and my stomach was twisted into a tight, anxious ball. All morning I'd been unsure of whether or not I could proceed with my submission. But then I'd heard that message, and my world wasn't so black and white anymore. That message had effectively made my decision for me. I was going to submit my design. For the next ten minutes, I operated like a robot. I shoved every emotion below the surface as I went about the motions I knew I had to do.

I loaded the letterhead into the printer beneath Alan's desk and pulled up the summary for my design proposal that I'd worked on over the weekend.

Once it was printed on the letterhead, I took a deep breath and forged Grayson's signature at the bottom of the page. There, in wet black ink, was visible proof that I was jeopardizing everything in my life by submitting my own design.

Would Grayson forgive me if he ever found out?
Would he ever find out?

What did it matter, anyway? Grayson had his own secrets to worry about.

Without another thought, I slipped the letterhead into the manila enveloper and sealed the top.

Done. There's no going back.

By the time I made it back up to the twentieth floor after slipping the envelope into the building's outgoing mail, I felt completely numb. I should have felt guilty, angry, sad, or at least somewhat regretful, but I couldn't manage a single thing.

I stepped into the office to find Alan, Mark, and Peter at their desks, chatting amiably. I watched Peter peel his satchel over his head and hang it on the back of his chair as Mark silently took his seat.

They didn't notice me at first, not until I was almost at my seat.

"Hey Cammie. I was wondering if you'd left your stuff here last night," Peter said, pointing to my purse on my desk.

"Nah. I got here a few minutes ago and then ran down for some coffee."

Peter glanced down to my hands, which were clearly *not* holding a cup of coffee.

"Drank it down there," I explained, though I should have just shut my mouth.

Peter nodded slowly and Alan turned to inspect me.

"Morning," I offered. He gave me a curt nod and took a seat.

I was the last one to sit down and as soon as my butt hit the chair, Alan began to drone on and on about the company's design submission.

"We're a little behind on our proposal and it needs to be in the mail by noon today," Alan said, reaching into a desk drawer to pull out our design packet.

I hid a smug smile. I'd done all of the design work on my own and I'd still managed to get it done, yet as a group, we were behind.

"I want you each to set aside your morning work and focus on this. We need to have everything together by 11:30 am at the latest. They pick up the mail downstairs at noon and we don't want to chance it."

We all agreed, and then Alan doled out tasks to each of us. Mark and Peter were both given actual design work but he put me on letterhead duty.

"They want a summary of our submission. Just explain our design and give a general idea for the project," Alan said, sweeping his hand to dismiss me to my work.

I opened my laptop and opened a blank word document. I was more than prepared to write our summary considering I'd just finished writing one for myself.

"And only go off of the things we discussed during our meetings. None of that other crap you tried to suggest," Alan added with a clipped tone.

I clenched my fists to keep from saying anything too disrespectful.

Any small flame of regret that was burning inside of me was effectively squashed by his attitude.

"Sure thing, *Alan*."

He glared at me from the corner of his eyes, but I was too busy typing bullshit to notice.

Chapter Twenty-Six

I obsessed about the message I'd heard on Grayson's answering machine for the next twenty-four hours. I tried to convince myself I'd heard the wrong apartment name, the wrong apartment number, the wrong words altogether. I tried to convince myself it'd been part of an elaborate dream, but in the end, I knew what I'd heard, and I knew that Grayson and I had a relationship that was muddied with deceit and lies.

I tried to pin Grayson down on Tuesday so that we could talk, but his schedule was jam-packed with design meetings. At 10:30 am, he had a meeting with Mitch. That meeting overflowed into his 12:30 pm meeting with Serenity. I watched her pace back and forth in front of his office, expelling an exasperated huff every few minutes so that we'd all know just how much of her time he was wasting. Finally, at 1:00 pm, Grayson's office door opened and I twisted my head to watch him say goodbye to Mitch and then turn to greet Serenity. He looked devastatingly handsome. His suit jacket was gone, probably hanging on the back of his chair. Everything else was quintessentially Grayson: shined shoes, cuffed shirt sleeves, gelled hair, straight tie, and killer smile. The killer smile was directed at me when he caught me staring up at him. My gut reaction was to smile back, and I did, before realizing how twisted our relationship had become in the last few days.

There was very little to smile about.

Did he have any idea that I'd broken into his office? Had I left anything out of place?

"Sorry for the wait," Grayson said to Serenity. "I have about thirty minutes before I've got to run to a job site."

"That's fine." She smiled. "You'll approve these designs as you always do. I know exactly what you like," she gushed. I rolled my eyes.

Grayson offered her a curt nod and then ushered her into his office, leaving the door slightly ajar. It was a thoughtful gesture, but I had too much on my mind to care that he was alone with Serenity.

"Cammie, I need you to stay late tonight. We're behind on a few projects because of that design proposal," Alan said, jarring my attention back to our table group.

"I can stay late too if you need it," Peter offered, meeting my eye.

I gave him a small smile, inwardly cursing Alan to the pits of hell.

"Fine," Alan agreed before picking up his phone and dialing out.

I stayed busy the rest of the day, nearly jumping out of my skin every time Grayson's office door opened. Finally, around 3:30 pm, he bid farewell to Beatrice and left the office for a job site. My phone vibrated with a text message a few minutes later.

Grayson: Had to run down to Malibu for a meeting. I might stay overnight depending on how late it runs.

Cammie: Ok. Good luck.

Grayson: Wish you were coming with me.

I didn't text back. I wanted to tell him about the voicemail, but then I'd have to admit that I'd broken into his office, and then I'd also have to tell him about my submission for the competition. My chest tightened just thinking about the mountain of lies building between us. I hadn't thought ahead enough to realize how far this one decision would throw my life off course.

Instead of deciding on a plan of action, I threw myself into work. Peter stayed late with me and we ordered in food from the deli down the street. The office was quiet and I ignored my buzzing phone. I'd sleep on it and wake up with a clear plan. I always did.

• • •

My plan didn't work.

The next morning, it still felt like I was in the eye of a tornado. By breaking into Grayson's office and by submitting my own design work, I'd set events into motion that I was helpless to stop. I hadn't considered it before, but the design committee would definitely be sending some kind of confirmation once they received our submissions; who they would contact, I hadn't a clue. I checked my email obsessively, hoping they would use the personal email address I'd provided for them, but on Wednesday morning, I still hadn't received a single thing.

I sat at my desk, refreshing my email over and over again, praying that I'd eventually find an email from the design committee. Nothing. In the proposal packet, they said they'd contact us no later Wednesday to confirm receipt of our packets.

I was royally screwed.

I stayed at my desk as people started to trickle into the office, dread gnawing at my stomach. I had five text messages and three phone calls waiting on my cell phone. They were all from Grayson, and I refused to check a single one until I knew what I wanted to do about us.

At 8:00 am, Grayson strolled into the office with a piercing gaze aimed right for me. I tried to ignore his approach by focusing on my work, but he completely read through my act.

"Let's go," he said, pulling my chair back so that I was forced to stand or fall to the ground.

"Stop," I hissed, aware of everyone's eyes on us.

"No. Let's go. You're talking to me. I've had enough of the silent treatment."

His voice warned me that he was not to be tested, but I wanted to test him anyway. *How dare he boss me around after what I'd heard on his answering machine?* I had every right to demand answers right then and there, to call him out for being an overbearing stalker, but we were interrupted a moment too soon.

"Just the two people I need to talk to," Alan spat from behind me with more venom than I'd ever heard before.

Grayson's blue eyes cut from me up to Alan, warning him away. "I'm busy right now, Alan."

Alan shook his head. "Not too busy for this," he said, slapping a piece of paper onto my desk. The font was too small for me to make out, but I knew it was an email. Just before Grayson snatched it up, I caught the committee's email address at the top of the page.

"Grayson let me explain—" I began, before getting cut off.

"What's going on?" Peter asked as he arrived at his desk, unaware of the hornet's nest he'd just walked into. Behind him, wearing a small smirk, Hannah stood watching the scene play out. Clearly, she wanted to be privy to the show as well.

I was about to tell her off when she held up a green post-it note. The note that had been missing from my desk a few days earlier. My eyes widened and she smirked, folding the note up and slipping into her pocket.

She'd sneaked into my room and stolen Grayson's address? That also meant she knew all about my design proposal. *Perfect.* My worst enemy, aka roommate, had my life in the palm of her hands.

"What is going on, Alan? What does this mean?" Grayson snapped, drawing my attention back to the piece of paper in his hand.

Alan punched my desk with his fist, making me jump. "I'll tell you what it means. Graduate Barbie here wanted to siphon some fame, so she submitted her own fucking design in the name of Cole Designs."

I stared between the two of them, watching my world crumble. I knew what was in that email; I knew I was about to have to own up to my actions, but I had no words.

Grayson rubbed his hand across his chin, staring me down with confusion, then fury when I failed to contradict Alan's accusation. Out of the corner of my eyes, I watched other coworkers stepping closer, hoping to catch a glimpse of the action.

"Is this true, Cammie?" Grayson asked, shaking the piece of paper in the air.

I mashed my lips together and stayed silent.

Alan pointed to the email. "That is an email from the competition's design committee stating that our firm has forfeited our spot in the Urban Park Design Proposal. Each firm is allowed to submit one submission, and yet somehow they received *TWO* from Cole Designs. What the hell were you thinking? Do you understand what you just lost for the company? That bid was worth millions of dollars, not to mention the fact that our firm's name would have been printed in every architectural magazine in the country when the design proposals were announced."

Grayson held up his hand to silence Alan's rant.

"Did you submit your own design, Cammie?" he asked, wearing a sad, yet hopeful look in his eyes. He wanted me to say no so badly, but I couldn't.

"Yes," I admitted, feeling a weight leave my shoulders as a heavy wave simultaneously crashed down over me. "I did."

Grayson crumpled the paper in his fist and squeezed his eyes closed for a moment. When he opened them again, there was only disappointment staring back at me.

"Why?"

I pointed to Alan. "Because he wouldn't listen to my ideas and I knew I had something better. His designs were shit, and everyone was too scared to speak up. So I submitted a design on my own."

Grayson threw the crumpled email across the room.

"Stupid girl," Alan spat.

Grayson shot him warning glance. "Alan, that's enough. Let's go into my office and get the design committee on the phone."

They turned and walked away from me without a second glance. Grayson didn't so much as look back at me and I wasn't sure if I was supposed to follow them or not, so I stood frozen, watching them disappear behind Grayson's door.

"Guess having a little affair with your boss isn't enough to get you out of this, is it, Cammie?" Hannah asked, loudly enough that in the quiet office at least a dozen coworkers overheard her.

"Shut up, Hannah," I said, grabbing my purse and pushing past her to head toward the stairwell.

"Guess you would have been better off sleeping with Alan instead," she called out after me. "Or maybe the whole design committee!"

I didn't bother turning around but I heard Peter's voice behind me.

"Don't you have work to do, Hannah? Why are you even over here?" he asked.

I'm sure she replied with something terribly catty, but I was too busy pushing through the side door into the stairwell to hear. The quiet wrapped around me and I stood with my back against the concrete wall as the last ten minutes began to sink in. Not only had I gone behind Grayson's back, I had also disqualified the entire company from the competition. Not to mention, Hannah had just all but convinced everyone that Grayson and I were having a secret affair.

I'd started my day as just another nameless rookie architect. Now, I was Cammie, the girl who sleeps around to get ahead and is stupid enough to jeopardize the company's reputation on a caprice. I was standing there, berating myself, when the door to the stairwell opened and I braced myself for Grayson. Instead, a pair of stiletto heels hit the concrete and I looked up to see Serenity stepping out of the office to join me on the stairwell landing.

"I thought I saw you come out here," she said, pulling a pack of cigarettes out of her small designer clutch. "Wanna smoke?"

I shook my head and then watched her shrug and light a cigarette for herself.

"I usually come out here to take a break, but lately you and Grayson have been stealing my spot," she said, staring at me out of the corner of her eye.

I swallowed. She'd known about Grayson and me all along, but never said anything.

Why?

"Are you allowed to smoke in the building?" I asked, to change the subject and to confirm my suspicions.

She pointed up to the wall, where the smoke detector should have been. Instead, there was a small circle of concrete that was lighter than the rest of the wall. *She'd removed the smoke detector off the wall.*

"Trust me, this building is in much less danger when I've had a few cigarettes," she said, taking a long drag.

I didn't really see her logic, but I wasn't exactly in a place to make anymore enemies.

"That was a foolish thing you did, huh?" she said, trying to meet my eye.

I rolled my eyes and crossed my arms tighter. The last thing I needed was a lecture from Miss Interior Design 2015.

"Do you realize how many asshole men there are in this business?" she asked.

I laughed, caught off guard by her candidness.

"Before I became the head of interiors, I worked for a crotchety old man named Mr. Winters. I knew that I had a better eye for design than he did, but I also knew that one day he'd step down and I'd get the final say in the department. I worked for him for four long years and I dreamed of doing what you did too many times to count, but I knew that it would get me nowhere."

I huffed, annoyed. "Where were you a few days ago?"

She laughed and took another drag of her cigarette, blowing the smoke away from me, down the stairwell.

"Was your design better than Alan's?" she asked.

The edge of my mouth hitched up. "A thousand times better. He's so out of touch with the original vision for the project."

She nodded and crossed an arm over her chest to prop up her elbow.

"Then when they fire you, you'll have no problem finding another job," she said, staring me straight in the eye. "But I wouldn't put Alan down as a reference."

With that, she bent to stub out her cigarette on the concrete and glided back into the office, leaving me with a whole new bomb to try to diffuse.

The Design

Chapter Twenty-Seven

I let myself stay in the stairwell until I was sure that everyone had gone back to their desks, bored with the drama. I knew I'd be the focal point of everyone's attention as soon as I showed my face, but I figured that at least a few people would pretend to be busy with their own work.

When I opened the door, I was pleasantly surprised to find that the office was all but deserted. I didn't see anyone, but then I heard the faint sound of voices coming from the conference room. I took another step and peered around the corner to see most of the Cole Designs staff packed into the conference room like sardines. I took a deep breath and moved to join them, when I heard my name.

"Cammie?" a voice called from behind me.

I turned to see a woman I faintly recognized as one of the company's HR representatives standing outside of Grayson's office door. Alan stood beside her with a scowl.

"Could we speak with you, please?" the woman asked, offering me a gentle smile.

I nodded and turned to join them before I noticed the small white binder clutched against her chest. *"Cole Designs HR Protocol"* was written across the front in thick letters.

Serenity was right. They're going to fire me.

When I approached the doorway to Grayson's office, Alan stepped aside to let me pass. It took all of my strength to stay silent as he glared down at me. I might have been in the wrong, but he deserved to be put in his place just as much as I did.

Grayson looked up from his desk when I entered, an indistinguishable expression on his face. Had we been alone, I would have hoped for some kind of greeting, but the HR woman and Alan followed me into the office and shut the door behind them. There was no hope for any privacy.

"Cammie." Grayson nodded. "Have a seat."

"Or stay standing, this shouldn't take long," Alan added with a sharp tongue.

Grayson glared up at him. "That's your final warning, Alan. I've had enough today."

Alan straightened his tie and cleared his throat, clearly embarrassed. The HR woman sat down in the seat beside me and flipped open her binder.

"So, Cammie, I'm Monica, and I'm here to supervise this meeting. As I'm sure you suspect, your actions concerning the design competition cannot be overlooked by the company—"

"Monica," Grayson interrupted, "If you don't mind, I'd like to do most of the talking. I understand that you have to be here, but Cammie should hear this from me."

I clutched my hands on top of my lap and stared down at my chipped nail polish as Grayson continued to speak. I tried to absorb most of it, but really only got bits and pieces while I tried to keep my tears at bay:

"...your actions were careless...",

"...jeopardized your coworkers' jobs...",

"...stolen company property...",

"...endangered the reputation...".

As I listened, I tried to pretend that I was hearing the speech from someone else's lips. I knew that Grayson was firing me. I knew that it was the only choice he had, but when he told me to gather my things and exit the building, I felt like a hot blade had pierced my chest.

I loved him and he was letting me go.

I loved him and yet I'd still betrayed him.

"You've left me no choice, Cammie." Grayson's eyes pleaded with me to understand.

I nodded and stood to head for the door before realizing that I should tell him the truth. I gripped the back of the chair I'd just vacated and met Grayson's eye for the first time since entering his office. I could have fallen so easily into his warm, trusting gaze, but I knew that couldn't happen anymore.

"Yes, I submitted a design behind your back and yes, I snuck a few pages of letterhead. I shouldn't have done it, and I realize that. The last thing I wanted to do was go behind your back, but I felt like I had no choice. I know that it was irrational, but I don't regret submitting my own design. I would have never forgiven myself if I'd let the Alans of the world walk all over me. If this is truly a meritocracy, just look at the two designs."

His frown deepened.

"Thank you for giving me this opportunity and I'm truly sorry for causing you to lose faith in me."

I was sure there were still things for us to work out, some kind of paperwork to sign before I left, but I turned toward the door and walked out of Grayson's office. They could mail me my final check. They could send me any exit paperwork. I'd be in another country soon enough, so what did it matter?

• • •

I took the long way home that afternoon. The sun was beating down overhead as I strolled down various LA streets, but I wasn't in a hurry to escape it. To go home meant that I had to decide what my next move would be. I'd wanted to travel, to leave for Paris and never look back, but I'd wanted to do it on my own terms. I hadn't saved up enough money yet and I wasn't ready to leave Grayson. It felt like we were right at the beginning of something good, and if we could only get through the storm, we'd have a real potential to end up together. Him and me.

However, if I wasn't making money, I didn't really have many options. I could get a part time job somewhere, just to prolong the inevitable, but I think deep down I knew that getting fired was the final kick in the ass that I'd needed to pursue my dream. I just had to figure out how I'd leave Grayson without tearing my heart out in the process.

Chapter Twenty-Eight

Amount saved for Paris: $3417 (plus $537 from my last Cole Designs paycheck and another $3250 from selling my car).

Items I have: a pumpkin spice k-cup I stole from my desk on the way out of the office.

Items I need: a list of hostels in Paris.

French phrases that I know: Non, je ne ai pas de travail. Puis-je laver la vaisselle?...which translates to: "No, I don't have a job. Can I wash dishes?"

"So, they canned you?" Brooklyn asked as we spoke on the phone later that afternoon.

I rolled my eyes and sat up in bed, suddenly feeling antsy. *Why had I called her instead of just moping solo style?* She had a way of making it seem like getting fired was a bad thing. I preferred to look at it like I was a badass, blazing my way through the business world and taking life by the horns.

"Cammie?" she asked again, this time a bit more impatient.

I sighed. "Yes, I am a jobless loser."

She laughed and then quickly corrected herself. "I'm sorry, Cammie. Why don't you come out to Montana and stay with Jason and I for a few days? LuAnne would love to see you and Cowboy Derek is still as cute as ever."

While the idea of Montana sounded very enticing, I knew I couldn't go. I had unfinished business in LA and as soon as it was cleared up, I'd be on my way to Paris. My gut twisted at the idea of boarding a plane—of leaving Grayson behind. Having him fire me was one of the most humiliating moments of my life, but leaving him behind would be ten times harder to bear.

"Thank you for the offer, sis, but I'm going to stick around here."

"For Grayson?"

I paused, wondering how much I ought to tell her.

"For a lot of reasons."

My entire life I'd had Brooklyn as a safety net to catch me whenever life got a little too hard. In the 7th grade, when Sarah Buchanan said that my eyes were so big that I looked like a fish in front of my entire English class, Brooklyn took me out for ice cream after school and then we egged Sarah's house on the way home. My senior year of high school, when Todd Jenkins was so drunk at prom that he tried to force himself on me in our high school's bathroom, Brooklyn picked me up outside the front of the school and then we egged his front door. *Hmm, my childhood had a lot of eggs in it.*

Most importantly, when our parents died, Brooklyn held me together as best as she could. It was a natural pattern for us to fall into, one that wouldn't easily be broken unless I put an end to it. I couldn't depend on Brooklyn for every little thing in life. Running to Montana and escaping my problems wasn't the answer.

A knock on the front door of my apartment jerked my attention from where I'd been twisting my bedspread between my fingers.

"B, I gotta go. Someone's at the door," I said.

"Ok. Be safe and don't worry about that silly job. You'll find something better and it probably wouldn't have been a good idea for you and Grayson to work together anyway."

"Yeah, maybe you're right," I said, just as I heard another knock from the front door.

"Oh, and hey! I sent you a hilarious picture of Jason sleeping on the plane the other day. I put pretzels under his lip like a walrus. Check your email, it'll make you feel better."

I smiled. "Will do."

Once I'd hung up, I threw my phone down onto my bed and went to check the door, praying it wasn't Hannah. I hadn't figured out what I was going to do about her yet. There's no way we could sleep in the same apartment anymore, not now that I knew how truly vile she was.

"Cammie, are you in there?" a deep voice boomed from the other side of the door.

I turned the lock to find Grayson waiting on the other side of the door. I swung it open and he pushed past me before I could even catch a glimpse of him.

"Good to see you too," I said, turning and pushing the door closed with my butt.

He spun around to face me looking more disheveled than I'd ever seen him before. His hair was standing on end like he'd tugged the strands all day hoping they would give. His tie was gone, the top two buttons of his shirt were open, and his eyes were wild, darting back and forth among my features.

"Why did you have to do it, Cammie?" he asked.

I pressed my palms together in front of my chest. "Save the lecture please. You already fired me. I spent all day moaning to Brooklyn because I have no job and no prospects. So please, take off your boss hat and put on your boyfriend hat."

His features eased, the wrinkles in his forehead going slack.

"Boyfriend?"

My eyes widened.

"It was a slip of the tongue. Besides, it'd take me like two hours to explain what we really are, so the label will have to do for right now."

The edge of his mouth hitched up. "I think the label should stay."

I wasn't sure if I agreed, not before we discussed the voicemail message.

"Was it chaos the rest of the day?" I asked, pressing my hands to his chest and leading him back toward the couch.

He shook his head. "No, Alan was under orders to keep the situation private. And I fired Hannah."

"You what?!"

He'd slipped in that detail so subtly that I almost didn't hear it. *He'd fired Hannah?* I couldn't say she didn't deserve it, but it still felt a little harsh.

I watched him sink down onto the couch and lean back against the cushions. It was probably his first break of the day. I cringed at the knowledge that I was the cause of his fatigue.

"Trust me, I'd rather have arsonists working for me than conniving gossips," he said, assuring me of his decision.

I rubbed the back of my neck, trying to comprehend how so much had changed in one day.

"I see."

"What will you do for work? I can't believe I had to fire you, Cammie. You left me no choice." His eyes pleaded with me to understand. "You know there was no other way, right?"

I nodded and offered him a solemn smile. I couldn't answer his questions about what I'd do because I didn't know the answers myself, so I just stayed quiet.

"Come here," he said, reaching his hand out to catch the tips of my fingers. A current of lust shot through me as our skin touched. It'd been the worst day I'd had in a very long time, but I had Grayson all to myself now and he looked so sweet and tired. I let him pull me down and then I straddled his hips with my legs. I hadn't changed out of my work clothes yet so my twist-tie dress slipped up my thighs with the help of Grayson's fingers brushing it higher and higher. His designer slacks rubbed against the back of my legs, tickling my skin.

"A boyfriend ought to make his girlfriend feel better after a long day." He spoke in whispers as one hand slipped beneath my dress. His other hand twisted my hair into a long rope and then he tugged gently, once, so that I was forced to tip my head back or suffer a shock of pain to my neck.

His lips found the juncture between my chin and neck, the sensitive little groove that when he kissed, shot goosebumps down my spine when he kissed it.

"I can't believe you fired me today," I spoke,.

"I can't believe you broke into my office," he said.

I shook my head, recalling the messages I'd heard on his answering machine. It was the perfect opportunity to bring them up and yet I couldn't make myself do it.

"I really didn't want to break into your office. I'm so sorry I did," I hummed, letting my fingers slide down his chest.

For the next hour Grayson and I made each other forget the horrors of the day. He kissed away my embarrassment and I brushed away his disappointment. Eventually, he picked me up and carried me into my room, but as we lay in bed later that night, I knew that things weren't cleared up. The chaos of the day had distracted me momentarily, but there was still so much I had to ask him about. A part of me knew that once I brought up the messages, we wouldn't be able to get back to this happy place—the place before I left for Paris and before he told me something I wouldn't be able to forgive.

Chapter Twenty-Nine

Later that night, I stared up at my ceiling, which was cast in shadows from the light streaming through the open blinds. A lone street lamp outside produced more light than I thought possible, but it wasn't the reason I lay awake. Grayson slept beside me, wrapped around me like a coiled snake, snoring gently and keeping me safe and warm. He seemed perfectly content, but I was still hanging in limbo, worried about what the next day would bring. We'd yet to discuss his voicemail messages, but I knew I'd have to bring them up tomorrow morning.

Knowing I wouldn't find sleep anytime soon, I extracted myself from Grayson's arms and pushed off my bed in search of something to distract me from another hour of tossing and turning. My options were limited since I couldn't leave my bedroom. I hadn't heard Hannah come home yet, but I didn't want to take my chances.

The soft light from my laptop charger caught my attention. My computer would have to do. I could put my headphones in and listen to Taylor Swift covers while pinning DIY projects I'd never actually get around to making. It was my favorite guilty pleasure.

I unlocked my computer and tilted the screen so that it wouldn't wake Grayson. Once my headphones were in place and I'd pulled up a few songs on YouTube, I switched over to my email, wondering if Brooklyn had sent the funny picture of Jason she'd promised me. I needed a good laugh.

After Gmail loaded up, I scanned the first few unopened emails and frowned, confused by the senders: Mitch@ColeDesigns.com, Alan@ColeDesigns.com, JimDwyer@DwyerConstruction.com. *Oh.* Grayson had logged onto his email a few days prior and I had yet to notice that he was still logged in.

I scrolled up to logout of his account, but before I got the chance, a folder on the sidebar caught my attention. It was the first folder listed and its name was only one word: *Cammie.*

Why did he have a folder with my name on it?

I glanced over my shoulder to check if Grayson was still asleep. He'd turned toward the wall, but when I pulled out my headphones, I could hear his soft snoring.

I turned back to the computer screen and contemplated my next move. I could sign out of his email and proceed to browse Pinterest until my eyes fell out, or I could scroll over and click the folder, just to see what he'd saved. It was probably something sweet.

In the end, my hand made the decision for me. It moved the curser to hover over the folder and my finger clicked once.

I'd expected a few email exchanges between us, maybe ones I'd overlooked during my short time at Cole

Designs. Instead, I found myself staring at a list of emails I didn't recognize. As I scrolled down, pages and pages of emails continued to load. Some of the them were dated back to when I was still in college, and then as I continued to scroll, I saw emails dated all the way back to when I was still in high school.

What the hell? Why are these emails categorized under my name? There wasn't a single email sent to me or from me.

A cold chill ran down my spine as I scrolled back to the very top of the page. I read the first few email addresses and their subjects. The most recent one had been sent just a few hours earlier.

> **Luke@GADesignGroup.com** - "Job for associate architect"
> **FrankJcomb@Whitmoorapts.com** - "Rent for Unit #450"
> **FrankJcomb@Whitmoorapts.com** - "Security System for Unit #450"
> **CarrieJohnson@gmail.com** - "Summer Internship"
> **GaryVaughn@hotmail.com** - "Recommendation for Cameron Heart"

I clicked a random email in the center of the page and waited for it load as dread began to take hold of me.

To: MichaelDMoore@AHLDesignBuild.com
From: GraysonCole@ColeDesigns.com

Hey Mike,

I understand that your summer internship program is competitive, but I urge you to reconsider Cameron Heart's application. She's more than qualified for the position and she's a personal family friend.

My firm has a few projects we're looking to pass on due to our current workload and I think your firm would be a good fit for a lot of these clients.

Let me know if you're interested in the work, and if you'll reconsider Cameron Heart for a spot as a summer intern.

Grayson Cole, *FAIA*
CEO Cole Designs
Principle Architect

My stomach dropped and my hand shook on top of my mouse as I reread the email again. I thought I'd interpreted it wrong the first time, but there was no doubt about it—Grayson had promised work to a design firm in exchange for my selection as a summer intern. I'd ended up interning with that company for three months before my senior year of college...and apparently I had Grayson to *thank* for that.

Sadly, that email was only the beginning. There were email exchanges between him and my professors, emails between him and my old landlords, emails about an anonymous academic scholarship I'd received throughout my four years in college. He'd even coordinated with the dean of my architecture school, all but promising free design services in exchange for my acceptance into their architecture program. Each email was more incriminating than the last and each one I read made my heart break a little more.

I scoured through them for hours, reading every last one until I couldn't stomach anymore. After reading them, one conclusion was painfully clear: for the last few years, Grayson had effectively played God in my life. I'd been a puppet for him to manipulate however he saw fit. I'd been a doll for him to play with.

I tried to comprehend his reasoning for interfering in my life. I'd had a rough time in high school and hadn't really found focus until my senior year. At the time, I'd assumed it would take a miracle to get me into the architecture program of my choice...but now I realized it had nothing to do with my talent and everything to do with Grayson pulling strings behind my back.

Every single defining moment I'd lived through in the last five years had been carefully crafted by Grayson. He'd given me unsolicited recommendations, unsolicited scholarships, unsolicited job interviews and internships. He'd even paid for a percentage of my rent in every apartment I'd lived in without me even realizing it. *How? Where the hell had my money gone?*

Seeing how much I'd unknowingly depended on Grayson for the last five years felt like someone had just ripped the rug out from beneath me. As I sat there in the dark, the glow of the computer screen illuminating my face, I realized that I hadn't earned a single thing my entire adult life. My designs had never been tested. My talent was nothing compared to the strings Grayson had pulled. Five years of work had been rendered worthless in the matter of hours.

Truth be told, it scared the shit out of me to consider what else Grayson had controlled in my life without my knowledge. *Did he read my emails? Did he listen to my phone calls?*

Without another thought, I pulled my tennis shoes out of my closet, grabbed my keys and left my apartment. I ran down the stairs as quickly as I could, pushed through the front door, and promptly leaned over and threw up all over some poor shrubs in front of my building.

An older couple walked past me to enter the building and I waved them on as they asked if I needed any help. The last thing I needed was for one more person to help me out. I was sick and tired of being coddled and manipulated. Grayson and Brooklyn wanted to be my heroes, and instead they'd morphed into my worst nightmare.

I wiped my mouth and walked through downtown LA with my arms crossed, my thin t-shirt doing little to protect me from the night chill. I had nowhere to go. Grayson was at my apartment. I had no other family in LA. I'd given up my key to Cole Designs before I'd left the building. I thought briefly of going to a 24-hour coffee shop, but I'd left my wallet in my purse back home.

Without intending to, I walked toward Brooklyn's condo. It felt like a bit of a copout, to seek refuge in her condo when I was trying desperately to stand on my own two feet, but I reasoned that it was only for one more night.

The bellman, Hank, recognized me and let me in without question, and I rode the elevator up to her luxury condo. I found her spare key hidden under a potted plant beside the door and let myself in. To say that stepping into her condo didn't feel like home would be a giant lie.

The smell was familiar, and the shoes lingering by the door were ones I'd borrowed dozens of times. I knew where every item of clothing was and where she hid a secret stash of chocolate. The refrigerator was empty since she and Jason were in Montana, so I got myself a glass of water and walked over to her computer desk. I typed in her password and smiled when I saw the picture of us that she kept as her desktop background. I'd put it up as a joke; it was a heinous photo of when we'd tried to put on each other's makeup with our eyes closed (we get bored late at night).

Seeing her smiling face made me long to call her and tell her everything I'd found on Grayson's email. I wanted her to erase the day I'd had, to whisk me away to Montana where I could forget all my troubles.

Instead, I pulled up Expedia.com and opened the top drawer of her desk—the one where I'd stuffed a note with my credit card information years earlier in an effort to make online shopping even easier. When the website was done loading, I looked up flights from Los Angeles to Paris. I clicked on the cheapest flight that departed the very next day and reserved my spot.

It was finally time to learn if I could make it on my own.

Chapter Thirty

When I arrived home the next morning, I pressed my ear to the door and slid my key into the lock. I had exactly two hours until I planned to be at the airport for my flight. Since I'd be traveling internationally, I wanted to get there extra early so that I'd have plenty of time to make it through security and find the correct gate.

My apartment seemed to be empty; I couldn't hear a thing from outside, so I took a deep breath and pushed the door open. The living room looked exactly as it had before I'd left. I checked Hannah's room first. Her door stood ajar, clothes strewn about everywhere. I figured she hadn't come home at all. *Smart girl.* I still wanted to rip her hair out.

I turned to my room next and that's when I heard a low groan followed by Grayson's sharp voice.

"I don't care what you have to do. I'm telling you she's missing and we shouldn't have to wait 12 hours before we start searching—"

Dammit. I flew through my bedroom door before Grayson requested sending the entire National Guard out looking for me.

"I'm not missing!" I yelled. Grayson turned to me with a face clouded in anger. He was standing in his boxers, bloodshot eyes hidden behind hard features. His dark hair stood in every direction and I wasn't sure if he was about to kiss me or strangle me. I'd say it was an even 50/50 for either option, so I stayed exactly where I was.

"Jim, never mind. She's here. Thanks," he said before tossing his phone onto my bed. He used too much force and the phone rolled off and thumped to the ground. He didn't move to grab it; instead he stared straight at me.

I held my hands up in defense. "Before you even start, just get out of my apartment."

My words wounded him. He flinched and took a step back, clearly confused.

"Where have you been? You look like you haven't slept at all," he said, scanning over me.

I crossed my arms. "I *didn't* sleep at all. I walked to Brooklyn's apartment and purchased a one-way ticket to Paris. But, wait," I said, with sarcasm starting to ooze out of every pore. "You probably already know that!"

"What the fuck are you talking about?" he asked, taking two steps toward me.

"Stop," I warned, holding out my hand again.

He raked his hands through his hair and bit down hard on his lip as if trying to keep it together.

"I'm leaving for Paris today. It's been my plan for a while. I just didn't tell you about it."

His eyes widened in disbelief. "Paris? What in the world? You didn't think that was something you should have told me?"

I laughed and turned to retrieve the travel backpack I'd purchased a few weeks earlier from beneath my bed. If I organized everything perfectly, I could fit everything I needed inside of it.

"Cammie, god dammit. You're being crazy. You need to slow down and talk to me," he said, reaching to pull the backpack out of my hands. "Where did you go last night and what's all this about Paris?"

"No! I don't owe you a damn thing!" I yelled, tugging the backpack out of his reach. "I saw your email, Grayson!" *There it was.* "You left your account open on my computer and I saw my little folder. All of your 'Cammie' emails. I read every single one. You're a sick son of a bitch."

He scrunched his face, trying to catch up and decipher my outburst.

"Your folder?"

I was beyond pissed.

"Yes." I spoke annoyingly slow to drive home my point. "The folder where you saved every single detail of how you've meddled in my life. Job interviews, test scores, rent, scholarships—every single thing you manipulated in my life. You are a fucking stalker, Grayson!"

"I'm not a stalker. Calm down," he protested. His eyes were completely dilated in anger and I knew that there was no going back. This was the fight that would end us. Except it wouldn't just end us. It would break us down until we were both casualties with nothing left to show but two broken hearts.

"After your parents died," he began to explain, "Brooklyn asked me to watch out for you. You and her had a rocky relationship then, and she felt like you had nobody to count on, so I stepped up and I did what I had to do."

"Bullshit," I hissed. "You did what you *wanted* to do, so you could be some kind of knight in shining armor. Can you even imagine how it feels to find out you've just been a fucking damsel in distress your entire adult life?"

"Tell me," he asked, stepping closer. "Tell me one thing I did that a devoted friend or big brother or father figure wouldn't have done! You had nobody, Cammie! Nobody to help you except for your sister."

"I didn't ask for your help!" I yelled. "I never asked for a big brother!"

"Because you're too proud," he protested, his rage boiling over. "You wouldn't ask for help unless you were seconds from drowning. And even then, you'd probably resent the life preserver! Fuck." He gripped his head and bent down, clearly struggling to make sense of the situation.

I gritted my teeth so hard that my jaw ached.

"Please get out of my apartment, Grayson."

"You're being ridiculous," he said, pulling on his jeans as quickly as he could. He turned back to me as he grabbed for his shirt. "I would have shown you the folder soon. I would have explained to you what I've done and you'd see my reasons. You'd understand why I stepped in when you had nobody."

I shrugged, digging my heels into my anger so much so that I couldn't find any bit of reason in his words.

"Yeah, well," I shrugged, holding back the flood of tears. "All's forgiven, because now it looks like I still have no one."

He glared back at me before tugging his shirt over his head. "And whose fault is that? You're running away to Paris, Cammie. Stay and fight with me. This is nothing.

This fight," he said, pointing between the two of us, "it's nothing compared to how I feel for you."

I turned away from him and my gaze found its way to my black computer screen. If I turned it on, his email would pop up. I'd be confronted by the overwhelming proof that he'd overstepped his place in my life time and time again. Maybe he would have told me about the folder, but maybe he would have kept it a secret forever.

"I need to pack," I whispered, unable to look back to him.

He growled, grabbed for his phone on my floor, and slammed my bedroom door shut on his way out. I squeezed my eyes closed until I heard my apartment door close and then I waited and wondered if he was truly gone—if that fight had been the end of us. In the romanticized version of my life, Grayson would have stormed back in and forced me to talk to him. But ten minutes later, when the apartment was as silent as when I'd first returned that morning, I began to pack up my things.

The plan was still on. I was going to Paris.

Chapter Thirty-One

Amount saved for Paris: After purchasing my ticket, I had about $5300 left to hold me over until I found temporary work, which wouldn't be easy to do considering I only had a tourist visa.

Items I have: a backpack filled to the brim, a carry-on purse, and a good book to get me through the flight.

Items I need: enough confidence to get me on the actual flight…

French phrases that I know: Pourriez-vous me diriger dans la direction de l' auberge la plus proche? et également un bar?…which translates to "Could you point me in the direction of the nearest hostel? And also a bar?"

"Where to, ma'am?" the cab driver asked as he loaded my heavy backpack into the trunk of the cab.

"LAX. Passenger drop-off, please," I answered, sliding into the backseat.

I had everything I needed clutched in the palm of my hands: my passport, my boarding pass, and my to-do list. I would have preferred to leave the states with a better plan, but in the end, life had forced my hand and I just had to make the best of it. I'd written down all the major things I had to get done.

Beneath "*FIND A SUBLEASE ASAP, YOU FOOL,*" I'd written, "*Tell Brooklyn you're in Paris.*" (There was a very real possibility Brooklyn would get on a plane to Paris and kick my ass once I'd told her I'd left the country. Either that, or she'd hire a French assassin to kill me for her.)

There was only one more item on my to-do list after that: find a hostel in Paris. I'd begun looking into my options weeks ago, but I had no clue if there'd be any vacancies or what kind of shape the hostels would be in when I actually got to one. It was too late to call ahead, so I'd just have to try and find one once I arrived. Worse case scenario: I could stay in a hotel for the first night and find a hostel in the morning. It'd deplete my savings a little bit, but it was better than sleeping on the streets of Paris.

"Here's your stop, ma'am," the cab driver spoke, drawing my attention away from my list. A quick glance out of the window confirmed that we were at the airport.

I'd come to the finish line.

I pocketed my things, and climbed out of the backseat just as the driver finished pulling my backpack from the trunk. He handed it over and I lugged it onto my back, cursing the weight. I'd packed up everything that was too important to leave behind in my apartment. There were photos and memories shoved between socks and underwear. It wasn't ideal, but it'd work until I arrived in Paris and had a little space of my own.

"You paying in cash?" the driver asked, subtly reminding me that I'd yet to pay for my fare yet.

"Ah, yes, how much was—"

"Cammie!"

I turned at the sound of my name, reached up to shield the sun from my eyes, and then saw Grayson hop out of a cab a few yards down from where I stood. He slammed the cab door closed and threw cash through the passenger side window before beginning to run toward me.

"What the hell, man?!" his cabdriver yelled back at him, but Grayson was already halfway down the sidewalk.

I wanted to cave then, to run to him and erase the past. We could start new and pretend there weren't any skeletons in our closet. But, I knew I'd never forgive myself if I caved.

He pushed through the crowd of travelers on the sidewalk, trying to get to me. I wasn't going anywhere. I was rooted to my spot, but he ran toward me like I was fleeing at the speed of light.

Before he reached me, I turned toward my cab and braced myself for the end.

"Cammie!" Grayson yelled.

I couldn't believe he'd come.

"Ma'am, the money," the cab driver reminded me, apparently unaffected by the romantic airport scene taking place before him.

"Oh. Uh," I fumbled for my wallet and tried to pull out exact change just as Grayson reached me.

"I've got it," Grayson said, reaching for cash before I held up my hand.

"No! No you don't have it," I argued, turning to the cab driver. "This should cover it."

"Whatever. Have a good trip." The cabdriver shrugged and fled the scene, wanting nothing more to do with us.

"Cammie. Please just wait a second," Grayson said when I turned to face the entrance of the airport.

"What do you want Grayson?" I asked, hitching my backpack up higher on my shoulder. The weight was already getting to me.

"You're actually going to leave?" Grayson asked, scanning over my backpack and passport sticking out of my front pocket.

"Yes, I'm really leaving," I answered.

He threw his hands up in the air, exasperated with me. "Because I helped you earn a scholarship? Because I gave you a job?"

I scanned the crowd around him, trying to do anything but meet his eye. "Because of everything. This is too much, Grayson. All the things you've done in secret—it's too much for me to ignore. The fact that you just tried to pay my cab fare proves that you still don't get it."

"Cammie. I would have told you about everything. You think it looks bad because it's all piled up in emails, but you have to just let me explain it."

He reached for my arm, gripping it securely in his hand so that I was forced to stay beside him, to stay with him. I glanced up at his face and immediately wished I hadn't. Sorrow was etched across every feature. His blue eyes threatened to tear me in two.

"Tell me the reason you're leaving me, Cammie."

He wanted an answer, but I couldn't give him one. I didn't quite understand my need to leave, but it was there, in the pit of my stomach, overpowering my love for the man in front of me. More than anything, I felt a need to flee, to get out and run as far away as I could. If I didn't do it now, at this moment, I knew I never would. I would be Grayson's puppet and my sister's charity project for the rest of my life.

So, instead of giving him the complicated version, I lied.

"It's all been a game to me, Grayson," I said with a steady voice. The words were a lie, but I was holding enough anger inside of me that they sounded real, even to me.

He frowned, his thick brows drawing together in confusion. "A game?"

I nodded.

"You don't meant that," he argued.

"Can't you see? It was a game to pass the time before I left for Paris. Can the ugly duckling, all grown up, score her childhood crush?"

His grip loosened around my arm and then his touch was gone completely. He took two steps back, stared at me for another moment, and then nodded.

"Yeah," he agreed. "Maybe this was all a game because I definitely feel like a fucking loser right now, Cammie."

I guess that made me the winner. Too bad I didn't feel like one.

Tears, hot and heavy, were threatening to stream down my cheeks. I turned and wiped my eyes before growing even angrier that I couldn't keep it together.

"Whatever." I took a deep breath. "Are we done here?"

My casual tone unnerved him. He flinched back and then lurched forward, stepping right up to me until our faces were inches away from each other.

"Do you think you're safe if you belittle our relationship? Hide behind the idea that it was all just casual sex?" he asked, his voice growing louder so that the passing travelers slowed around us to listen.

"What's your goal here, Grayson?" I cried. "I'm leaving for Paris! And you're staying in LA to run your company. Just let it go!"

He shook his head and gripped my arms, his final resolve coming to life. "You once called me a liar. Do you remember that? You jabbed your finger into my chest and you called me a fucking liar."

"What's your point?!"

"You're a hypocrite!" he yelled. "You're scared and you're running because of it."

I laughed sarcastically, a shrill sound that sounded terrible even to my own ears.

"Yup. You've figured it out. That's the exact reason I'm leaving. Now let me go."

He threw up his hands. "Okay. Fine. I'll let you go if you tell me you're getting on that plane for the right reasons, that you won't regret your decision to leave the second it takes off."

Of course I couldn't tell him that, not if I was being honest, but then his indiscretions flashed through my mind like a horrible daydream. The emails, the jobs, the internships, the subsidized rent…but most importantly, the fact that nothing in my life had been accomplished by my own two hands. Grayson had acted as my god for far too long. I couldn't separate my love for him from my hatred for what he'd done in my life. I had to get out. I had to leave.

I gripped my backpack strap and took a step back. The small separation was enough to break my resolve.

"Goodbye Grayson. Take care of Brooklyn."

"Cammie!"

I walked through the airport doors, and did my best to ignore the tears clouding my vision.

• • •

As luck would have it, my plane was delayed twice because of mechanical issues. I sat in the crowded terminal and watched plane after plane take off, wondering when my turn would come. Each hour that passed made it that much easier for me to question if I was making the right decision. I was still in LA. I could walk out of the airport at any time. If I was on a plane or in Paris, the waiting, the wondering, the second guessing would be put to rest.

I sat between a family traveling to Paris for vacation and a couple anxious to start their honeymoon. There were a few passengers traveling for business, but they were focused on their work, unencumbered by the noise around them. I sat at the crowded gate, people watching and feeling wholeheartedly alone.

In an effort to distract myself from the sick feeling in my stomach, I'd pulled out my sketchbook and started drafting simple designs on the last few pages. The process helped pass the time and gave me something to focus my mind on.

Finally, after four hours of delays, they announced that our flight was boarding. I was rushing back from the bathroom, the effects of two cups of coffee starting to become unbearable. Just as I arrived back at the terminal, my boarding group was lining up and I scrambled to gather my things.

"Miss?" someone spoke behind me as I felt a tap on my shoulder.

I turned to see a middle-aged man pointing over to where I'd been sitting.

"I think that's yours?" he said.

My sketchbook sat on the ground, flipped upside down with its pages splayed out.

"Oh! Thank you!" I said as I rushed to gather it up. I flipped it over to dust off the pages that'd been on the floor, and my stomach clenched. Grayson's soulful eyes stared back at me as I gazed upon a sketch I'd done of him years ago, when I was still in high school. The sketch was on one of the first pages, long forgotten. Even the graphite from the pencil had started to fade. I remembered sitting in my room and sketching furiously while I listened for any sign of footsteps, praying Brooklyn wouldn't come in and catch me in the act. The entire first half of the sketchbook was practically a shrine to him.

"Everyone in boarding group B, please line up!" the flight attendant instructed over the speaker system, jarring me from my reverie.

"What's taking you to Paris?" the man asked as I moved to join the line. "Business or pleasure?"

He eyed me with a tentative smile.

I closed my sketchbook and turned toward the boarding door. Down that dim hallway there was a plane waiting to take me to Paris. There was no turning back.

"Neither," I answered as my gaze held steady on the future.

It was the first honest answer I'd given all day.

Chapter Thirty-Two

"Cammie, get your ass back to the United States or I will get on a plane and drag you home myself. Seriously, what were you THINKING?! Grayson called to let me know you'd left. Thank god for him. How could you leave the country without even telling me? Haven't you seen *Taken*?! Don't you know what happens to pretty American girls when they go abroad? No, Jason, I will not hang up. She needs to know how insane she is. No, seriously—"

Brooklyn's message cut off after that, so either her allotted message time had ended or Jason had forced her to hang up. There were three more messages waiting for me after that one, all from Brooklyn and each over a minute long.

Instead of listening to them, I shot a selfie and paired it with a simple message: "I am FINE. Please don't worry. I'll call you soon."

I'd been in Paris for two days and was in no rush to call Brooklyn. I was just getting my bearings and calling her would throw me back to square one—back to when I'd first stepped off the plane and felt the crippling grip of homesickness around my neck. I'd pushed through it, ventured out, and managed to find a small hostel on the edge of a relatively nice arrondissement to establish as a home base.

Each guest at the hostel had a small bunk to themselves with storage space beneath to lock up any valuables. My bunkmate was a Russian girl with cropped black hair and a tattoo of a tiger along the side of her neck. Across from us was a bunk with two teenage guys from Australia. The last two nights they'd arrived back at the hostel at nearly 5:00 am and slept well into the afternoon. I hadn't had the chance to meet them, and the only reason I knew they were Australian at all was because they both talked in their sleep (mostly about wallabies and sheilas, heh).

In an odd way, everything seemed to be coming together. I spent my first few days wandering around Paris and trying to blend in with the locals. I tried out three different crepe cafes before I had to cut myself off. If I wasn't careful, I'd blow my entire savings on desserts.

Money was constantly on my mind. I knew that I had the trust my parents had left for me, but I didn't want to touch it. That wasn't Paris money. That was money for purchasing a house and settling down. Besides, the whole reason I had flown to Paris was to see if I could stand on my own two feet. If I budgeted right and found a decent job, I could live in Paris indefinitely.

On my third day in Paris, my bunkmate, Kiki, told me about her job teaching English to adults in the evenings. She said the program was constantly looking for new teachers, especially people who knew American English well. I agreed to accompany her to the program's offices that afternoon. After a short interview process where they confirmed that I did in fact speak English, they hired me and set me up with a preliminary class schedule.

It wasn't my ideal job. I wanted to design and use the degree I'd worked so hard to get, but teaching in the evenings left me with plenty of time in the mornings to take my sketchbook out and wander around Paris. I dreamed of perfecting my French, applying for a work visa, and trying to land a job with a Parisian architecture firm. If I found a large enough firm, chances were they'd need to have architects fluent in English.

So I settled into a simple routine. The hostel was great, but roommates came and went every few days. I was constantly surrounded by people—sleeping in a room with six bunk beds ensured that fact—and yet, I always felt alone. As soon as I'd get to know someone in the hostel, they'd jet off for their next destination. Kiki stayed in Paris for the first two weeks I was there before she packed up and headed off to Germany. She had plans to meet up with her boyfriend there and then the two of them would travel together through Europe, teaching English as they went.

About three weeks into my stay, I realized that the hostel couldn't be my permanent home. It encouraged a transitory lifestyle, and I was in Paris for the long haul. A part of me yearned to find a Parisian apartment of my own. Nothing special, just a small, one-bedroom place where I could start to lay down my roots.

Though I dreamed of an apartment, I was in no rush to actually find one. The hostel let me pay per week and I had the freedom to leave at any time. That freedom helped me sleep at night. When homesickness threatened to break my resolve, I'd tell myself that I was just on vacation and it seemed to help a bit.

One day about a month into my stay in Paris, I found a small cafe and sat outside, sketching and reading off and on. I was midway through a sketch when the wind whipped the pages of my notebook, flashing back to the sketch of Grayson on the first page. I slapped my palm onto the pages, overpowering the wind and forcing the pages to lay still, but the damage was already done.

My dream, the idea of being in Paris and living on my own, was starting to fray. I loved being in the City of Light. I loved exploring the ancient buildings and exploring structures I'd studied for hours on end in my architecture classes. Yet at the same time, in the back of my mind I was starting to wonder if Paris was really where I belonged.

I'd wanted to break the chains I'd felt in LA and leaving for Paris seemed to be the best way to do it.

Well, I was standing on my own. I was in Paris, completely isolated from everyone I loved, and most of time, I felt depressed and scared. It was a humbling thought to acknowledge and the first few times it surfaced in my head, I'd quickly squashed it.

Paris was my dream.

I belonged here.

But, didn't I belong with the people I loved?

Those people held me back. They were my crutch.

But maybe that wasn't their fault.

Chapter Thirty-Three

I waited another two weeks before I called Brooklyn. I counted down the days, stubbornly believing that the longer I waited, the more independent I was. In the end, the moment I heard her voice, I broke down into sobs.

"I don't speak the language. I don't know how to use the subway. I hate most of the people in this dumb hostel. My bunkmate hasn't showered in two weeks. Do you know how smelly someone is when they don't shower for two weeks?!"

I rambled on and on and Brooklyn silently listened.

"I thought Paris was your dream?" she asked quietly.

I sniffed. "I thought it was. I really thought I'd be happy here. Happiness for me is a moving target, I guess."

She hummed, mulling over my confession. "Were you happy in LA?"

I didn't even have to think about her question. "Of course I was happy there, but that's because you were in charge of every difficult thing in my life and Grayson was paving and paying the way for me. I never had anything to challenge me. How could I not be happy?!"

"Wait," she interrupted, "What are you talking about with Grayson? Just because he was your boss doesn't mean he paved the way for you."

I laughed, a cruel, sarcastic laugh.

"Oh, yes he did."

I told her about everything Grayson had done, about all of the emails I'd found and the way he'd gone behind my back. I relished getting to talk about him, even if it was in negative light. For the last month and half I'd had no one to discuss him with. He'd been secluded away in my thoughts. *And boy, did I think about him.* The good. The bad. The ugly. The beautiful. I couldn't stop thinking of him.

"You know this is very similar to what happened with me and Jason. When our relationship got tough, I left Montana with things still in limbo with us. I should have stayed and listened to him. Just like you should have stayed and listened to Grayson."

I scoffed, wiping residual tears from my cheeks. "This is nothing like that. I left because I wanted to. It had nothing to do with Grayson. I had a dream of coming to Paris and I knew I wouldn't forgive myself if I never actually did it."

She laughed. "So, you're fine with everything you found out the night before you left? You're fine with the fact that he fired you and you're fine with the fact that he hasn't shown up in Paris yet?"

I swallowed those questions, knowing I'd have to digest them later, when I was alone and could really delve into my feelings.

"Y'know, I'm peachy. In fact, I've hardly thought about Grayson while I've been here. It feels like all that happened ages ago."

"So you don't think you should have stayed and worked things out?"

"Those are two different questions, Brooklyn. I honestly don't think there's any way it could have worked out between him and me. If our paths cross in the future it'll be good to see him. We'll say hi and he'll introduce me to whatever girl he's dating. I'm not sure about a lot of things, but leaving and starting fresh felt like the right move."

"You sound so calm about everything," she said, disbelief clear in her tone.

I shrugged, though she couldn't see it through the phone. "So why were you crying when you first called?" she asked.

I bit down on my lip, trying to keep my emotions at bay. "I think I just realized that I'm not the person I thought I was. I wanted to be the cool girl who could travel around Europe and experience the world. I've been here for a month and a half and I think I made a huge mistake."

"So are you going to come home?" she asked tentatively.

"I'm not sure."

"Well, I have something that might convince you…"

"What?" The elation I felt at the idea of going home to LA was practically tangible. "What is it?"

"Jason asked me to marry him last week."

"WHAT?! ARE YOU FREAKING KIDDING ME? You let me ramble on about dumb Paris while you were sitting there freaking engaged? Are you completely insane?

Send me a picture of the ring. No, wait. Tell me how he did it. No wait, have you picked a date yet?"

She laughed. "Alright, settle down, you weirdo. We haven't picked a date yet but we know we don't want to wait long. It was a really simple proposal. He and I write on the upstairs balcony at his ranch—you know the one I'm talking about?"

I tried to envision Jason's ranch from my stay a few months earlier. It basically looked like a ski lodge transplanted into the Montana forest. It was breathtaking and the balcony she was talking about was the focal point of the entire house.

"Yes, I remember what it looks like."

"Well, we were out there writing a song and he paused right in the middle and dropped to one knee. He'd been carrying the ring around in his pocket for the last month, trying to think of what the most special proposal would be. When we were out there writing, he told me that there wasn't a moment that would feel more right to him. That balcony, and that house, hold a lot of memories for us and he thought it was only right to add one more."

"Holy shit. J-fresh is so romantic! You did good, sis. Now send me a picture of the ring or I'll kill you."

She laughed.

"Well actually, before I hang up, there's one more thing. Jason and I were thinking of having an engagement party in a month or so. I was going to ask you to help host it, but since you're across the world, I guess that's not possible."

I flinched at the hurt in her voice. I'd completely left behind all of my responsibilities in LA. My big sister—AKA the only family I had left—was getting married, and I knew I should be there with her, helping her plan her wedding, not halfway across the world.

I bit back my regret and spoke up.

"No. No. I can help plan it while I'm here. I'll search for some invitations and email you the links so you can pick your favorite."

"And do you think you'll fly back for it?" she asked.

I thought of my bank account and how little it had grown since taking the teaching job. The program paid me enough to live and eat, but I hadn't saved a dime since arriving in Paris. If I went home for the engagement party, chances were that I wouldn't have enough money to fly back to Paris.

"I'm not sure yet, but I'll let you know soon," I answered, not wanting to get her hopes up.

The Design

Chapter Thirty-Four

Traveling to Paris was supposed to solve my problems. I had dreams of establishing a home base, working my way up in a firm, and coming into my own in the City of Light. Instead, I felt like I'd carried all of my problems with me overseas. I didn't feel any more self-sufficient than before. I was still mad as hell that Grayson had gone behind my back, meddling in my life time and time again. I'd lied on the phone with Brooklyn: I missed him like crazy and the real reason I wasn't enjoying Paris was because I didn't think I was meant to be there without him. I wanted to be sampling crepes with Grayson. I wanted to be exploring the architecture with him by my side. I wanted him to take my hand as we strolled across the gardens and direct me into a hidden cafe so we could share an afternoon cappuccino while we rested our feet.

I thought of him every day, but most of all, I thought of him when I visited the Eiffel Tower. I sat on the grass, marveling at the monument's immense structure, and the only thing it reminded me of was the way Grayson had looked during our interview. The way his blue eyes had held me captive from across the desk, stealing my heart as if it was the simplest thing he'd ever done.

Two months without seeing him was enough time for me to go back and forth about my feelings time and time again. One day I'd wake up and miss him so much that I'd lay in bed pulling up old text messages and rereading every word he'd ever sent to me. Other times, I'd remember an email about a scholarship or an interview he'd negotiated, and I'd feel so angry with him that I had to stop myself from dialing his number and berating him. Most days, I fluctuated between loving and hating him at least thirty times (and that was all before I'd had my coffee).

It was perplexing to work through such polar opposite feelings for one person...especially when at the end of the day, Grayson was the one human on the entire planet that I knew I couldn't live without. He was intimidating and passionate, creative and intense. He taught me to love architecture and he inspired me to pursue my dreams, so why couldn't I forgive him for overstepping his bounds?

Why couldn't I realize that being with Grayson wouldn't mean that I was completely giving up my independence?

I missed him so much that a week before I was scheduled to fly back to LA for Brooklyn's engagement party, I'd even managed to convince myself that his actions were somewhat noble. It wasn't as if he'd been secretly sabotaging me. He'd been a guardian angel of sorts, ensuring that there weren't any obstacles blocking my path. *Could I really hate him for that?*

Maybe a little, but not enough to stay away any longer.

● ● ●

Arriving back home in LA felt similar to when I'd first arrived in France. I had no place to call home, no money to my name, no job, and Grayson and I weren't speaking. As terrifying as all of that was, the final detail was by far the hardest to stomach.

It felt just about as shitty as you could imagine to return home having failed at my dream. All I had to show for my two-month stint abroad was a smattering of French words and a purse full of Parisian chocolate. Some people would have been ashamed, but I was above that. You see, I had consumed copious amounts of alcohol during the long, long flight home and I couldn't actually find the will to care about anything, let alone the fact that I was a giant loser with no job and a boyfriend who wasn't actually a boyfriend, but rather someone I hadn't spoken to in two months.

"Cammie! You made it!"

I looked up to see Brooklyn and Jason standing at the bottom of the escalator with open arms. One quick scan around them let me know that Grayson was nowhere to be found.

"What the hell is the point if it's just you two and he's not here and just—" I'd made it to the bottom of the escalator and all but tossed my luggage at Jason. "Just take that because it's heavy and I bought way too many Parisian scarves. Who the hell wears that many scarves? And berets? No one wears them. If you wear one you look like a buffoon. Just an FYI."

"Wow. Alright, looks like they served some drinks on the flight over," Brooklyn said, exchanging a knowing glance with Jason.

"I see what you're doing. Stop being telepathic with each other and just take me to the airport lounge so that I can wait for Grayson to pick me up."

"Grayson?" Brooklyn asked, her bright blue eyes meeting mine. She looked so innocent and sweet with her golden blonde hair and designer clothing. I hated her for seeming confused about why I wanted Grayson to pick me up from the airport.

"Yes. Grayson. The person I'm in love with. He needs to pick me up from the airport." I shook my head, annoyed that I had to catch her up to speed.

"Listen, why don't we go home and we can finish setting up for the engagement party tomorrow. Maybe Grayson will come over after that?"

That sounded reasonable, so I let Jason and Brooklyn lead me out of the airport, a cloud of booze following my every step.

Chapter Thirty-Five

Grayson didn't come over while we set up for the engagement party. He didn't call or text me. He knew I was back in town: I'd overheard Brooklyn on the phone with him earlier that morning, confirming my arrival and my presence at the party. I guess we really weren't on speaking terms or he would have at least called me himself.

I yanked a long-stem rose out of a bucket of water and started plucking off the leaves. The engagement party was due to start any minute and I still had a few last minute flower arrangements I needed to throw together.

Brooklyn had stressed the fact that she wanted the decorations to be tasteful, so I'd skipped balloons in favor of flowers and large framed photos of her and Jason placed around the room. We'd spent all day transforming Brooklyn's condo for the party and it was finally coming together.

Three long tables were set up for dinner. A catering company was hard at work in the kitchen, whipping up hors d'oeuvres and a four-course meal for the small gathering.

I'd invited thirty guests. Everyone from Brooklyn's publicists to Jason's friends from Montana would be in attendance, and I couldn't wait to deliver the speech I'd been working on for the last few days.

"Cammie! I can finish doing that, you go get dressed!" Summer, Brooklyn's spunky assistant, demanded as she pulled the rose from my hand. I hadn't seen her in a few months, but she looked as awesome as ever. Last time I'd seen her she'd dyed her hair purple ombre. Now, it was a bright pink.

"I'm almost done!" I protested.

"Nope. No. The guests are arriving in five minutes and you're still wearing pajamas."

I glanced down at the flannel pajamas I'd stolen from Brooklyn that morning. I hated to hand over the reins, but Summer had a point. I couldn't greet the guests in plaid sleepwear.

"I've got this. I swear. Go get ready," Summer insisted, slapping my butt and pushing me toward Brooklyn's bedroom.

"Fine! But those flowers had better be perfect when I come back out," I teased.

Summer flipped me her middle finger as I stepped past Brooklyn's doorway. I was still laughing when I all but collided with Jason as he made his way out of the room.

"Woah," he said, reaching out to steady my shoulders so that I wouldn't topple over.

He was already gussied up in a designer suit and I paused for a moment to admire him. Jason Monroe was more leather boots than shined shoes, but he pulled off a suit as well as Grayson.

In an instant I was flooded with emotions. This was my future brother-in-law, my sister's fiancé, and he was one of the best men I'd ever known.

"I'm really happy my sister found someone like you," I said, meeting his gaze and trying my hardest to keep any tears at bay.

"Aw, you're gonna make me blush, Cammie," he quipped.

"I'm serious! Brooklyn is the best person in the entire world. She's seriously a baby angel and she deserves the world. Do you hear me, Monroe? I will take you down if you hurt my sister."

Clearly, my emotions were starting to jump around. I'd never threatened someone so soon after complimenting them before.

"Woah," he laughed. "Alright. I swear that your sister is in good hands with me."

"Pinky swear," I said, holding out my hand with utter seriousness.

He laughed, but when my hand didn't budge, he stuck his out to join mine.

"I do solemnly pinky swear," he said with a sincere tone.

"Cammie!" Brooklyn yelled from her bathroom. "Jesus, stop scaring off my fiancé and come get dressed!"

"I'm watching you, Monroe," I teased, as I pointed the same pinky from my eye to his, then moved to step past him.

He laughed. "I wouldn't expect anything less."

After that, Brooklyn and her makeup artist rushed to help me change into my dress and touch up my makeup and hair. I was wearing my favorite color: a deep royal blue. The dress was stretchy and easy to move in. The hem cut off at mid-thigh and the strapless bodice was fitted with a hidden corset so that I didn't have to worry about pulling it up all night. I was borrowing some of Brooklyn's cream-colored Louboutin heels that I'd worn dozens of times before. *I mean, they were basically mine at this point.*

Since the hairstylist had curled my hair earlier, I left off a necklace in favor of layering gold bangles on my wrist. It offered a little bohemian touch to an otherwise fancy outfit.

"You look gorgeous!" Brooklyn said, meeting my eye in the mirror.

I laughed, unable to fully look at her without going blind. *Literally.* She looked absolutely stunning. She was wearing an ivory Grecian-inspired dress that was belted around her waist with embroidered crystals. Her hair was down, just like mine, and the only accessory she needed was the giant rock sitting on her left ring finger: a princess cut stone that was big enough to knock someone out. *Good work, Monroe.*

"Ready?" I asked, taking her hand in mine.

She smiled and nodded. "Let's go."

• • •

I stood in the corner of the room, sipping on a glass of champagne and watching as Brooklyn and Jason moved around the room and greeted guests. I smiled at the way Jason looked at Brooklyn with stars in his eyes. He was completely enamored and I knew that my sister was in good hands.

A waiter circled by me with a tray of delicious smelling hors d'oeuvres and I shook my head, knowing that I couldn't stomach any food until I saw Grayson. He was due to arrive any minute, but every time the door opened, I'd feel a pang of disappointment as another one of Brooklyn or Jason's friends stepped inside instead of him.

"Have you tried the salmon balls yet? They are fucking amazing," Summer said, joining me in the corner with two champagne flutes.

"Not yet. But, oh, I already have a drink," I said, holding up my champagne.

She laughed. "Don't flatter yourself little C, these are both for me."

I laughed and shook my head. Summer had worked for Brooklyn for years but her shock factor had yet to wear off for me.

"There aren't many eligible guys here tonight. I mean, that waiter is pretty hot, but I gave up waiters for Lent," she said, waggling her eyebrows at the young waiter across the room.

I thought about her comment for a second. "Summer...Lent isn't going on right now. What are you talking about?"

Her eyes lit up and a slow smile broke out across her lips. "If you'll just excuse me then," she said, all but bee lining for the spiky haired waiter she'd been ogling for the last few minutes. Just as she reached him, the door to Brooklyn's apartment opened and more guests flooded in.

There was an older couple that walked in first, leaning on one another for support. After them, I recognized Brooklyn's manager, strolling in on his cell phone, probably trying to cram in five more minutes of work. He continued on the phone while reaching for a glass of champagne as it passed by him on a tray. *Impressive.* I watched him for another second before a glimpse of dark brown hair pulled my attention back to the open door.

Grayson.

I froze and stared as he walked through the door. It'd been over two months since I'd last seen him but it felt like no time had passed at all. He looked just as handsome as he had when I'd left him at the airport. He was wearing a navy suit with polished brown shoes. A crisp white shirt laid beneath his fitted jacket that he filled out oh so well. His lips were spread into a wide, easy smile, and his dimples were just as appealing as they'd been two months ago.

I took a step forward to greet him, and then my eyes finally fell to his side, to the petite redhead touching his arm.

He brought a date to Brooklyn's engagement party?
He brought a freaking date?!

The Design

Chapter Thirty-Six

I managed to pull it together as best as I could as Grayson strolled around the party with his date, introducing her to anyone he could find. I stood against the wall, watching them and trying to recall whether or not I knew any spells or hexes off the top of my head, before remembering I wasn't a witch. *How hard could it be?* Surely Brooklyn had a voodoo doll or some eye of newt lying around somewhere.

He finally looked my way and I froze. The petite redhead was trying to get his attention, pulling hard on his arm, but he held my gaze for a moment. I recognized the cool indifference in his eyes from my days at Cole Designs, but I wasn't prepared to see it aimed at me.

I cocked a brow and raised my glass in a silent salute. *Well played, asshole.* He narrowed his eyes and turned back to his date. Adrenaline had flushed through me when our eyes locked, but when he turned away, I was left with the aftereffects. My hands were shaking and my mouth felt dry. If my champagne flute had been cheaper, I would have already shattered it into a million pieces.

"Cammie, are you almost ready to give your speech?" Brooklyn asked, coming to stand beside me. "I think most everyone is here, so we should get started."

"Yes. Perfect. Great. Let's do that speech now," I said, scanning the room for any eligible bachelors I could pay to be my date for the night. There was a fourteen-year-old kid playing Nintendo DS on Brooklyn's couch. Hmm… I could tell Grayson he's a prodigy with that Benjamin Button disease so he ages backwards. *Yeah, that could work.*

"Cammie? Are you good? I saw that Grayson brought a date, and if you don't want to do the speech, you can just—"

I laughed a twisted sort of laugh and then waved her off. "Oh, please. I totally have this," I said, whipping out the folded piece of paper I'd used to jot down the important points of the speech. It'd been wedged between my boobs and was now a little damp, thanks to Grayson's holy hotness making me sweat.

"Oh, um, alright then," Brooklyn said, trying to decipher my erratic mood.

I ignored her and made eye contact with Summer so that I could give her the go-ahead to get started. *Why not give the speech now?* The sooner I said my spiel, the sooner I could get the hell out of there.

"Ladies, and gentlemen," Summer yelled, clanking her champagne flute a little too hard. "If you'll give us your attention, the maid of honor and the best man would each like to give a short speech in honor of the bride and groom to start off tonight's party."

Best man? I hadn't realized he was giving a speech as well. I scanned the room, wondering which one of Jason's friends he'd chosen for the coveted spot. *Maybe Derek or another friend from Montana?*

When Grayson stepped forward through the crowd, beelining in my direction, I had to force myself to close my gaping mouth.

Oh, hell freaking no. Jason made Grayson his best man? Bastard.

"Cammie?" Brooklyn murmured beneath her breath. "Say something."

Everyone's eyes had turned to me after Summer's introduction and I'd yet to make a move. I cleared my throat and stared down at my sweaty notecards just as Grayson fell into place beside me. His suit jacket brushed my skin as he spun around to face the crowd and I almost reached out to push him two feet away from me. The scent of his aftershave hit me and I closed my eyes, trying to compose myself as best as possible.

"Right, so, hello," I stammered, forcing my gaze up to meet the crowd. "I'm Cameron Heart, Brooklyn's sister and I'll be giving a speech…um, right now."

My palms were sweating so badly that I was forced to wipe them on my dress.

"They know you're giving a speech," Grayson whispered.

I shot him a death stare, but he shrugged it off, offering a diplomatic smile to the crowd. *Asshole. Asshole. Asshole.*

"As some of you may know, Brooklyn and Jason had quite the whirlwind romance," I began, smiling over to where Brooklyn and Jason were wrapped around one another, listening intently. "They were both content to work on their solo careers. They weren't looking for someone to stand next to on stage, but their record label had a different plan for them.

"You see, I spoke with Brooklyn just after she and Jason met for the first time. It was an awkward encounter to say the least, but I knew she was enamored by him. Jason was a challenge for Brooklyn, something she wasn't used to. As many of you know, she's good at getting what she wants."

I paused while the crowd laughed.

"Sounds like someone else I know," Grayson whispered just loud enough for me to hear over the laughter. I tried to ignore him.

"In the beginning, I was worried that Jason would break my sister's heart. All signs pointed to him being a musician with a big following and an even bigger ego, but Jason took me by surprise. He loved my sister fiercely, despite their rocky start, and in the end, he showed her just how loyal, passionate, and long-lasting his love for her was."

Grayson cut in, "And she was smart enough to give him a second chance when she knew he deserved it."

I shot him a glance while trying to keep my cool. A few guests laughed, but most of them were too confused to do anything but stare at us. *I will not let Grayson ruin my speech.*

"Pardon the interruption. Anyway, I brought a little something to read for you all. It's a letter Jason gave to me on the day I graduated from college. He'd shown up at the ceremony to surprise my sister and at that point, I was still doing my best to protect her from him. This letter was his way of letting me know I could trust him. So, here goes:

"*'Dear Cammie,*

I propose an alliance.

You care for your sister, you stick up for her through thick and thin, and you always want what's best for her, but now you aren't alone. I'm going to love Brooklyn every second of every day. Every time you think she needs someone in her corner, I'll be there, standing by her side and putting her needs before my own.

I plan on asking your sister to marry me soon, but by asking for her hand in marriage, I'm also asking for your approval. I've never had a little sister and I'm sure it'll take some time for me to get it right, but I'm prepared to put in the work. The Heart sisters are more than worth it.

Let me know if you accept my proposal. We'd make a pretty great team. We could even have nicknames. How about C-Stacks and J-Money?

PS. Don't tell your sister. I want the proposal to be a surprise."

I folded the note back up and glanced at Jason. He had tears in the corner of his eyes and a giant smile on his lips. I knew I'd made the right decision in reading the letter.

"Obviously, I accept your alliance," I told him. The room erupted in laughter and I held up my glass of champagne. "Jason, welcome to the family. I'm so happy you found my sister. Cheers!"

All the guests clinked their champagne flutes together and took little sips. My nerves were shot and I'd kept in my tears as best as I could. The worst part was over...and then Grayson stepped forward and I realized that I wasn't out of the clear just yet.

"The thing that I admire about Brooklyn and Jason is that they both fought for their love," he began, his deep voice commanding the room. "Some of you may not know, but the two of them faced quite a few obstacles in the beginning of their relationship. They had more than enough opportunities to walk away when the going got tough, but they stayed and fought for their relationship. Not everyone chooses to do that," he said, his gaze cutting over to me. *I get it, Grayson. I hear you loud and clear.*

"Yes. But luckily, Jason and Brooklyn didn't have any truly divisive problems," I clarified, smiling out toward the crowd. *Had I really just said that out loud?*

There was a moment of silence and then he spoke up again.

"No," Grayson argued. "When you love someone you don't flee the country. You stay and you fight."

By this point, the crowd was starting to get confused.

"Is this still part of the toast?" an elderly woman whispered to her friend beside me. A few other guests cleared their throats or coughed, proving that we were straying a little too far off topic.

"Yes, but Jason didn't just let her go. He flew all the way to LA to get Brooklyn back," I retorted with a giant fake smile. The crowd sighed at the sweet gesture.

"Yes and what a way to show his devotion to her," Grayson agreed, before veering off topic again. "But maybe if Brooklyn had flown halfway across the world without so much as a courtesy call to let Jason know she'd arrived safely, he would have thought twice about following her."

"Jason loved Brooklyn enough to follow her anywhere," I argued, turning to face him so he could see my built up fury.

"Yes, but I doubt Brooklyn told Jason that their love was just a game," he answered, taking a step toward me so that his fiery blue eyes were only a few inches away from mine.

"Well, I bet Jason would have been smart enough not to bring a date with him. I mean, seriously Grayson, what the hell—

"Alright, well," Summer yelled over me, panic written across her face. "Wow! I don't know about you guys, but I have *never* heard such sweet toasts before. I mean, wow, so much love. So let's just, everyone, raise your glasses to the bride and groom!"

Half of the room raised their glasses to Summer's toast, and the other half continued to gape at Grayson and me, confused about what the hell had just happened.

I felt my cheeks redden with the embarrassment of ruining Brooklyn and Jason's night. I should have kept my mouth shut, but Grayson had a way of bringing out my *passionate* side. Without a word, I moved toward the door of Brooklyn's condo and dropped my champagne glass on a table on the way out. I needed to leave. Brooklyn would understand. She'd probably even feel better once I was gone.

The night should have been completely about her and I'd just nearly ruined the whole thing. *What had I been thinking? Did I honestly think Grayson was going to waltz into the party and beg to get back together with me? Had I thought he'd welcome me back to the states with open arms?* I'd left him at the airport and he had every right to hate me for it.

I flew down the stairs, skipping the elevator in favor of a quicker, more private getaway. Once I hit the bottom level, I pushed through the exit door, wrapped my arms around my chest, and inhaled the chilly night air.

It's done.
He's with a new girl.
Drop it.

Fuck. He's with a new girl.

"I have to admit, that was an all time low, even for me," a voice spoke behind me.

I spun around to see Grayson standing in the open doorway, his mouth hitched up in a half-smile. He must have followed me down the stairs, but I hadn't noticed his footsteps.

"I can't believe we just did that," I replied. "I mean, of all the times to get into a fight."

"It needed to happen," he said, stepping out of the doorway and letting the heavy metal door shut behind him. "But that wasn't how I had it planned."

I nodded. The blame was definitely a burden we'd have to share.

I took a seat on the edge of an abandoned wooden palette near the backdoor. We were alone in the small alley next to Brooklyn's condominium building. A lone streetlamp afforded us a gentle layer of light, just enough so that when Grayson took a seat beside me, I could see his subtle frown.

"I wasn't prepared to see you with another girl," I admitted, keeping my gaze on the layers of brick across the alley. "I could have handled it better."

He nodded, taking a while to respond. "That was a dumb move on my part."

"Does she mean something to you?" I asked, peering over at him from the corner of my eye.

"The girl? No," he answered, picking up a stray rock from the ground and tossing it along the concrete as if he were skipping it on water. "I met her in the elevator on the way up and just stuck by her after we walked in just in case you had a date. I think she's Jason's cousin or something."

"Are you serious?" I asked.

He laughed and nodded, staring down at the ground in shame.

I nodded slowly, processing his message at the same time that my brain bombarded me with questions. I had so much I wanted to know and yet, it felt good to just sit beside him in silence. I knew the moment was fleeting. As soon as we began to talk, I'd inevitably ruin whatever peace temporarily hung over us. He must have felt the same way because for the next few minutes, the two of us just sat on that palette and stared out into the alley. I listened to the passing cars, the chattering groups of people as they walked by, and the way the wood creaked whenever we shifted our weight. It was a moment I'd be able to hang on to when I was alone later, one last moment of peace with Grayson by my side.

I dropped a finger to the dirt and made circles, realizing it was time to tell him the truth.

"I think a part of me thought you'd come to Paris. I even waited by the Eiffel Tower thinking that if I went there every day at the same time, eventually one day you would be there," I admitted, feeling tears burning the corners of my eyes.

"I wanted to be there, Cammie. I bought three tickets, but each one inevitably went unused," he replied with defeat.

"Why didn't you come?" I asked, watching my finger creating circles in the dirt.

"There were a lot of reasons, but most of all there was the fear that you'd reject me once I arrived. You didn't exactly leave me much hope at the end."

I cringed at the memory of walking away from him at the airport.

"Anyway, did you like it? Paris?" he asked.

I wanted to tell him the truth, but instead a lie came out.

"Oh, yeah. It's great. I'm heading back soon."

Lie. Lie. Lie.

Grayson nodded, visibly impressed. "Wow. That's good to hear."

"Yeah, I think I just fit in there."

"And how do you like the people? Do you have a guy you're seeing?"

A slideshow of terrible prospects flashed through my mind. There'd been the hobo who'd peed next to me on the subway, my bunkmate who thought bathing was optional, and a slew of French guys who thought that any American girl traveling abroad was down for an easy lay.

"Oh, I've just been playing the field. Y'know, don't want to tie myself down with anyone early on."

I peered over to see him smiling, a bit too smug for comfort.

"What? Why are you smiling like that?" I asked.

He corrected his features right away. "Oh, no. I'm just happy everything is working out so well for you. Seems like heading to Paris was the smartest decision you've ever made."

"Oh, yeah," I agreed emphatically. "Definitely."

What was I saying? Why couldn't I just tell him the truth? Why couldn't I tell him that I'd majorly fucked up, that leaving him was the worst mistake I'd ever made?

"So when do you head back?" he asked.

Never. I had like $50 to my name.

"Hmm, maybe in a few weeks. Brooklyn has missed me, so I don't want to rush off."

He nodded and stared off in the distance, that same smile begging me to decipher his true intentions.

"I'm sure you're really anxious to get back. We must seem like uncivilized brutes compared to all of your French friends."

I lingered on his appearance: the sharp, regal features paired with his suit and cuff links. Grayson was anything but a brute.

"Oui. Le chien a mangé le beignet."

His eyebrows rose. "See, you're already fluent."

I smiled, completely unsure of what I'd just told him. Something like "The dog ate the donut."

"Do you have plans tomorrow morning or are you too busy planning your return trip?" he asked, shooting me a playful glance.

"Tomorrow morning?" I confirmed.

He wanted to see me again?

He nodded.

"Yeah. I think I have time. What do you have in mind?"

He pushed himself up off the palette and reached for my hand.

"It's a surprise."

Chapter Thirty-Seven

The following morning, Grayson sped down the streets of LA while I tried my best not to spill my coffee all over his leather interior. I'd picked out a cream blouse that I hoped fell between "I STILL REALLY LOVE YOU, PLEASE NOTICE ME" and "Oh? This old thing?", but neither message would matter if it was completely covered in coffee.

Grayson hadn't told me where we were going when he'd picked me up a few minutes earlier, so my curiosity was getting the better of me. Every time we turned a corner, I tried to decipher what landmarks we were near. *Was he taking me to his place? Was he taking me to breakfast at a special restaurant?*

By the time he slowed his car to park, I was completely turned around. I knew we were somewhere north of downtown, but the buildings didn't look familiar. They were old worn down industrial warehouses with caving roofs and garbage cluttering the ground around them.

Wow. Very romantic, Grayson.

"Do you recognize this address?" he asked.

I shook my head. "No?"

He killed the engine and pocketed his keys.

"Hop out really quick. I want you to see something."

I dropped my coffee into his car's cup holder and trailed out after him. His gait was easily twice the length of mine, so I had to hurry to catch him. Just when I got close, he reached back for my hand, and like an old habit, I let him take hold. The desire to never let go was too much to handle.

He pulled me after him as he circled the side of the building. We walked along the fence to the very front, where large gates blocked the entrance to the old abandoned warehouses. In front of the gates there was a large, wooden sign. I recognized the type of sign from various construction sites around LA. Usually the signs boasted future hotels or trendy eateries, but this sign was different. As I rounded to the front and Grayson let go of my hand, I realized why.

It was a sign announcing the future site of a municipal park, and the design pictured below in full color?

It was mine.

"Your park design won the competition," Grayson announced.

My hands flew to my mouth. "You resubmitted it?"

"I did," he replied, moving to stand in front of me so that I'd be forced to look him in the eye. "But I promise you it will be the last time I ever interfere in your life without your permission."

"Are you kidding me?!"

He half-smiled. "Are you mad? I can't tell."

"Grayson! I WON THE COMPETITION. This is my design! They picked *my* design!"

"Of course they did," he nodded. "It was by far the best one and you had some stiff competition. You should have seen Alan's face."

I shook my head, trying to connect the puzzle pieces in my head.

"But I thought we were disqualified? I thought both of our submissions were thrown out?"

He nodded, stepping to the side so that I could see a glimpse of my design once again.

"They were, but I had a meeting with the design committee and I requested that they trash the original Cole Designs submission and instead take your design into consideration. They weren't happy about it, but when they saw your plan, they decided to bend the rules a little."

I shook my head in disbelief and then stepped up to the sign to get a closer look. The Cole Designs logo was printed at the very bottom, but above that, there was a small gold plaque.

"The winning design for this municipal park project was contributed by:
Cameron Heart, Associate Architect, Cole Designs."

"Holy shit," I whispered as tears began to slide down my cheeks. The competition was open to every architecture firm in California. The committee must have received hundreds of submissions, yet my name was printed on the plaque. *I'd won.*

"And before you ask," Grayson said, stepping up to meet me in front of the sign. "I had no hand in who won the competition. The panel of judges had no clue who you were. They chose your design because it was the best. You won this on your own, Cammie. You're a damn good architect and you deserve recognition for your work. Please know that anything I did to help you along the way was nothing compared to the things you managed to do all on your own."

I nodded and kept my hand pressed to my mouth in an attempt to conceal the fact that I was all but hysterical.

"I can't believe you did this," I said, turning to wrap my arms around him.

My face smashed against his chest, his cologne enveloped me, and he held me there as I cried tears of joy. Every single failure I'd endured in the last few months was nothing compared to that moment. Paris, Alan, Hannah—nothing mattered in that moment because I'd made it on my own. I was going to be the designer of a major multimillion-dollar park.

"There is one thing…since you aren't a licensed architect yet, I have to supervise the build, but I won't make any decisions without you by my side."

I leaned back so I could meet his eye. "Does that mean I have my old job back?"

He smiled. "I was actually thinking of something better," he said and then he slowly slid down to the ground, holding his weight up on one knee.

What? WHAT?

"Grayson! What are you doing?!"

"If you change your name to Cameron Cole, then that would technically make you a partner in my company, right?"

"Grayson!" I exclaimed as he pulled a small, simple gold band from his pocket. It was delicate and thin, understated and unique.

"I let you leave me once, Cammie. I let you leave and I had no choice but to watch you board that plane to Paris. I let you go because I thought that's what you wanted, but now I'm going after what *I* want, and I want to marry you. I want you by my side in life and in business. You're a visionary, Cameron. I admire your drive and tenacity. I admire your passion and determination. If you want to go back to Paris, we'll go to Paris. We'll live wherever you want, just as long as we're together."

I laughed at the idea of us living in Paris, but Grayson took it the wrong way. His smile faded for a moment as he processed the fact that I'd just laughed at his proposal.

"No! Grayson. Wait, not 'no' to the proposal. Yes! Yes, to that."

He smiled as I tried to unscramble my speech.

"But no, we cannot live in Paris. We'll stay in LA and we'll oversee the building of my park. Paris held nothing for me without you there."

He grinned.

"So is that a yes?"

I laughed. "That's a hell yes."

He slipped the delicate ring on my finger, stood up, and kissed me. I lifted up onto my tiptoes and wrapped my hands around his neck. It'd been two months too long since our last kiss. I'd been so wrong about leaving. I'd thought I needed to leave behind the people I depended on so that I could learn to stand on my two feet, but Grayson had proven to me that I could do it all on my own, right from where I was. Sure, Grayson would probably still try to be a controlling and Brooklyn would always worry, but I'd tell them how I felt, we'd adjust, and they'd give me room to grow.

After I managed to stop crying and my face was a little less blotchy, Grayson and I stood in front of the sign and snapped a photo of our smiling faces with my ring on full display.

When we got back in the car, I stared down at the photo. It was hardly the best photo I'd ever taken, but I'd never seen myself look happier than I did right then. Grayson and I were wrapped around one another and our cheeks were crushed together so that our giant smiles were slightly lopsided. Since Grayson had attempted to snap the photo himself, our foreheads were, of course, cut off, but Grayson's eyes were in focus and there were tears hovering in the corners. My cheeks were flushed and the wind had whipped my hair all over the place. I'm sure a photographer would have balked at the execution, but the emotion? The love? *It was right there, plain to see.*

I attached the photo to a text message and sent it to Brooklyn with the caption: "I said yes!"

She replied within seconds.

Brooklyn: ARE YOU KIDDING ME???? DOUBLE WEDDING?????!!!

Epilogue

Amount saved for our wedding: $10,345 (which will cover like one-fourth of my dress. Ha, just kidding.). Grayson keeps trying to convince me to let him pay for the wedding, but I've insisted on paying for half. Clearly, I'm still working on convincing him that he doesn't have to be in control of everything!

Items I have: a beautiful strand of pearls my mother left me. I'll wear them on my wedding day. For her.

Items I need: DJ, caterer, photographer, officiant… basically everything. Oy vey.

French phrases that I know: Mon fiancé a un mégot mignon…which translates to: "My fiancé has a cute butt." ;)

Amount saved for our house: $125,405. *Wondering where that money came from?* Grayson took most of my rent from over the years and invested it. When I found out, it of course sparked a heated argument between us, but in the end, I couldn't hate him for wisely investing my money.

He swore (under penalty of death) to never meddle like that again and I promised to use the money for our house, something we'd share.

A few short months after my sister's engagement party, I stood at the front of her wedding reception as the chatter started to die down. It was time for my maid of honor speech and my hands shook with nerves—no thanks to the little ensemble Brooklyn had surprised me with.

"Some of you may be wondering why I'm standing up here wearing a sombrero and a clown nose." I spoke into the microphone so that all of my sister's wedding guests could hear me. "Well, during a certain speech a few months ago, Grayson and I may have gone a bit off topic. In an effort to pay me back, my sister decided that we had to wear these fetching ensembles while delivering our speeches this time around."

I adjusted the bright pink sombrero so that it wouldn't fall off.

"Obviously her plan failed because she didn't realize how killer I look in a sombrero."

The crowd laughed and I twisted my engagement ring around my finger, a habit I'd developed in the last few months.

"As most of you know, my sister is older than me by a few years, and because of that, I've always looked up to her." I scanned to where Brooklyn sat, looking like a freaking Disney princess in her wedding gown. Her blonde hair was twisted into a complicated up-do and her makeup was flawless as usual. "When I was little, I'd follow her and her friends around, listening in on their gossip and stealing their makeup whenever they weren't looking. She put up with my antics and convinced her friends to let me hang around with them even though I could hardly keep up."

Brooklyn smile and pressed her hand over her heart.

"As we got older, I continued to idolize her and she continued to be my greatest teacher. She taught me how to paint my nails, how to throw a curveball, and how to run from a doorstep after you've just egged a house. While those are skills every young girl should know, it wasn't until our parents passed away that she was forced to step in and teach me the most important lesson of all. Brooklyn taught me how to grieve for our parents while still understanding that we had a lot of life left to live. She taught me that we couldn't waste life just because they were gone—we had to honor their memories any way that we could.

"I see Brooklyn honor the memory of our parents everyday in the way she loves Jason. I watch the way she treats him, the small acts of love and kindness she bestows upon him everyday, and I see my parents in them."

Brooklyn glanced toward Jason with tears brimming over in her eyes.

"I know how it feels to be unconditionally loved by my sister, and I have to say, Jason, you are one lucky man."

"Here, here," Jason said, raising his glass and stirring a few laughs around the banquet room.

"I've also seen how much joy Jason brings to Brooklyn's life. He treats her as if she's the most precious gift he's ever received."

Brooklyn and Jason turned to one another and he dipped his chin to give her a quick kiss. I turned to my left, to where Grayson was standing, wearing the same clown nose and sombrero I was (though pink really wasn't his color). He'd already delivered his speech, but he stood by my side, pressing his hand to my lower back for support and nodding for me to continue.

"So let's raise our glasses to Jason and Brooklyn. May they always remember to cherish one another and may we all find a love as lasting as theirs. Cheers!"

"Cheers!" everyone sang, clinking their glasses together and taking sips of the champagne.

Grayson clinked his glass with mine, but before I could take a sip, he leaned forward and stole a kiss. Our sombreros collided and his pushed mine off the back of my head, down to the dance floor.

I laughed and pulled back to stare up at him. The man had a clown nose on and he still looked adorable.

"Are you laughing at me, Cameron?" he asked with a wink.

I squeezed his clown nose and then pulled it off.

"Ah, much better. Now I can actually see my fiancé again."

Grayson reached to pull my clown nose off as well.

"Gorgeous," he smiled.

"Can you two stop being adorable?" Brooklyn asked as she bumped her hips with mine. "Jason and I need to do our first dance."

"Yeah, yeah, yeah." I smiled and tugged Grayson off the dance floor beside me. The house lights dimmed and a spotlight hit the newlyweds as they took their positions. Jason wrapped his arm around Brooklyn's waist and she cozied up to him with her head resting against his chest. Love surrounded them.

A slow jazz song swept over the speakers and the DJ announced that Brooklyn and Grayson would be enjoying their first dance together.

"Don't forget your mom wants us to come over for dinner tomorrow," I reminded Grayson as Brooklyn and Jason danced slowly across the floor.

"It's a wonder she even wants me there. These days it seems like she only has eyes for you," he teased, pinching my waist.

"That's because I reply to her texts much quicker than you!"

I left out the fact that Grayson doesn't gossip with her about The Bachelor. No need to wound him—we both knew I was her new favorite child. (*Or soon-to-be child.*)

"Yeah, yeah," he mumbled, nuzzling my hair.

"Do you think anyone can tell that Brooklyn's been drinking sparkling juice instead of champagne?" I asked as we turned our attention back to the newlyweds.

"Nah. No one suspects a thing."

I smiled. Just two weeks earlier Brooklyn had found out she was expecting her first child with Jason. The news was still fresh, and with the paparazzi hounding their every move, she was keeping the announcement private for as long as possible.

I leaned against Grayson and let him support me as I watched my sister dancing with her new husband, the father of her child.

"We need to think of what song we want to dance to at our wedding," I said, tipping my chin to look up at him.

Without pausing, he answered, "'You Shook Me All Night Long' by AC/DC."

I laughed. "Yeah right, you're dreaming."

His gaze tipped down to me, his eyes sought mine, and we stayed like that for a moment, watching each other. Then, finally, the side of his mouth hitched up and he nodded. "Yeah. I think I am."

The Design

The End

Just kidding.

MORE Epilogue!

Grayson and I traveled to Paris for our honeymoon. We spent three days in a hotel near the Eiffel tower and each afternoon, we walked the entire perimeter of the monument. There was a bench I used to sit on, and it was where I'd dream about Grayson coming to find me in Paris. I showed him the bench and we sat there each day, talking and people watching. On our final day, Grayson sneakily carved our initials into the wood. He told me it was so I could always have a little piece of myself in Paris.

Brooklyn and Jason had a baby girl named Jillian and I, of course, purchased an infant sized guitar as a joke. But who are we kidding? That baby is learning to play guitar before she walks.

My park project took two years to build and once it was complete, the entire city was invited to the grand opening. Food vendors lined up along the basketball courts, and a local cinema set up an outdoor screening that started just as the sun set. It was exactly what I'd envisioned.

Grayson scaled back his business after we found out I was pregnant with our first child. I thought it'd be hard for him to do—after all, Cole Designs was his first love—but he was actually the one to suggest the change. He passed on most of his large-scale industrial jobs to other firms in the area, and he and I turned into a design duo. Along with a few interns, an assistant, and an office manager, Grayson and I tackle three to four high-end residential projects a year. Our very first project was our own house—which needed a nursery and a room for our son, Caiden, by the time we finally moved in.

Life moves fast these days, but I haven't felt that itch to pack up and leave in years—not like I used too—but why would I? Everything I could ever want is under one roof, waiting for me at the end of each day.

Acknowledgements

(I put this in every book, because it's SO important.) To every reader that takes a chance on an indie author, thank you so much. It means the world to me that you took a chance on this book.

To Lance, who as I write this is making me laugh…Nothing changes.

To my family, thank you for everything.

To all of my friends (readers and authors included) in the indie community, thank you for being awesome!

GIANT thank you to my street team!!!! R.S. Grey's Girls is the best group I belong to and it's because of all of the wonderful people in it! Thank you for being such supportive friends.

Jennifer Flory-Van Wyk, once again I am using this little section of my book to confess my love for you, haha! THANK YOU for everything you do and for basically running my street team for me!

Big thank you to my proofreaders: Chanpreet Sigh, Amanda Daniel, Miranda Arnold, Lindsey Boggan, and Christine Wicklund!!

Patricia Lee, thank you so much for everything you do.

Jamie Taliaferro & Gabbs Warner – I love you both so much!! Thank you for the amazing support!

Thank you to all of my fellow indie authors (within Author Support 101 & Write Club). I don't think I'd have the energy to write without the help from all of you ladies. Thank you for providing support and a sense of community within a crazy world!

Thank you to everyone who accepted an ARC edition of this book and hanging with me for all the tweaks and changes!

Other Books by R.S. Grey:

The Duet
Adult Romance

When 27-year-old pop sensation Brooklyn Heart steps in front of a microphone, her love songs enchant audiences worldwide. But when it comes to her own love life, the only spell she's under is a dry one.

So when her label slots her for a Grammy performance with the sexy and soulful Jason Monroe, she can't help but entertain certain fantasies... those in which her G-string gets more play than her guitars'.

Only one problem. Jason is a lyrical lone wolf that isn't happy about sharing the stage—nor his ranch — with the sassy singer. But while it may seem like a song entitled 'Jason Monroe Is an Arrogant Ho' basically writes itself, their label and their millions of fans are expecting recording gold...

They're expecting *The Duet*.

Recommended for ages 17+ due to language and sexual situations.

Available on: AMAZON

Scoring Wilder
USA TODAY BEST-SELLER
New Adult Sports Romance

What started out as a joke-- seduce Coach Wilder--soon became a goal she had to score.

With Olympic tryouts on the horizon, the last thing nineteen-year-old Kinsley Bryant needs to add to her plate is Liam Wilder. He's a professional soccer player, America's favorite bad-boy, and has all the qualities of a skilled panty-dropper.

* A face that makes girls weep - check.

* Abs that can shred Parmesan cheese (the expensive kind) - check.

* Enough confidence to shift the earth's gravitational pull - double check.

Not to mention Liam is strictly off limits. Forbidden. Her coaches have made that perfectly clear. (i.e. "Score with Coach Wilder anywhere other than the field and you'll be cut from the team faster than you can count his tattoos.") But that just makes him all the more enticing...Besides, Kinsley's already counted the visible ones, and she is not one to leave a project unfinished.

Kinsley tries to play the game her way as they navigate through forbidden territory, but Liam is determined to teach her a whole new definition for the term "team bonding."

Recommended for ages 17+ due to language and sexual situations.

Available on: AMAZON

With This Heart
New Adult Romance

If someone had told me a year ago that I was about to fall in love, go on an epic road trip, ride a Triceratops, sing on a bar, and lose my virginity, I would have assumed they were on drugs.

Well, that is, until I met Beckham.

Beck was mostly to blame for my recklessness. Gorgeous, clever, undeniably charming Beck barreled into my life as if it were his mission to make sure I never took living for granted. He showed me that there were no boundaries, rules were for the spineless, and a kiss was supposed to happen when I least expected.

Beck was the plot twist that took me by surprise. Two months before I met him, death was knocking at my door. I'd all but given up my last scrap of hope when suddenly I was given a second chance at life. This time around, I wasn't going to let it slip through my fingers.

We set out on a road trip with nothing to lose and no guarantees of tomorrow.

Our road trip was about young, reckless love. The kind of love that burns bright.

The kind of love that no road-map could bring me back from.

Recommended for ages 17+ due to language and sexual situations.

Available on: AMAZON

Behind His Lens
Adult Romance

Twenty-three year old model Charley Whitlock built a quiet life for herself after disaster struck four years ago. She hides beneath her beautiful mask, never revealing her true self to the world... until she comes face-to-face with her new photographer — sexy, possessive Jude Anderson. It's clear from the first time she meets him that she's playing by his rules. He says jump, she asks how high. He tells her to unzip her cream Dior gown, she knows she has to comply. But what if she wants him to take charge outside of the studio as well?

Jude Anderson has a strict "no model" dating policy. But everything about Charley sets his body on fire.

When a tropical photo shoot in Hawaii forces the stubborn pair into sexually charged situations, their chemistry can no longer be ignored. They'll have to decide if they're willing to break their rules and leave the past behind or if they'll stay consumed by their demons forever. Will Jude persuade Charley to give in to her deepest desires?

Recommended for ages 17+ due to language and sexual situations.

Available on: AMAZON

CPSIA information can be obtained
at www.ICGtesting.com
Printed in the USA
LVHW091032140419
614124LV00002B/654/P